PUTTING OUT

PUTTING OUT

Neil Ferguson

HAMISH HAMILTON · LONDON

HAMISH HAMILTON LTD
Published by the Penguin Group
27 Wrights Lane, London W8 5TZ, England
Viking Penguin Inc., 40 West 23rd Street, New York, New York 10010, U.S.A.
Penguin Books Australia Ltd, Ringwood, Victoria, Australia
Penguin Books Canada Ltd, 2801 John Street, Markham, Ontario, Canada L3R 1B4
Penguin Books (N.Z.) Ltd, 182–190 Wairau Road, Auckland 10, New Zealand

Penguin Books Ltd, Registered Offices: Harmondsworth, Middlesex, England

First published in Great Britain 1988 by
Hamish Hamilton Ltd
Copyright © 1988 by Neil Ferguson

British Library Cataloguing in Publication Data

Ferguson, Neil
Putting out.
I. Title
823'.914[F]   PR6056.E61/

ISBN 0-241-12291-0

Typeset in 11/12½ Sabon at
The Spartan Press Ltd,
Lymington, Hants.
Printed and bound in Great Britain by
Butler & Tanner Ltd, Frome and London

For Eighty-Eight

1

Swish. Swish.
Almost silently the tiny roar of sealed nylon bearings rotating inside skate-trucks swish in a counter direction to the swish of nylon wheels against the black-topped surface of the boulevard through the Park. On boards and skates bronzed and athletic bodies swan and pavane with exquisite nonchalance. Acrobats sidesurf, pirouette, cruise in and out of each other's swaying perfect balance and that of the occasional statuesque loner for whom the strip is deserted. Roller-disco dancers – juggling lovers – execute faultless arabesques and pliés to the funk pumping through their personal music systems. This way, that way. Swish. Swish. The supple limbs of boys and girls, young men and young women, teenagers and pre-teenagers, of every shade of skin-pigmentation, are revealed beneath the finest cut-away designer sportwear: perfect gluteus and trapezius muscles, chests, breasts, ankles and napes of the neck. Black thighs in bright white Schwinn shin-socks, ice-blue raked-satin Cobra shorts – blond-haired pairs, slender in luminous leotards, lycra leggings, numbered Adidas team tops, Swedish sweat-bands, matching lilac and magnolia Ikawa tracksuit creations, brand new white leather Bauer skateboots with Veriflex plates and All Black toe-stops, rush by with the hushed sound of seafoam breaking on a pebbled shore.

Swish. Swish.
It's the early morning workout on the Mall before the sun

softens up the asphalt, before the Upper East Side joggers start to head across the Park to their midtown offices, before anything of any importance has happened in the day. A slender dawn-gilded young woman pedals by, no hands, on a chrome-plate Cinelli mixteframe bicycle. It has immaculate titanium Campag 3-DIM gear-changers and a sexy Vitesse chain-set. She has short spiked purple hair by Carlton Laplace and a Malayan reticulated python draped around her shoulders, embracing her waist, its throat supported on the crown of her head with an expression on its mouth that belongs to a species which has successfully tamed one less intelligent than its own for the purpose of getting about town. A couple of lovers straddle the center of the strip, touchingly intimate. She is a pretty woman in a silver Bonwit Teller dance outfit. Her face is familiar – maybe you saw her on a t.v. commercial recently. He, of course, is Bo, the famous Broadway midget actor, cool in Cartier mirror-reflecting shades. He skates backward in the opposite direction to her on custom-miniaturized trucks, assured, his upper arm wrapped around the inside of his girlfriend's silver thigh. Her hand rests on the nape of his neck. Nobody gawks at them. Why should they gawk? Here, nobody gawks at anyone. Here, every person is famous or at least familiar-looking, someone capable of defying gravity. Here, a man turns on a dime as if he owns a million dollars. And he probably does. You don't look at him and he doesn't look at you, although you can see that he is dressed in a one-off Henri Ribèc doublet-and-slacks skatesuit built out of some shimmering silky lapis lazuli-colored fabric. Henri Ribèc probably cut it from a bolt of silk last night with his own pair of scissors. It is wittily slashed and ruched for expert skating maneuvers. Without moving, the man turns through three hundred and sixty degrees with an ineffable grace. You – assuming you have the poke to be there in the first place, that is – skate by without paying him any attention.

But if you had the poke and you did pay him some attention you would see that he is watching the VDU of a cute SONY portable micro-video which he is holding in his left hand. On the screen is displayed the outside of a newly-styled corporation-type building in an old block that could be just about anywhere in any part of the midtown section of the city. After a short time a police prowl car draws to a stop in front of it. A scene from a cop drama, it looks like. The building on the screen has one of those orthogonal steel-and-glass boutique façades that cost about eight million dollars. Inside the portico someone – an old bag person? – is lying under sheets of newspaper. Two police officers in pressed marine blue cottons climb out of the prowl car, slow and easy, the way they do, and politely urge the old bag person to keep moving. They don't even have to take their hands – let alone their nightsticks – off their hips. Eventually the bag person – he is wearing an unfashionable two-piece tan herringbone suit, crumpled – ups and gathers his worldly possessions and hits the road and the two cops climb back into their vehicle and disappear from the screen.

The young man in the Henri Ribèc skatesuit continues to pirouette and watch the screen, both, although now the screen is empty of people. There is just the building. He presses one of the mode-change keys – he's bored with this movie – and the picture abruptly disappears. Coincidentally the earth shudders under a dull explosive thud which most of the beautiful skaters, even those immured inside the thudding of their personal music systems, are aware of and react to. If you were there, you would probably look round to see what the fuck's going on the same as everyone else.

The front of the steel-and-glass boutique has disappeared from the screen of the man's SONY, blown upwards and outwards in a cloud of smoke and dust, masonry and other construction debris. For a moment the screen goes white with smoke. Nothing happens until, from within the building itself, bits of lifeless bodies begin to appear, tumbling out of the smoke into the street. Arms – legs – hands – feet. The street is suddenly strewn with fragments of the building shell, modular office furniture, porcelain toilet bowls, mixed together with limbs torn from mutilated torsos, severed elbows and knees, colorful pieces of clothing fluttering from them. When the smoke clears, the severed heads of women, cock-eyed, blond- and dark-haired, lie still among the destruction as the dust settles on them. Only the expressions on their faces remain intact.

Nearly all the skaters pause to wonder about the explosion and to pass some remark concerning the mushroom of black smoke sprouting up a few blocks south, right close by.

Holy Jeezus!

What'ya maka that?

It muss be on Sixth. . . .

Seventh. . . .

The smoke plume rises straight up and then collapses under its own weight. You all watch it, the purple-haired woman on the chrome Cinelli and the purple-haired woman's reticulated python, the midget Broadway acrobat actor, Bo, and his pretty familiar-faced girlfriend.

Oh boy! Did you see that?

I juss don' believe this!

Holy smoke!

Meanwhile the young fella in the exquisite lapis lazuli silk suit – daringly cut on the bias, you can't help noticing, snagging the oblique early morning rays of sunlight – skates along with the crowd, half-watching the plume drifting across the clear blue sky, half-watching on his cute hand-sized computer the pretty blonde Channel Eleven anchor-ette introducing the Early Bird News program, his pair of off-white Canal Street snakes swishing against the black road surface.

Swish. Swish.

'MAGIC! PURRR MAGIC! . . . .' the man said. 'Is what I'm saying youda seen, you were there las' night at the Shea Stadium! The Mets doolin' with their ol' rivals from 'cross the River. Game five of the Series, probably the most thrillingly atrocious con'est ever perp'trated on a World Series. . . .'

The sound of the television woke Professor Summers at 7:05. The usual time. The excited voice of the Channel Nine anchor, Harvey Walker, first vibrated the tympanum of her middle ear –

'. . . The Mets, looking pretty good in their new tie-fronted tabard jerseys from Zhorrer. . . .'

– then passed along the spiral fluids inside her cochlea to where the auditory nerves deciphered the vibrations for her brain to make sense of – what all the excitement was about.

'. . . Have finally gotten away from the frou-frou image that dogged them all last season when they were with Osca Selzer. Las' night they looked much more like a baseball team. The essentially loose and romantically structured coordinated collection mixed together seriousness and wit. There was a polished untricksy finish to their turnout. To the kind of East Coast refinement you use to expect from this team before its excursion into whimsy, Zhorrer has brought a quiet sensuality expressed in very simple designs but made up of the *slinkiest* fabrics! Cashmere and silk, crepe de chine, lycra. . . .'

The smiling face of Harvey Walker cast its reflection, back to front, on her eyelids before striking her retina upside down. The optic nerve, the only section of the retina which could not register the image – her blind spot – conducted Harvey Walker towards the opposite hemisphere of her brain for it to unscramble.

'. . . The discreetly scrolled peplums at the trim of their warm-up jackets were just right! And habitually soigné pinch hitter Chris Karan, looking his most restrained, brought the park to its feet with his witty tribute to the old Doge, Vincent Torelli: extravagant butterfly revers in laminated acetate plastic! But it was Karan, in fact, who

5

killed the inning by grounding out, stranding two men on the corners. . . .'

The sound of the television, particularly of the voice of Harvey Walker, was the only alarm the Professor had found which was guaranteed to shake her and wake her from her dreams, get her up, out of bed, into the shower and on with her life. She was nearly always – in her dreams – deep in the heart of her favorite jungle where she was stalking and being stalked, embracing her peril, experiencing the alternate sensations of being both very small and very large. Giant insects copulated with her while, simultaneously, they bit each other's heads off. She possessed vast nacreous wings, compound eyes, a chitinous carapace. She had a proboscis and ovipositor with which to hunt prey, evade predators, mate. She was a huge assassin bug that has just sighted its favorite species of tree leaf-hopper. She was also the tree leaf-hopper that the assassin bug just sighted.

Out of one eye Delia watched the Yankees pitcher – Mel Gomez, it looked like – peering over his shoulder at the man on first before going into his windup, and then Chris Karan bunting the grounder to the nearest infielder.

It was one hell of an awakening.

Without moving more than her lower left arm and her finger tips she zapped channels. Channel Eleven had pretty blonde Bonnie West, the most personable of all the morning news presenters, summing up the latest opinion poll for the Mayoral Election – currently the big news story – due to take place tomorrow. The two main rivals were running each other neck and neck. On Seven there was a portrait of candidate Rocco Da Silva – a feature-length advertisement. Thirteen, to coincide, was running the same for the other contender, Tina Rauch. Eight, of course, had Kiddies Time cartoons. Cheapo Four had a cheapo archive clip of Tina and Rocco dancing a merengue with each other in the good ol' days. You couldn't get away from them, whichever channel you tried. Rocco and Tina, between the two of them, had bought up almost all the available time.

Resigned to the fact, Delia returned the picture to the ballgame on Nine and slid out of bed and headed for the bathroom, on the way pausing to say good morning to the pair of dead-leaf-shaped Bolivian bush crickets which she had installed in a slatted bamboo Malayan cicada cage and suspended at eye-level from a length of cord. In the half-light it took her a moment to distinguish them from the dead leaves inside the cage. Both insects – the male Simón, and Conchita, the female – were akinetic against their habitat and as far apart from each other as they could get, no different than any other old married couple. Or – it was even possible – they weren't able to distinguish one Bolivian bush cricket from a dead-looking leaf either. Delia Summers – for the sake of the species they belonged to – sincerely hoped this was not the case.

She sat on the lilac-tinted seat in front of the t.v. screen just as Romeo Moschino, in a saddle-shouldered lycra jersey with striped team-color rib-knit trims, paralysed by the crowd's roar, let Calvin Laroche's lazy two-out grounder go untouched between his feet – forcing the Mets to accept the winning run. Oh boy! Delia laughed all the way down to her belly. The sphincter muscles of her bladder wall relaxed while, reflexly, those in her urethra contracted, releasing the pressure on her kidneys. Exquisitely. She pissed the bottle of Château Margaux – now voided of its taste, color, body, alcohol content – into the lilac ceramic bowl. It was a slow and satisfying experience. Almost as slow and satisfying as it had been drinking the stuff last night in the first place.

'. . . Well, for their part,' the voice of Harvey Walker was saying over the picture, 'the Yankees looked as assured as we've come to expect them to – right down to their stirrup stockings. Clean lines. Sober colors. Spartan. Their traditional neat no-frills cropped bolero jackets were a sensation. So what's new? And the box-pleats concealed inside the pinstripe of their uniform trousers, well it said everything about the reverence in which this team holds the traditions of this great game. Fact, at times the severity of the dark and white look of the Yankees seriously aggressed the dawn blush of the Mets' pastel blue and orange combinations. It was an ol' fashion tussle 'tween classic New York minimalism and dare-you-do New York flair. Some like it cool, some with spice. Course, y'all going to have your 'pportunity tomorrow to express your own preference. . . .'

Delia Summers took her shower and let herself forget about the Mets' freak win over the Yankees. The commentators wouldn't waste any time telling her what it was going to mean as far as the Mayoral race was concerned – the effect the win would have on Tina Rauch's supporters. And, for that matter, on the Yankees' major shareholder, Rocco Da Silva. Instead, she lowered her eyelids and let the hot downpour recall her dream of freak tropical rainstorms in turbid hydroglyphic forests. It was a sound she loved. She had heard it once – during her research spell in Brazil – for real.

She rubbed down and powdered her body. Across the bathroom the Yankees' right fielder was playing a single with his chest for an error and so letting the Met get to third. Shaking her head in disbelief, she lifted the lid of the autoclave and took out a sealed paper sachet which she tore open without examining. She extracted a warm sterilized set of robin-egg blue bra and panties and stepped into them, her eyes on the play. It was unbelievable! The Yankees were going all out to play worse than the Mets! How do you blow a two-run lead in the bottom of the 11th with two outs and nobody on base? Harvey Walker was right. It was rivetingly bad baseball. Delia unfolded and zipped herself into a pressed pair of lichen and taupe combat fatigues, cool and crisp as a nurse's uniform, just as Cody La Renta – of all people – was bollixing the seventh sacrifice bunt attempt of the game. If that's what they wanted to call it.

Returning to the living area – showered, dressed, faintly amused – Delia took a slow-motion Di Maggio swing with the knotted towel in her hand at the bamboo sphere containing the silent pair of Bolivian bush crickets, accidentally making contact with the cage and sending it spinning on the end of its cord. It was unbelievable! The species was down to a handful of members and here were these two, Simón and Conchita, acting coy. Or, maybe they thought, what the hell? Now that there was no Bolivian bush left to speak of, they had decided it wasn't worth the effort any more.

She hand-adjusted the electronic jalousie which was set into the glass comprising the entire far wall of the living study area. A reflection of the finger of sunlight creeping down the rear of the tall building opposite filled the apartment. Below lay the lush canopy of the atrium, almost the tropical forest of her dreams, a controlled wilderness of greasy greens and hidden gold: flies, spiders, beetles, small amphibians, various reptiles. It was the domain of her research, and monitoring the delicate balance between the various environments it contained was her responsibility, what she was paid for.

Ignoring the blank IBM VDU, she crossed the length of the window toward the lighted fishtank where the vividly-colored male guppy was already displaying to the female, flashing his flank in front of her eyes. For her part, the female, gravid with eggs, looked rather unimpressed. Delia Summers was interested in the enormous amount of time certain polygynous males were prepared to put in before females responded. She would have liked to have known for certain, for example, what advantage the female gained by mating preferentially with the most splendid males, the ones with the most vigorous courtship display. She wasn't convinced that such a male was necessarily the fittest. Display had little to do with general ability – to mate, find food, avoid predators. Not in her experience, anyway.

She turned.

As she turned to reach for the plastic canister of ground fish-meal which she used to feed them –

The fishtank exploded

– to stop them feeding on each other, the blast –

The television screen and that of the IBM library imploded

— threw her across the living area, along with the furniture, the old La-Z-Boy recliner, the fishtank and its contents and most of the glass from the viewing wall with the built-in electronic jalousie, a shard of which collided with her right thigh, another with her forehead. Her turning gesture had saved her life.

Professor Summers lay on the floor of her apartment, conscious and stunned, watching the colorful little South Seas fish gyrating in front of her eyes on the damp carpet next to her face. They reminded her of the two candidates for the Mayor's office dancing a merengue with each other. She lay there in a waking dream, paralysed – her own blood running into her mouth from the wound in her head – until the fish gradually ceased gyrating and just twitched and then became completely still. And then – in the absolute silence that followed – Simón, the Bolivian bush cricket, started up the high-pitched continuous stridulation which the male of the species customarily emits to alert any female in the vicinity that he is there, at hand and at her service.

THE BACK room of Max Faraday's house on Cross Bay Boulevard looked out onto the deserted Bird Sanctuary that looked across Jamaica Bay to the deserted airport. It was one of those old pine-shingled wood-framed two-storey houses that line both shores of the isthmus route to Rockaway. The property had been rejoisted and renovated by the previous owner and was probably in better shape now than the day it was built. The back room, on the second floor, gave out onto a wooden deck where there were some white plastic chairs and a table with a red and white Martini umbrella which had come with the house. The deck projected over wild timothy grass that stretched all the way to the mudflats. On summer days you could see cranes out there without even opening the french windows. Facing north, the back room was cool and shady. It was unfashionably furnished with articles from a random assortment of periods and places. On the floor there was a worn Afghan kilim and several dhurries, in the corner a chrome and emerald green 1940s 78 r.p.m. jukebox that looked like a 1940s idea of a spaceship about to take off. There was an antique round English center-legged oak table, every available space on which was covered with periodicals and papers and a brand new-looking 1947 black enameled office typewriter bearing the trade name of the small arms manufacturer. There were pieces of figurative china on the mantel, hardcover books in bookshelves, framed fragments of nonrepresentational embroidery on the walls and – incongruous on the glass table near Faraday – a modern television.

'. . . Coming out of their primaries with big victories behind them, the two Mayoral candidates are still neck and neck in the run up to Election Day. At their respective press briefings yesterday, Tina Rauch and Rocco Da Silva were both in confident mood, each claiming they already have the endorsements they need to win outright. A number of constituences have still to pledge their support one way or the other, however, and both candidates admitted that a lot will depend on who puts up the best performance during their scheduled t.v. clash on the Robbie Robson Show at the St Regis-Sheraton Hotel tomorrow. On Channel Eleven. Starting at eight o'clock. . . .'

Max Faraday – he was reclining with his back to the t.v. in his antique mahogany manager's chair, the kind that swivels and pivots at the same time – swirled black coffee inside a chipped white Wedgwood porcelain tea cup, listening with half an ear to the Early Bird News Show while he tried to picture in his mind's eye what outfit the news-presenter was wearing today. Was it her cheerful Toe Knee Girl lowcut denim blouson or her grave Bill Rodgers grosgrain skirt with strapless piqué top? It would depend, of course, on the quotient of gravity or cheer in today's main story. Over his coffee Faraday, for the hell of it, tried to gauge from the content of the news item she was presenting the form in which it was being presented. Inside the still unlit back room the colorful reflection of the television screen flickered against the wall in front of him, fractured, pretty, like a video of ghosts recalling each other's past lives – a wistful reverse reflection. Blues and creams smudged into each other, apparently synchronous with the cadence of the newscaster's fractured pretty intonation. She was wearing her cornflower blue and white crepe dress, he decided, the one with the Eton collar. Unless she had gotten something new recently that he had not seen yet.

'. . . Speculation is growing every minute, of course, concerning the Rocco-Tina clash . . .' she said. 'This special edition of the Rob Rob Show – sponsored by *Vogue Magazine* – will make an exciting climax to the season and many voters have indicated that they are going to hold their option until they get a good look at the two candidates and what they stand for. . . .'

The voters, in other words, would watch the two candidates with their fingers on the electoral facility in their t.v. remotes until they couldn't bear it any longer.

When Faraday couldn't bear it any longer he swiveled the chair round to face the t.v. and looked for himself.

The young woman on the screen paused, batted her eyelids slowly as she glanced down towards the flowers on the otherwise featureless desktop in front of her. She might easily have been an elementary school teacher acknowledging the small token of adoration from one of her pupils. A brief shy smile traveled across her lips, momentarily producing the illusion that it was him, Max Faraday, that she was smiling at. It was his attention she was seeking to engage. Faraday found himself smiling too. It was by such small intimate gestures that he knew her. He and forty-five million other people.

Today she was wearing her cornflower-blue silk crepe summer dress, the one with the white Eton collar, perfect like a problem in geometry. And for a change she had her hair up in a French pleat, revealing the curve of her neck. Her smiling lips had been dusted with a soft pinky-purple lipglow that subtly echoed the single spray of pinky-purple sweet-pea in the fluted vase on the desk top. She looked terrific. The combination of guiltlessness and sincerity that she projected was irresistible. Anyone would have believed anything this young woman said. The uncomplicated sexuality radiating from her was that of a younger sister. Most of the time Faraday didn't think about it but when he did it provoked in him innocent and pleasurable frissons of guilt. In Faraday and in forty-five million other people.

'. . . For those of you who just joined us, Hi! I'm Bonnie West and this is the Channel Eleven Early Bird News you're watching – the first with the Latest! Brought to you today courtesy of the Raxell Communications Company. . . .'

The gentle slopes of her intonation, rising and falling like soft snow following the contours of solid ground, communicated her sincerity. The timbre of her voice rang true like honest china, made only more credible by the human imperfections of her grammar.

'. . . News is just coming in of an explosion that rocked the Garment District this morning when a bomb went off inside the Torelli Fashion House on Seventh Avenue. Although this was only a short time before shoppers and workers would normally be in the area, miraculously there were *no* casualties . . .' Bonnie West said. 'We understand, however, that a number of new Torelli creations were destroyed. So far. . . .'

Behind Bonnie West's voice pictures illustrated the unhappy consequences of the terrorist attack. Yellow-helmeted firefighters were wading among the debris while police forensic officers, some of them in uniform, were examining the charred torsos, the slumped mutilated bodies, of the destroyed mannequins, upon the blistered limbs of which fragments of Signor Torelli's gowns still clung in shreds. It wasn't a very pleasant sight. One officer was shown cradling the remains of a slender lower arm, the delicate fingers still intact – you could just make out the nailpolish on them. The t.v. camera clos ed onto the mildly surprised expression on the pretty face of a blond-haired completely severed head. Then it moved onto the tiny pathetic shape of a child's body which a female officer was in the act of salvaging from the mess, its colorful cotton overalls unscathed. One of the legs still had a brand new white Nike sport shoe on its foot while the other leg was missing the foot altogether.

'. . . So far the police have been unable to provide an explanation for the attack. But Signor Torelli, apparently, was due to launch a private showing of his newest original designs later today. Some of these had been expected to sell for hundreds of thousands of dollars. Many international personalities were expected to attend at the building only moments after the bomb detonated. The police, however, are not prepared to comment on who of these might legitimately be considered a terrorist target. . . .'

Faraday couldn't help smiling at Bonnie West's turn of phrase: how *anyone* could legitimately be considered a terrorist target!

On the screen a calm disorder reigned. Nobody was rushing around. The firefighters were rolling up their hoses. The fire was out. Forensic experts sifted among the destruction like archaeologists who had all the time in the world. They would piece the fragments together in the laboratory later. A balding overweight precinct detective – his gun on his hip – punching out numbers on a handphone was about the most frantic thing taking place.

Faraday lowered the white chipped Wedgwood cup into the white Wedgwood saucer and placed the saucer with the cup onto the glass table next to the white handset. He had his hand on the handset at the very moment that it began to peep. On the screen the face of Bonnie West returned.

'. . . Well, we'll get back to you soon as we have any developments in the Torelli bombing,' she said, her voice modulated to suit the gravity of the occasion. 'But don't go away now. We have more coming up soon. . . .'

Faraday's handset chimed. Reluctantly he killed the sound of Bonnie West – now in a canary silksatin short skirt and scarlet cloqué shirt – promoting the products of the Raxell Communications Company.

'Morning Captain,' he said into the phone without waiting for the caller to announce himself.

'I – ah – din't get you outta bed or nothing, did I?' Captain O'Duff said pleasantly.

'Not at all, Captain,' Faraday said. 'I was just watching the Early Bird Show.'

'I'm sorry, Lieutenant! I didn't mean to disturb you while you were – ah – *working*. . . .'

Faraday bared his teeth at the t.v. image of Bonnie West. He enjoyed his boss's sarcasm. 'Don't worry about it, sir,' he said. 'What can I do for you?'

It was a joke they enjoyed sharing. Faraday's method of working – so far as the tough overweight precinct detective was concerned – consisted of attending art gallery preview parties, reading the society pages of the overpriced glossy fashion magazines and, above all, watching t.v. Whereas Captain O'Duff was paid to run down dark alleys after crims with his gun. The joke was one they cherished and kept alive. They had no alternative. It was about the only thing they had in common.

'Then I guess you already worked out the whole story.

What happened, who did it, why and how?' O'Duff snickered at his own jibe.

Faraday said nothing.

'Vincent Torelli's factory was hit early this morning. Bombed out. Could be a straightforward torch job or something with a bit of finesse. Torelli is a big noise in the couture end of the fashion market.'

'I know.'

'I know *you* know!' O'Duff growled. 'Me, I only found out ten minutes ago! I figured *you*'d know! Fact I was wondering if I could persuade you to drop by, you got the time, and give the Department the benefit of some of your expert knowledge.'

'You sure you need me? The forensic team can probably sleuth this without any help from me.'

'Shake your ass over here, Faraday!' O'Duff murmured. 'Toot sweet.'

Tall in her peep-toe stiletto sling-backs, slender in her very short slinky skirt, her hair nonchalantly wind-tossed, Bonnie West riveted the eye. Disarmingly sexy, she probably had no idea that the equation of her anatomy, the garments adorning it multiplied by her personality, was being used to sell Raxell Communications hardware. She probably sincerely believed every word she uttered concerning the superiority of their product.

'I'm on my way, Captain.'

Maxwell Faraday, Lieutenant, second grade, of the 19th Precinct, the most senior semiotician on the homicide squad, lowered the handset into its cradle.

2

It was as if a bite had been taken out of the side elevation of the old ten-storey midtown building. A geological section of construction techniques from different periods in its history had been revealed by the explosion. Between the elegantly dressed masonry of the exterior and the attractive pastel-colored gesso walls inside, it was possible to distinguish the supportive structures, decorative panels, utility membranes, the severed vermicelli of generations of heating and ventilating conduits. The ancient rubble that had lain for so long between the courses of the original walls was now mixed up with the more recent rubble – a poignant reminder, Faraday mused, of the rubbish that is nearly always concealed inside the structure of otherwise elegant, outwardly organized statements.

Faraday hoped that Dinah Lazlo, the chief forensic officer in conversation with Captain O'Duff, would find what she was looking for, but the building held no interest for himself. The magical paradox between within and without – from a semiological point of view, one of the qualities that distinguishes human constructs from natural phenomena – had been removed. 700 Seventh Avenue, as a building, no longer existed.

Amid the ruined masonry Dinah Lazlo was being discreetly filmed by the News syndicate crew. She looked good in her tailored sta-prest cotton navy zipsuit, the shiny white patent leather of her gun holster-strap accentuating her waist. She looked good standing there with one hand on her hip and the other holding fragments of the blast, charred fabrics whose luminescent colors had been singed dramatically. An analysis of these would lead her towards discovering who had planted the bomb – and how. Dinah Lazlo was a forensic scientist. The best. She would be able to calculate the position of the bomb from the angle of the debris, and the signature of the manufacturer from its construction. If she let them, the t.v. crew would follow her as far as the Department laboratory where her staff would make their tests. By the end of the week she would be a minor media star. And she looked the part in her gold-framed Dior tinted lunettes, although Faraday suspected that she wore these not because contacts were incompatible with her corneas, as she claimed, but because eyeglasses made her look more like a forensic scientist. The lunettes were an item of functional jewelry.

Faraday knew that it was something that puzzled O'Duff that he had never been able to come to terms with Dinah Lazlo, who was a good cop of her kind. The best. Nevertheless, she got on his nerves. Whereas he was quite fond of Faraday who – almost everyone was agreed – wasn't much of any kind of cop. This didn't puzzle Faraday, however. Anyone could see that O'Duff was impressed by Dinah Lazlo's efficiency and alarmed by her sexuality. He respected her and he feared her. It got on his nerves that someone could be so neat and clever and also so attractive and desirable.

'. . . If the person or persons who planted the device was out to knock off thirty of the finest Italian female-shaped mannequins, they did a great job,' Dinah Lazlo was saying to O'Duff as Faraday approached. Overhead a pale blue SkyPol helicopter hovered low in the sky, motionless over the remains of the building while, incongruously, one or two brightly colored butterflies congregated in patches of sunlight around the yellow helmets of the fighters. '. . . The first floor has gone, and most of the second and third. That means the workshops and the demo-stage. The manne- quins, apparently, were decked out with Mr Torelli's new gowns for the models to jump right into soon as they arrived. . . .' Dinah Lazlo consulted her molded white natural rubber Tissot chronometer. '. . . Any moment now.'

The police Lieutenant with the PhD nodded in Faraday's direction – out of respect, perhaps, for Faraday's own qualifications. O'Duff made no acknowledgement of his arrival at all. As far as the Captain in homicide was concerned, the Lieutenant semiotician didn't have any qualifications.

All around them water was steaming from the puddles in the warm sunshine. Wet slivers of broken glass slewed and crunched underfoot. It was like walking on thawing ice except that the temperature was already up in the eighties. O'Duff was in his shirtsleeves. He had his jacket hooked over his shoulder, his gun-holster frankly admitting to the world – which is to say the t.v. audience – his identity as a plainclothes law-enforcement officer – in Faraday's opinion the main function of that particular accessory. Another piece of functional jewelry.

'These gowns,' O'Duff asked Dinah Lazlo. 'How many Ks they fetch?'

Dinah Lazlo prudently glanced at Faraday.

'About a small briefcase-full,' Faraday said. 'Apiece.'

'Oh hello, Lieutenant! Glad you could make it.' O'Duff grinned menacingly.

'Max is right,' Dinah Lazlo said. 'You want to run your eye down the guest list for today's preview. Film stars. Sport personalities. Politicians. You'll have heard of nearly all of them.' She inflected her emphasis to mean: Even *you*, Clarence O'Duff, will have heard of nearly all of them.

'I wouldn't bet money on that,' O'Duff muttered. 'But show me anyway.' He took Lieutenant Lazlo by the arm and guided her away from the t.v. cameras. 'Oh, and Lieutenant . . .' he said to Faraday over his shoulder. 'Whyn't you go talk with Mr Torelli. I understand you two speak the same language.'

Faraday picked his way among the disembodied limbs that were entangled with the wreckage. Heads and torsos of varying hair and skin color lay in contorted attitudes of pain and ecstasy that recalled a medieval picture of Death. Any moment now the pieces were going to be joined together to be Judged for the Last Time. The scene imparted a peculiar feeling that was both tragic and hilarious. Exotically colored fragments of lawn and faille and crepe de chine snared the eye and provided camouflage for the butterflies.

Dinah Lazlo's assistant, Sergeant Kriwazcek, posted outside the glass door leading from the showroom to the chambers in back — presumably to keep the t.v. crew from penetrating too far into the building and stumbling on the truth before O'Duff did — nodded at Faraday and stood aside to allow him to pass, politely indicating where he would find the owner of the premises. Faraday passed along the ghost of a corridor until he emerged from the shell of the old block into the modern central well behind it. The building abruptly gave way to a verdant mass of tropical vegetation. He paused. Billowing overhead, a canopy of tall evergreen leaves, palm fronds and tree-ferns reticulated the light onto his face and his hands. Rivulets of clear water trickled out of a carpet of mossy liverworts and dense clumps of horsehairs and fern thalluses. Faraday shivered, apprehensive to find himself suddenly in an environment entirely bereft of human signs. It was a moist, succulent, primitive world in which creepers hugged and tugged each other and blades of sunlight slashed at shield-shaped leaves in a silent stationary pitched battle. Only the concealed jets of mist spraying the air and the hum of the helicopter hovering immediately over the shattered roof of the atrium gave any indication that this was not a piece of West African jungle.

'Yes?'

The single human utterance traveled through the dense foliage in Faraday's direction, its rising intonation barbed with suspicion like a poisoned dart. Faraday froze, unnerved to be sniped at by a speaker whom he could not see in a tropical jungle otherwise devoid of speech. He turned very slowly, warily, as he imagined a reptile might turn at the approach of a predator. He allowed his eyes to swivel inside their sockets.

Silence.

Faraday waited, peering in the direction from which the voice had come. Leaves and the shadows of leaves were layered impenetrably over each other, slits of sunlight blinking through them at him. He saw only merging greens and the flash of a small luminescent blue butterfly.

'What do you want?' the voice – behind him now – enquired. Faraday, taken by surprise, jerked around, at the same moment that a young woman stepped out of the foliage. She was wearing a light cotton foliage-colored pantsuit slashed with grey, and dark soldier-length hair. She stood watching him, her eyes brimming in the reflected sunlight. In her right hand she carried some kind of fine gauze net.

'. . . And, if I may ask, who the hell *are* you?'

'Max – well, ah – Faraday. Lieutenant. 19th Precinct,' Faraday stammered. He fumbled for his buzzer and when he found it held it open in his hand. The woman turned it the right way up to examine it. She had a smooth-skinned attractive face with a strong symmetrical mouth. Open stitch-plaster criss-crossed a recent flesh wound on her forehead.

'I was hoping to talk to Mr Torelli,' he said.

'He spoke with the detective already,' she said, handing his buzzer back to him, closed. 'Answered all his questions.'

'I don't want to ask him any questions. I just want to talk to him.'

'Why?'

Faraday shrugged. 'It's my job. I work for the Police Department.'

'I know. 19th Precinct. Lieutenant, second grade. You're a cop.'

'Part cop, part semiotician.'

'Ah – someone with an interest in signs?'

Faraday nodded.

'. . . Codes? The social aspects of language?'

He nodded again.

She took a step in Faraday's direction, holding as she did onto one of the plants in her way, bending it toward Faraday for him to take a close look at. The soft leaves had fine-toothed edges and they were covered with minute yellow egg-shaped protruberances.

'These are signs, Lieutenant. What do you think makes them?'

'Some kind of insect?' Faraday hazarded. This wasn't really his territory.

'Not bad. But you're mistaken. In fact these are identical to the eggs of the heliconius butterfly. This plant is a passion flower. It manufactures these nodules to deter the female butterfly from laying her eggs on the plant and its larvae, when they hatch, from chewing it up. The female heliconius will see them and find some other passion flower to lay on rather than submit her offspring to more competition than she has to. Neat, huh? So you see, Lieutenant Semiotician, signs can sometimes be deceptive. These are made by a plant to look like they were made by an insect.'

Faraday grinned. 'And you are a biologist.'

'Part biologist,' she said. Her strong symmetrical mouth half-returned his smile. Beads of sweat had gathered in the little indentation over her upper lip. 'Part arachnologist.'

'Someone with an interest in spiders?'

She nodded. 'I hold the chair in Arthropod Behavior at the Sherman Fairchild Center for Life Sciences.' She held out her hand towards Faraday. 'Delia Summers. I also switch-hit as Mr Torelli's personal assistant.' She gestured with the net. 'I'm in charge of all this.'

They shook hands. When Faraday was about to withdraw his hand from hers she held on to it. 'This is a sign, Lieutenant. Is it the kind you interpret?'

Faraday – he had no choice but to look the woman straight in the eyes – felt uneasy. He had a horrible suspicion that his mind was being read. His carnal reaction to her was being registered.

'The handshake has its, ah, semiology, sure,' he said.

'And its biology also,' Delia Summers said. She gave him back his hand as if it were an old glove he had mislaid.

'I guess I deal in more conventional signs,' he said. 'The

languages of people. Clothes, hairstyles, fashions. . . . That's why I'm here. I want to talk to Mr Torelli about his collection.'

Delia Summers grimaced. 'There isn't much left of it,' she said. She lifted the fine green gauze net for Faraday to see for himself. Inside a fold in the gauze, gathered against her hand, a large black swallow-tailed butterfly with purple and vermilion chevrons on its folded wings struggled against the walls of the net. 'Most of the collection that wasn't zapped outright by the explosion escaped through the. . . .' She raised her eyes toward the shattered glass dome-roof of the atrium. 'You want to see it?'

Faraday followed Delia Summers into the undergrowth until they came to a green-painted wooden pavilion inside which an assortment of non-native butterflies flapped around or else clung to the perforations in the zinc panels. Delia Summers crouched onto her haunches next to the muslin trap entrance set into the side of the pavilion. Behind the zinc panels rows of larvae were stacked in ranks from framed hooks onto a central pillar, identically symmetrical according to their species like gridded computer circuitry. They reminded Faraday of mummies embalmed inside sarcophaghi waiting inside a pyramid to emerge into the presence of Horus.

'We don't have any place else to put them right now,' Delia Summers said. 'This is just an emergency measure till we can seal the breach.'

Her left hand slid into the folded net and gripped the swallow-tailed insect expertly at the point where the wings joined onto the thorax, drew out the butterfly and transferred it into the pavilion through the muslin trap where she released it. Faraday, standing over her, became conscious that he was watching the pallor of her skin at the point where her neck, lengthened by the shortness of her haircut, was released into the darkness of her tunic.

'The detective . . .' she said.

'O'Duff.'

'. . . Was very considerate. It was he arranged for the

SkyPol chopper to maintain altitude over the atrium. He figured it might create a fast cool turbulence that would discourage the butterflies from staging a mass getaway. He could see it was the only thing Vincent cared about. It might even work.'

'That doesn't sound like we're talking about the same Captain O'Duff,' Faraday said.

'The Captain assured us . . .' she looked up at Faraday over her shoulder, '. . . that we would *not* get disturbed. We have a lot of work to do here.'

'I guess he just wanted to keep you away from news-starved t.v. crews. They'd be crawling over this place, you gave them the chance. Captain O'Duff was saving you for himself.'

'I see.' Delia Summers stood up and turned around to face Faraday. Tiny shadows freckled her nose. She wore no makeup except perhaps a touch of liner. She didn't need to. Her skin was perfect. 'The Captain, sounds to me, would be at home in the insect world,' she said. She shook her net loose.

'O'Duff? He's a preying mantis!'

'It's *pray* with an *a*, you know that? And it's mantid with a *d*. And it's only the female of the species you want to watch out for. She takes the shape of someone at prayer when she is devouring the male – in the act of copulating with him.'

Her mouth formed into a smile for him. He felt a sudden urge to make a closer inspection of it, but the import of what it had just uttered deterred him from venturing.

'Vincent Torelli is this way,' she said, immediately striking out into the jungle, brushing aside palm fronds which closed behind her. Faraday followed before she disappeared completely.

A concrete causeway led them circuitously through what must have originally been the central well of the surrounding buildings. The tamarinds and bamboo gave way. A shaft of sunlight speared down through the bomb-shattered roof, collecting in the fragments of glass lying over the ground in jagged puddles that reflected the sky and which Faraday carefully avoided. By the time he had caught up with the biologist she had disappeared. He stood alone in the sunny glade looking for her. Delia Summers – like the princess in the fairy story – was nowhere to be seen. A cobalt butterfly approached the gaping labia of a splendid creamy-purple lily-orchid, circling it several times, dithering fetchingly. The butterfly eventually settled onto the fleshy blue calyx of the flower and, putting out its proboscis, began to imbibe the nectar. Max Faraday watched, horrified, as the beautiful petals closed very slowly over the intoxicated insect which realized too late the peril of its situation and beat its wings pathetically against the closing walls.

He picked his way between the fragments of broken glass and clumps of wet moss toward the tinkling sound of water falling over rocks. The level of the atrium floor dropped and sloped towards a narrow concrete culvert through which a stream flowed. On steps cut into the bank opposite to where Faraday was standing, Delia Summers sat next to a white-haired old-timer in a khaki tank top and white shorts held up by elasticated suspenders. On his feet he wore a pair of old white canvas sneakers without laces or socks. The old-timer and the biologist appeared to be examining something he was holding in his hand. Faraday climbed halfway down the bank until Delia Summers looked in his direction and slowly nodded. It was the solicitous gesture of a nurse toward a visitor to a patient in her care. He paused.

'Vincent, there's a police detective here,' she said. 'Lieutenant Faraday – would like to talk to you.'

The old-timer glanced up from the colossal turquoise butterfly that was lying half-open in his palm like a tiny exotically rigged beach yacht. He looked at Faraday without appearing to focus on him, with no expression on his face. Faraday offered his hand across the culvert toward Torelli who, likewise, leaned across with his own, but instead of taking Faraday's hand, carefully placed inside the outstretched palm the corpse of the butterfly.

'An African Sorcerer, Lieutenant,' he said.

25

The almost weightless insect completely covered Faraday's hand. The silver-blue of the wings, the long intact trailing tails, shimmered with a dusty sheen like – of course! – like a Vincent Torelli evening gown! It was the effect no other couturier had ever succeeded in achieving. Faraday's attention was drawn onto the black pupils staring at him out of blue irises set against brilliant white circles, unblinking and fearless. It baffled him that such gorgeous tensile beauty – the heart-breaking serenity of a desert sunset – could be constructed on a scale so vast and at the same time so minute.

'BANG!'

Faraday jumped backwards, stumbling against the rising gradient of the steps behind him. For just a fraction of a second he regretted having deliberately left his gun at home, in the sock drawer of his bureau.

'. . . BANG! . . . You're dead!'

The old-timer in khaki shorts was standing over Faraday, two fingers of his right hand pointing at his heart, the thumb cocked. There was probably something funny about the situation, but if there was Faraday found himself unable to laugh at it.

'Make sure you don't miss the point, Lieutenant!' Torelli said. 'Those eyes are not meant to frighten you. Just the reverse. They are there for you to look into, fall in love with and, maybe, want to destroy – even though they are false. And probably toxic. Any predator goes for them will be in for a surprise. And ever you get taken by surprise in this world, you're good as dead. Those beautiful eyes are an invitation to attack a non-vital part of the body.'

Faraday recovered his balance, if not his dignity, which was still smarting from the invisible bullet which had just winged him.

'Delia said you're a police officer,' Torelli went on with only a hint of irony in his intonation.

'Meant to be,' Faraday said. Why did no one take him seriously? He glanced in the direction of Delia Summers who, he saw, was watching him with amused skepticism, and handed the African Sorcerer back to Torelli. He was looking at her, into her eyes, when he said: 'You're saying their only purpose is to deceive?'

Torelli chuckled. 'It's the only purpose of *all* clothing. Ask Delia. She'll tell you. This little critter is dressed to *kill*!'

'Was,' she reminded him. 'It's dead, Vincent.'

Faraday accepted the invitation of their example and seated himself on the concrete step opposite them. He watched the old Italian couturier whose latest collection of fabulously priced gowns had been subjected to a terrorist bombing while he discussed the emergency with his personal biologist.

'It's not good,' she told him.

'How bad is not good?'

'We've lost nearly all the small-winged varieties – the European hesperides, the vanessas, the heliconids. . . .' She reeled off the names without emotion like an adjutant reporting which regiments had been destroyed in the engagement. Torelli was listening to her with his eyes clamped shut as if, in pain, he were the general who had ordered the charge. 'Those that weren't zapped outright by the blast escaped through the. . . .' She jerked her thumb up towards the noxious city atmosphere. 'But I have engaged a company of architectural artificers who say they can throw a temporary impermeable membrane over what was the roof. They should be here any moment.' Delia Summers paused. 'That's the bad news. The good news is we shouldn't forget, Vincent, that we have almost the entire stock in pupate form. With the exception of one or two varieties – such as the African Sorcerer – we should be able to replace those we have lost. Eventually. We just have to wait – and see whether we have sufficient genetic variance.'

This piece of information raised the old-timer's spirits visibly. Faraday noted the intimate glance he exchanged with his biologist.

'How do you feel about your other collection?' he said.

Torelli looked across the culvert towards him as if he had never seen him before.

'He's talking about your new designs – that were in the workshop when the bomb detonated,' Delia Summers said. 'Your gowns.'

'Feel? Not a thing. Why should I *feel* anything? A few fancy clothes aren't going to make any difference to the history of the world one way the other.'

'I understand they were worth. . . .'

'Listen Lieutenant. Let me tell you something. A bomb has gone off, right? Nobody was killed. Nobody was maimed. So what matters? Some expensive clothes? Allow me to worry about what is worth worrying about: an environment that supported a multitude of ecological systems has been destroyed. Insects have been killed and maimed. . . .' His voice faded away and then, with more power, returned: 'I don't know as I'm not even pleased the designs *have* gone – disappeared before any rich woman dressed herself up in them, sat down in them, poured wine over them, threw them over the backs of chairs. They haven't baited any traps or broken any hearts. They have existed – briefly. Isn't that enough? Nothing lasts for ever! At least they can't end up in some bank vault to be used as a piece of collateral in some shady real estate deal! Don't you understand? Now they don't exist, they have acquired a different kind of significance. They are worth more than any of the garments I have ever made! They exist only in people's imaginations!' Vincent Torelli grinned. 'Fact, they must be the most exclusive collection of women's clothes ever made!'

'WELL . . . ?'

Captain O'Duff, now with his jacket on, slid his backside onto the high wooden stool next to the one Faraday was already sitting on.

'. . . What did you find out?'

With two fingers of his right hand the Captain semaphored a short signal to the barman – two of the usual – who was standing some ways down the bar, under the television and in front of a row of upturned glasses. The barman put down the glass he was polishing and, with just one finger, returned the conventional counter-salute: check! He approached the two men without saying a word and dealt a pair of fresh coasters onto the bar in front of them.

'From today *papilio fulgurans* – the rare African Sorcerer swallowtail butterfly from Burkina Faso – is officially extinct,' Faraday said. 'The last pair of specimens were zapped by the blast this morning.'

O'Duff – Faraday watched him in the mirror – glanced sideways at him. 'Oh, I see,' he said. 'It's like that, is it?'

Faraday nodded.

'That's bad,' O'Duff muttered. 'Real bad news.' He shook his head.

Faraday nodded again. Neither of them spoke, the news was so bad. They observed a minute's silence for the demise of the African Sorcerer.

The barman – an ex-cop from the 19th Precinct by the name of Danny Keach – reappeared in front of them and placed onto the coasters two glasses of black beer. The outsides of the glasses were already coated with a cloudy film of condensed water-vapor and the tops of the beer with a thick creamy white foam which you could probably write your phone code in. 'Two o' the usual,' he said with a voice from which twenty-five years in the squadroom had removed whatever expression it had once possessed. He sauntered back down the bar and picked up the next glass in the row. He was wearing one of those old-fashioned white bib-aprons that tie in a bow behind, the kind you hardly ever see anymore. Mild-mannered, quiet-spoken, Danny

Keach ran a mild, quiet bar. Faraday found it hard to believe some of the stories the older guys at the 19th told about him.

Right now the bar – except for themselves – was empty. And tranquil – except for the hum of the big window-fan set high up over the door, level with the sidewalk, churning in the city fumes. Hardly any of the lights were switched on. The juke box was inactive and the t.v. screen flickered with replays of last night's ballgame, without the sound. Slowed up and at normal speed, it looked as if the Yankees were teeing off the Mets but, everyone now knew, they were in for a surprise. Faraday began to relax. The current of colliding oxygen and hydrocarbon molecules stirred up by the window-fan produced the illusion of a pleasantly refreshing breeze.

O'Duff lifted his glass and spoke.

'Max. . . .'

He took a sip out of the ice-cool black beer and waited until it hit the spot.

'. . . You know, I know you and me, we like to kid each other around. Agree to pretend that one of us is the Dumb Cop and the other is the Professor. Right? We like to score off each other. But you know something. . . .'

O'Duff looked across towards Faraday, a white mustache of foam on his top lip.

'. . . You ain't *so* dumb.'

'Thanks, Captain,' Faraday said, wary at O'Duff's use of his given name. 'I do my best.'

'Fact, I don't know what I'd do without you – to remind me that we're only dealing with terrorist bombings, murders, political assassinations, that sort of thing. I forget that there are things more important – like extinct butter-flies and what kind of dress Tina Rauch will be wearing on the Robbie Robson Show tomorrow night.'

'Oh, I see,' Faraday said, unable to conceal his surprise. 'It's like that, is it?'

O'Duff nodded.

'I been doing some semi-logical detection work myself. Hope you don't mind. I unnerstand Tina Rauch was on that guestlist to attend at the Torelli House for the private viewing or whatever it was. Not part of her public schedule. I unnerstand she was going to try on her new dress, the one she plans to wear on t.v.'

'Figures. Torelli gowns are her trademark. She looks pretty good in them too,' Faraday said.

'You don't say?'

O'Duff stared at the image of himself in the mirror on the other side of the bar but without appearing to see it. Gray-haired, balding, running to fat, he didn't look like a man who gave a damn how good Tina Rauch looked in her new Torelli gown. His mouth drooped sadly under his graying mustache.

'You know, when I was your age – a bit younger maybe, before I joined the Department,' he said, 'I use to be a good-looking boy. Rode a Harley-Davidson 1000 c.c. Silver Hawk. Ever heard of a Silver Hawk?'

Faraday shook his head – although of course he had heard of it.

'It was a mark of motorbike. It had class. Lotsa class. They don't make 'em anymore, goes without saying. They don't make anything with class anymore. But what that bike had was classy. Women, they couldn't stop themselves from getting their leg over it. And me, I was hard. I was tough. . . .' He tugged the skin where his jowls ran into his double chin. 'You can ask Danny Keach. Hey Danny! . . . Was I tough or was I not? Back inner ol' days?'

Danny Keach gave the one-finger salute: check!

'Now,' O'Duff went on. 'I guess now I'm not even tough to bluff.'

There was a short poignant silence in which both men sipped their beer. What was there to say? It was one of those moments of intimacy in a bar, teetering on the edge of awkwardness, an older and a younger man pausing on the fulcrum of their rivalry to reflect on the ancient conundrum: Time versus the old vanishing trick, Youth.

'You want me to talk to her?' Faraday said.

'Who?'

'Tina Rauch.'

'I want you to talk to Rocco Da Silva, you dumb shit!' O'Duff said, rousing himself. 'If that bomb would've gone off an hour later he might of been without a rival for the Mayor contest! One I'd put money on to win.'

'I didn't think you took that much interest in politics.'

'Is that what they call it? A pair of clothes-hangers jostling for who looks best in a repro biker's leather-look jacket?' O'Duff pshawed. He shook his head, disgusted either at the way city politics had gone or at the image of himself in the mirror, remembering the way he looked before he joined the Department, in his own genuine leather-and-chrome-studded original. 'Me, I call it something else.'

'Take it easy, Captain. You're beginning to sound like a semiologist. Like I keep trying to tell you, it isn't the content of a statement that is important but the idiom by which it utters itself.'

O'Duff looked askance at Faraday. 'Everything you say, Lieutenant,' he said, 'is either genuine horsesense or just plain horseshit. I can't make up my mind which it is.'

Faraday shrugged. 'It's pretty obvious stuff. Maybe it's both.'

'Well, whyn't you try it on Rocco Da Silva? See how far it gets you?'

'You think they'll let me get near him?' Faraday said. He sensed that the Captain was going to try and dump the case in his lap because there were no bodies in it, nothing to interest *him*. And he didn't relish the prospect of approaching Da Silva, such a big face in the style world, in order to ask all those dull polite police-type questions. He had counted on returning to the atrium and talking some more with Torelli's biologist, Delia Summers. Her struggle to seal off the butterfly environment was so much more attractive. It was on a much more heroic scale than the issue of ascribing responsibility for the attack. The police angle, as usual, seemed to miss the point.

'Why the fuck shouldn't they let you near him?' O'Duff swiveled on his stool and looked Faraday up and down, appraising his marled earth-brown crimped seersucker suit.

'*You* speak his language, *I* don't. Me, I wouldn't know what the fuck to say to him or unnerstand what the fuck he would be saying me.'

'I mean, do you think I have enough authority?'

'Christ, Lieutenant! You may not dress like a law enforcement officer or even think like one but that – so please the NYC Police Board – is what you are! Detective. Second grade. And you're responsible to *me*. And *I*'m responsible to the Commissioner, "Black Fats" Liebman, who is responsible to the Mayor. Citizen Da Silva has a prima facie motive for planting the bomb that wrecked 700 Seventh Avenue. No harm you go find out what kinda alibi Da Silva has. Routine police work, like they taught you at the Academy!'

'What if they don't – ah – let me get near him?'

O'Duff – he tilted back the glass to finish the rest of his beer – said, 'Show them your fucking gun!' Then – the glass still poised in midair – he added: 'Oh no! Don't tell me!' He glanced again at Faraday's outfit, this time with his special X-ray vision. 'You don't *have* your gun!'

'Sorry, Captain. I can't help it. It ruins the line of my jacket.'

'One these days, Faraday! One these days you going to find yourself cuddling up some hoodlum down one those alleys off 32nd. I'd just love to know how you aim to persuade the party to come along quiet.'

'How about my famous charm?'

'Hee! Hee! Hee! . . .' O'Duff wheezed loudly, trying not to laugh. 'Oh, no! Please don't make me laugh! It makes me break wind. . . . Oh no. . . . And you, you could start talking your semi-logical shit at him. Anaesthetize the poor bastard! Hee! . . . Hee! . . . Hee!' Captain O'Duff, wheezing, laughing, broke wind – a steady low obbligato to his higher-pitched cachinnation.

On the t.v. screen over the barman's head the ad promoting the seventh game in the World Series merged into the midmorning News Roundup. The screen framed a familiar blonde young woman. She had changed out of her cornflower blue dress with the Eton collar. Now she was

33

wearing her silver lamé halter-top with pleached chrome-wire trims.

'Turn the sound up on this, will you Danny?' Faraday called to the barman. To O'Duff he said, 'You know, we should watch this, Captain. Find out how they're running the story.'

'. . . New developments in the explosion that destroyed a fashion house in the Garment District this morning. Fifty pound of high explosive was apparently placed near the entrance of the storefront, damaging a large part of the building,' Bonnie West said. 'Chief Forensic Expert of the Lower Manhattan District, Lieutenant Dinah Lazlo, was at the scene of the bombing. . . .'

Dinah Lazlo – wearing red lipglow and a short dress, the two top buttons undone – was standing outside the ruined Torelli premises. She had removed her lunettes.

'*Lazlo*! . . . You dumb broad!' O'Duff started. 'Wait till I. . . .'

Faraday shshed the Captain quiet.

'All the garments that were inside the Torelli Building at the time of the explosion were destroyed,' Dinah Lazlo said to camera. 'Among these was the much-publicized gown Tina Rauch was due to wear for the *Vogue* Election Ball tomorrow night. Naturally we're carrying out an analysis of the blast debris. . . .'

A picture of Dinah Lazlo entering the PD Forensic Laboratory on 29th Street.

That was all they let Dinah Lazlo say. The t.v. picture returned to Bonnie West.

'So far the police are no nearer to an explanation for the explosion,' Bonnie West said. 'The building belongs to Vincent Torelli, one of the small and exclusive group of couturiers who design for some of the world's most beautiful and wealthy women. . . .'

Behind Bonnie West's voice a sequence of still pictures of some of the world's most beautiful and wealthy women came onto the screen. The First Lady. A couple of t.v. soap actresses made up to look like European princesses. A couple of European princesses made up to look like t.v. soap actresses. Then, looking like herself, Tina Rauch.

'As Lieutenant Lazlo just indicated, there seems to be some speculation about Ms Rauch's new gown. Tina was to have been a guest at a private viewing at Torelli's this morning only moments after the explosion. She was expected to collect the dress she plans to wear during her clash with rival Rocco Da Silva on the Robbie Robson Show tomorrow night. . . .'

On a signal from Faraday, Danny Keach killed the sound.

The window-fan hummed.

O'Duff was the first to speak. 'What d'you make of it, Sergeant?' he said.

'The Torelli bombing?' Danny Keach said. 'I hope you collar the bum 'at did it, is all. Cost me a couple dozen glasses and a bottle of Roses.'

'I mean, what d'you make of it when the boys and girls in the white coats start talking to the television cameras, acting like fucking filmstars? Who they think they are, for Crissake?'

Danny Keach shook his head at the newfangled practice, lost for words.

'I guess – thanks to your colleague, Lieutenant – you ain't going to need your gun after all,' O'Duff said to Faraday. 'Da Silva and his gangsters'll be expecting you.' He pushed his empty beer glass away from him – disgusted, he had had enough – and slid his backside off the high wooden stool, adding as he did: 'You're worried, take along Officer Conway to hold your hand, or Officer Tornova – or both, all the good they do you.'

Officers Conway and Tornova were the two probationary police cadets, trainee semioticians whose training it was Faraday's responsibility to provide. O'Duff made no secret of his feelings about their presence on his beat.

'You want my opinion, Cap'n,' Danny Keach said, twirling yet another glass in the white cloth, 'the Lieutenant, he oughta take his gun with him just the same. A cop never can tell when he might need a gun.'

35

FARADAY INVENTED a pretext with which to disregard the Captain's suggested line of enquiry and instead – now that it was evidently his responsibility to solve it – returned to the scene of the crime. For a second time he waded through the debris of 700 Seventh Avenue, past the images of disaster that were in the process of being recorded to be piped, edited, onto television screens throughout the city. He crossed the no-man's-land between the cameras and the action, conscious that he would himself become a transient cypher of the signal being transmitted, and entered a zone which the t.v. audience so far remained in ignorance of: the pierced hermetic environment of Vincent Torelli's private collection of lepidoptera. 'The explosion that rocked the Garment District,' as reported by Bonnie West, signified something to the city at large and something completely different to Maxwell Faraday.

The pretext for his return had been no more than some routine police questions to put to the Torelli staff. The names of the clients for whom the destroyed garments had been destined. Their political allegiances. Questions Faraday probably would not have had much difficulty guessing the answers to without anyone's assistance. Already the public chain of circumstances, the betrayals and jealousies behind the attack were of no interest to him, and routine police work, like O'Duff said, would reveal what they were. It was the hidden reality behind the public image of the attack which the semiologist was attracted towards: the degree of intimacy between the old fashion maestro and his young biologist, between the garments he made and the insects she raised, and, above all, the lost world of their secret garden where beautiful things devoured each other alive. Vincent Torelli's single-minded fight to save the insects from annihilation reflected a scale of priorities that was so minute, so utterly pointless in the context of this vast city where everything had the same point – to make as handsome a profit as possible – that Faraday was touched by the romanticism of the enterprise.

The atrium was now a hive of busyness. Technicians

came and went, warily pooling their specialist skills in a common aim: to restabilize the system. Faraday, from a quiet spot in a dense area of the jungle, concealed, watched Delia Summers direct the team of architectural artificers whom she had hired to seal off the shattered roof from the open sky. The artificers' bright vermilion and black zipsuits flashed among the pale and dark green foliage – an invasion of dangerous spiders, throwing their invisible web of commands and counter-commands over the atrium, as if the satisfaction of the young woman in pale and dark green fatigues directing operations with the butterfly net were the prey they were intent on ensnaring. The circumflected intonation of their low voices as they checked and double-checked with each other over their communications system contrasted with Delia Summers' higher-pitched, more auth-oritative voice, amplified only by the urgency of the situation. At intervals, from ventilation engineers sweating out of sight, she took readings of air pressure, humidity level, heating and cooling capacity. It was a situation she was in total control of. Absorbed in her professional capacity, the last thing the arachnologist would want – Faraday could see – was to converse with a city cop in *his* professional capacity.

Observing her – as she had observed him earlier – framed through a square gap in the leaves, was like watching someone on a screen. Like watching Bonnie West read the News and being unable to communicate with her. This wasn't the moment to try. He didn't belong among this team of clever athletic young men and women. He didn't particularly feel like a spider either, dangerous or otherwise. He felt like a male member of the same species that Delia Summers belonged to.

Through the leaves over his head Faraday glimpsed flimsy tensile derricks lowering sheets of impermeable film over those sections of the polyhedral roof that had blown in, fractionally opaquing the blue of the sky. Below, all around Faraday, butterflies of every size and shape and color described their whimsical double helix two-step in the air like intoxicated ballet dancers, happily ignorant of all the time and money that was being expended removing the peril they were in, ignorant even that any peril existed, that a benevolent intelligence greater than their own was working on their behalf. Faraday smiled. It made them seem almost human. In a short while the war on the rim of their cosmos would be won. He was surprised to realize how relieved he felt about this and not only because it was something that mattered to Delia Summers. It mattered anyway.

Cautiously Faraday stepped backward – it needed will-power – like a man waking from a beautiful dream, retreating with instant nostalgia towards the things he had to do. He would just have to wait a little longer for the woman he had already waited for all his life. He backed through the undergrowth, conscious of the foolishness of his situation. Was this what love was? Heading rear-first to a crossroads in a jungle? Damp palms and horsetails slapped against his face and cuffed the back of his neck, leaving beads of water rilling down the dry fabric of his sleeves and trousers.

'*Ho-up there*!'

Faraday turned through ninety degrees to face an old-timer in a khaki tank-top and oldfangled elasticated suspenders holding his pants up.

'You know, you'll find it a whole bunch easier, you turn around and use your eyes, Lieutenant, to see where you're going. That's why they're placed where they are and not in your backside,' the old-timer said, adding acerbically, 'I'da thought a police officer would have known that!'

Faraday grinned, no doubt foolishly, at Vincent Torelli, who was standing in front of him behind a lightweight plastic wheelbarrow, the two shafts raised in his hands like the reins of a pony he had just ho-upped.

'You looking for something particular?' Torelli said. He lowered the shafts of the wheelbarrow and winked at Faraday. 'Or is something particular looking for you?'

'My bearings, I guess,' Faraday muttered. 'I'm sure they're around here some place.'

'You were an insect in *this* world, Lieutenant, you wouldn't be for long. Can't afford to lose your bearings. Some hungry frog would have bit your head off by now.'

'Oh yeah. . . ?' Faraday straightened up in the clearing. He shook some of the water droplets from his clothes. 'And who gets to bite the frog's head off?'

Torelli's wheelbarrow, Faraday now saw, was piled with the carcasses of dead butterflies and moths – albescent blues and marbled scarlets, wasp yellows, silvers and golds, and blacks that were neither this nor that but every color simultaneously, like rhinestones. It was a dragon-eyed iridescent jumble.

'Why – the *snake*, of course!' Torelli said with a certain amount of glee. 'Only snakes, as a rule, don't bite off heads. They prefer to swallow their prey whole. So you can take your pick. Or were you planning to use your gun?'

Vincent Torelli was a wicked old man. He was enjoying himself at Faraday's expense. The peak of the emergency must have passed.

'I was trying to find out something,' Faraday said. 'That I didn't know.'

The old man nodded as if Faraday had finally said something that made sense. His eyes flashed. He wasn't a world-famous couturier, Faraday decided. He was a garden gnome. 'The interesting thing,' he said, 'for you to work out, Lieutenant, is how you came to find out you didn't know it.'

It was a curved ball that Faraday let go for a strike. Dazzling himself at his own lazy insight, he said: 'I guess I was trying to find out the connection between your butterflies and your gowns.'

'Who said there was a connection? I wouldn't say there was a connection, exactly. Far as I'm concerned they're the same thing!'

From his pants pocket he fished out a thumb-sized oblong cotton ball and let it rest in his palm for Faraday to look at. 'The chrysalis of the butterfly of the family *Lycaenidae*,' he said. Then he leaned over and lifted from the jumble of colors in the wheelbarrow a plain chalky-blue butterfly. 'The caterpillar hangs around ants of the genus *myrmica* until it gets itself picked up – literally – and carried off to the anthill. Spends the night with them – if that's what you want to call metamorphosis. They look after her until it's time to change into this. Then she flies off to find a mate of her own choosing.'

'Why do the ants do it?' Faraday said, appalled at the altruism. 'If they were human beings in *this* city, they wouldn't be for long.'

'Because they are attracted to her. They like how she looks, how she smells! She intoxicates them! So she takes them for a ride? As far as the ants are concerned, *she's got what it takes*!'

'You're saying Tina's gown has the same kind of effect?' Faraday said.

'Bó!' Torelli shrugged, the expressive Latin shrug which can mean whatever you want it to mean. Don't ask me. Let's wait and see. Who cares? Then: 'The voters, yes, in many respects behave in similar ways to ants. They don't need Tina any more than *myrmicae* need the Large Blue butterfly. But they *think* they do.'

'I thought the gown was destroyed,' Faraday said, pleased that he had found a police question to ask.

Torelli shook his head. 'Tina will be wearing it tomorrow night for her t.v. show appearance, don't worry. Here. . . .' He handed the chrysalis to Faraday. 'Take it. As a souvenir.'

Faraday accepted the almost weightless bundle. The miniaturized mummy lay in the flat of his hand, a conundrum of relativity, like Einstein's railway carriage traveling at the speed of light, in which the sleeping traveler arrives younger than when he left.

'Whatever it is this little thing is dreaming about,' Torelli said, lifting up the shafts of his wheelbarrow. 'It's the stuff my gowns are made out of.'

3

After a pleasantly fast drive uptown from West 35th Street to Washington Heights on the Henry Hudson Parkway – almost half the length of Manhattan – Sergeant Kriwaczek took Riverside Drive through Fort Tyron Park, cruising slowly as far as the quiet Deco town houses of Inwood, where he deaccelerated his vehicle in front of the 'NO UNAUTHORIZED ADMISSION' warning staked outside the gate of the perimeter fence just below the sign advertising 'THE SCHRYER BUILDING'. Both signs, even in the middle of a summer's afternoon, were illuminated. The anti-prowler camera mounted over the check-in bay slowly tracked the vehicle to a halt. From the air-conditioned cool of the police limousine, Faraday looked out toward the immaculately trimmed garden on the other side of the fence, shadowless in the July heat, as perfect and as hospitable as the surface of Venus.

'Don't try to take us in, Sergeant,' Faraday told Kriwaczek. 'It'd take a long weekend to check this through. I'll walk it. Make my own way back. Thanks for the ride.'

He climbed out and Kriwaczek backed his vehicle away from the fence. The camera hesitated a moment, then left the vehicle and followed Faraday to the check-in bay. After his identity had been scrutinized by the processing technology and returned to him, Faraday continued on out through the self-opening glass doors. He strolled through the immaculate garden towards the ten-tier pink-stone ziggurat that called itself 'The Schryer Building' – 'The' in case

41

anyone had any doubts about its unique qualities. His feet crunched the raked gravel path that ran between shin-high hedges of mauve-flowering perennials bordering an authentic-looking lawn, so authentic it might have been astroturf. As he approached the unadorned smoked-glass front of the building, its tiers overflowing with green tendriled plants, he recognized the expensive contract horticulture some security firms specialized in. The creepers festooning the balconies were not intended to look rural any more than the dwarf ornamental fruit trees were intended to bear fruit. It was a style. Like most styles it had its own language. What this one, deconstructed, said to the world was: 'DON'T EVEN THINK OF TRYING ANYTHING!' The creepers were there to conceal the building's defense weapons-systems and surveillance gadgetry, the fruit trees to afford them both a clear a line of fire and offer as little cover as possible to any intruder. A hefty slice of the monthly it took to buy into a condo such as The Schryer would go towards the privacy insurance necessary to maintain an effective security-web around it. Behind its verdant outer defenses the building was as fortified as the keep of a medieval castle.

Faraday smiled and waved, real friendly, in the direction of the old man in blue work pants and red plaid shirt who was occupied hosing down the lawn, taking his time. The old man seemed to make a reciprocal gesture with the hosepipe but Faraday could not be sure, the way the sun was back-lighting the expression on his face. Anyone with sufficient curiosity might have wondered what the old man was doing out there at all instead of a conventional automatic sprinkler-system, but Faraday didn't. He already knew. He merely wondered where exactly on the autonomic handyperson the video camera was located.

The cool uncluttered interior of the lobby was deserted except for the usual polished evergreen plants set in the usual concrete containers and, seated behind a molded lilac polymer reception desk, the usual security employee thinly disguised as a reception clerk. The place had the antiseptic welcome of a privately endowed museum of Art. The negatively ionized air tasted brand new. Organisms with difficult Latin names and cataloged by Linnaeus had been extracted by powerful contract-cleaning equipment. Faraday couldn't help grinning, as he passed the small Max Ernst bronze sculpture on a plinth, at the irony of how even the most revolutionary art ends up as interior decoration.

'Lieutenant,' the security clerk – Vergil Wymann, according to the name slotted into the little frame in front of him – said, looking up from the newspaper propped between the pair of VDUs. 'Can I do for you?'

He was a dark-skinned white-haired middle-aged black man – a retired police officer, Faraday would have bet money on it – with the kindly family-man sort of face that would never have gotten anywhere in any authoritarian organization, especially if the organization was the Police Department. He would have logged traffic violations all his working life until he drew his retirement check and was put out to graze. Faraday offered him his shield to look at, although the particulars on it were probably still showing on one of the two screens, and at the same time let him have a glimpse of his gun holster. It told him that they were both law enforcement officers. They were in the same business. The holster was empty, of course. For Faraday, the semiotician, it wasn't the content of a sign which was important so much as the form it took.

Vergil Wymann put on a pair of metal-framed eyeglasses and brought Faraday's hand holding the shield into focal distance.

'19th Precinct, huh? You know an officer name of Keach? Sergeant Danny Keach?'

'Sure do,' Faraday said. 'Tough as they come, so they say. One of the old school. Of course, he's retired now.'

'He damn ought to be! Me and him was rookies together! I drove the wagon, Danny Keach rode shotgun. Started the same day! Only Danny, he made it to Sergeant. He had what it takes. Not me. Ammunition Super with a bad case of hemorrhoids was far as I made it. Sitting on my black ass for thirty-five years! Can I do for you Lieutenant?'

'I'd like to ask you two small favors, Vergil. Well, one small favor and one not so small.'

Vergil Wymann carefully folded away the newspaper he had been reading, for a moment revealing the headline screaming across the front page: BOMB BLASTS GARMENT EMPEROR'S CLOTHES FACTORY, and filed it away in his desk as if it were some important document, such as a crime sheet, and said: 'Ask Lieutenant!'

'You have a recording of my arrival.' Faraday nodded in the direction of the video screen.

'Sure.'

Vergil Wymann tapped out the appropriate instruction and Faraday saw himself appear on the screen, a man in his late thirties in a well-cut lightweight brown seersucker suit, shades, white Sicilian leather shoes, approaching the lobby across the lawn from the point of view of the old gardener, smiling, throwing a real friendly salute at him. Wymann pressed some more keys and the image advanced so that Faraday's head and shoulders filled the bullseye of the target markings of the screen and he was able to read the insincerity of his own smile.

'I could of erased you right there and then,' Wymann said. He leered pleasantly. 'You tried anything.'

'That's the first favor. How about you erase the recording of my arrival from the old man's memory?' Faraday said.

Wymann thought about it. Then he said: 'You're in O'Duff's homicide squad, right?'

Faraday nodded. There was enough truth in this statement for it not to be an out-and-out lie. O'Duff, if he could help it, kept Faraday away from any case that actually involved homicide.

Wymann tapped some keys on the terminal which had the effect of removing the image from the screen. 'As a matter fact the old guy's been having these memory-lapses recently,' he said. The lawn became deserted. 'He's getting past it, I reckon.' Then: 'And the second?'

'I'd like you to afford me entry to the apartment of one of

44

the Schryer's residents,' Faraday said with standard police prolixity.

'Which one did you have in mind?'

'Tina Rauch.'

There was a short silence.

'You want to see Ms Rauch, you make an appointment through one of her staff,' Wymann said. '*I* can't do that'.

'You don't understand. I don't want to *see* her, no. And she's too busy to see me. All I want is to take a look round her place. Just poke my nose in. Won't take more'n five minutes. In and out.'

Vergil Wymann hesitated.

'Of course, I would want you to accompany me,' Faraday added. 'We wouldn't like for any string of pearls to go missing, anything like that.'

'I don't want to ask what this is all about,' Wymann said, although it was obvious that was just what he did want to do.

'I'd like to tell you Vergil. You know how it is with police work. Less you know the better.'

Vergil Wymann looked stern and showed Faraday the palms of his hands, either to tell him that he did not have to say any more or to indicate that they did not conceal a weapon. So he must have used his foot – as he would for a guest of a resident on his or her way in – to open the elevator gates set flush into the long wall in back of Faraday.

Wymann accompanied Faraday to the tenth-floor apartment – at the apex of the ziggurat, it occupied the entire top floor – and used his pass-number to trigger the privacy-catch on the door.

Faraday walked past the security guard into a spacious lighting showroom. It was dazzling.

'What do you call this?' he said. 'The ballroom?'

'We call this the reception salon,' Vergil Wymann said, deadpan.

The reception salon of Tina Rauch's apartment had the kind of interior decoration Faraday sometimes saw featured in *Better House & Garden*, if not the *Architectural Review*: a

45

paragon of recent taste sculpted out of costly substances and ingenious construction techniques and from which lesser – which meant less expensive – ambience therapists would leach their inspiration. This one – Ben Croxley, Faraday seemed to recall reading someplace – had made use of the reflective properties of transparent materials to create a space inside which walls, floor and ceiling appeared to disappear into each other, as if the three-dimensionality of the place were just some trick of the light, nothing to be taken too seriously. A lucite staircase suspended in the air from stainless steel rods connected the split-level living spaces with the walls and the dropped ceiling which housed the subtly-angled spot-lamps. More or less furnitureless, the space created gave the illusion that you were in a museum of contemporary art in which you, the visitor, were the exhibit. One of the things the highly intricate geometric patterns reflected, besides each other, was the occupant's interest in aspects of illusion and reality. The light modulating between the carefully placed mirrors had a kaleidoscopic quality. Every small gesture that was made inside the room altered the overall design completely, creating a shimmering, unstable, fragmentary world, but one momentarily personalized by the individual making it. It was – Faraday saw at once – a clever simulation of the Heraclitian vision of reality which informed much of Tina Rauch's style and was so appealing about the image she projected to the world: life as an ever-fluctuating stream into which individuals must throw themselves for the moment that was allotted to them. It was the attitude totemized in her fabulously expensive Torelli butterfly gowns, worn for a day and then cast aside. Just the opposite of the severe enduring classicism of her rival's tuxedos.

'Kind of classy, don't you think Vergil?' Faraday said. He was standing in the center of the reception salon, so called. The earth-brown of his suit had become diffused throughout the room, subtly permeating the fittings and the walls. Just how this had been effected Faraday did not know. Probably an application of the New Physics: lasers beamed through optic fibres, he surmised, laced into the translucent fabrics of the construction. The blue of Vergil Wymann's uniform progressively marbled into Faraday's brown as he stepped forward. The room became a merged extension of both men.

'Classy, but not what you'd call cosy,' Wymann said. 'No place here I'd care to put my feet up, plant my ass, read the sports page.'

Faraday smiled. It wasn't cosy, that's where the retired police officer was right. Where he was wrong was in thinking that it was ever intended to be. The importance of the décor lay – like any other style – in the statements it made about reality.

Tina Rauch was on the point, maybe, of getting herself elected Mayor of the city. If she succeeded it would be because she had the ability to put her finger on the pulse of what the majority of the people in the city required from a fashion leader. On one level her style articulated the kind of personality – the clothes, the accessories, the personal imagery – that most citizens responded to at this particular moment in their history. She expressed their fantasies about themselves. On another level she was an embodiment of the *zeitgeist*, resonating with the serious epistemological preoccupations of the age – how the world was best viewed – and she challenged Rocco Da Silva's claim to do that same. Frivolous or academic, you could take your pick.

'You want to see the rest?'

Vergil Wymann led Faraday under the lucite staircase and into the adjoining chamber. Here the drapes were open and midafternoon sunlight exposed a conventional unpretentious boudoir, a place where a woman dressed and undressed. A patterned hand-loomed cotton coverlet over the hip-high hardwood platform bed. Articles of clothing on the floor and furniture. A scarlet draped panné velvet sheath with sculpted shoulders. A marocain and satin slip, ruched and piped with rose and pistachio petals. A white worked-silk bra. A pair of fine gauge *film noir* silk stockings. Faraday crouched and scrutinized, without disturbing, the crumpled heaps of clothing. There was something touching about the shapeless shapes abandoned on the floor. They seemed to have lost their meaning, their magical efficacy, without having changed into anything else, like pressed flowers in a book. Here was the form of the woman – not the woman herself but something that expressed her essential nature. Faraday held his breath, unwilling to alter anything. Surely this was what archaeologists experience when they break the seal and enter for the first time an ancient royal tomb where children's toys and workmen's lunches still litter the floor. A past that history has not interfered with.

'You – ah – looking for something particular, Lieutenant,' Vergil Wymann said behind him. 'You got 'bout three minutes left of your five to find it.' He sounded nervous.

'I never look *for* things, Vergil,' Faraday told him. 'My job is to look *at* them. That's all.'

He peered into the empty cup of the laced-silk bra which described in reverse the shape of the breast – exquisite in the paradox it offered and simultaneously withheld. Why, he asked himself, did the bra convey a completely different order of information, tell him more about Tina Rauch, than the bared breast itself ever could? Like the woven Berber motif on the whorled coverlet that still held the shape of the woman who had slept inside it, its significance did not lie in any forensic statements it made about her – such as Dinah Lazlo might have been interested in – but in its linguistic content. It expressed her as eloquently as the discarded husk of a chrysalis did the perfect imago.

Straightening up, he threw a glance over Tina Rauch's collection of blushers, lip gels, liners on the capacious vanity-table: *Hibiscus Rouge à Lèvres, Plus Qu'invisible Poudre translufine, Ocres les 4 ombres*. He wondered whether he had found, as Vergil Wymann had put it, what he was looking for. He had learnt something about the subject – sure – more than he ever would have learnt from interviewing her, assuming he knew the questions to ask. But was it enough? If he succeeded in cracking the code of the sign-system of Tina Rauch's style he might, just might, be in a position to decipher what she was trying to tell the world. Her myth. But was that what Captain O'Duff wanted?

Vergil Wymann coughed explicitly. Faraday turned and nodded – the five minutes were up – and they left the bedroom and returned to the reception salon. As they were passing underneath the steps of the lucite staircase Faraday asked him, 'Where does this lead to?' and – at exactly the same moment that he did – saw on the other side of the staircase a woman move her head and look in his direction, her image split into sections by the horizontal tiers of the translucent steps. Reality filleted by illusion. Wymann edged him into the room and they all stood there, appraising each other's presence – the woman, the cop and the ex-cop.

'To the Studio,' the woman said.

For some reason they all three glanced up the staircase to where the Studio was. Faraday felt like a prospective buyer inspecting a piece of realty. No, this wasn't quite what he had in mind, thank you. The room became filled with the mobile colorings emitted by the three people in it, only now the blues and browns were aflame. Sunlight flashing on oil and water. Dragonfly's wings. It had the effect of putting the three people in instant harmony with their environment and, without the use of hallucinogens, with each other. It was the corollary of the studied alienation of Rocco Da Silva's colorless realism.

She said: 'You a friend of Tina's, or what?'

'Not exactly. But not necessarily an enemy either,' Faraday said. 'How about you?'

'I'd know if you was one of her friends. I got them all on file. Every one of them.' She tapped her head with her finger as she said this, as if to indicate where she kept her files. She was a young bob-haired blonde woman in her twenties, slightly built, five ten, in cling-fit kingfisher-blue stretch pants and an open-collared cerise cotton shirt. A shiny white plastic belt held it all tucked in. She had a pretty over-made-up heart-shaped face which exactly suited her outfit.

All she needed was a bottle of Coke in her hand, a Corvette Stingray to lean up against, and she would be perfect. Every Korean War GI's dream. A real life-size Barbie Doll. It was the kind of witty eclectic historicism you came to expect from people in Tina Rauch's entourage. As long as you kept within the bounds of good taste you could be who the hell you liked. Tomorrow you could be someone else completely. In such a selfconscious world, the young woman's outrageous come-on might even be some kind of ironic post-feminist joke.

'This is Tracy Wilder, Lieutenant,' Vergil Wymann said. 'She has access. Comes and goes as she pleases. She cleans for Miz Rauch.'

'Vergil! You make me sound like I was the help!' she said. 'Which I ain't. I just straighten out her clothes. Hold the mirror. She trusts me, right? I'm her *con-fi-dante*!' And to Faraday: 'He called you Lieutenant. You a police officer?'

Faraday nodded.

'Well, I never would have guessed!'

'That's because I'm not wearing a uniform. I'm a plainclothes police officer. I'm meant to be in disguise.'

'Let me see your gun, then,' she said. 'At *least*!'

'Sorry. It's 'gainst regulations to draw a weapon except in the course of duty. That means except I have reason to think I will need to fire it.'

Tracy Wilder giggled.

'I was – ah – hoping to ask Tina some questions,' Faraday lied. 'But I can come back.'

'You looking for Tina, you'll have to go to the Convention Center. She's selling herself to the full Assembly of the City Labor Unions – DC 37. You can't miss it. It's that big building between 11th and 12th.' Tracy Wilder grinned. 'Whyn't you ask *me* your questions?'

Faraday shrugged. 'I was wondering what Tina plans to wear tomorrow, now that her gown has been destroyed in the Torelli bombing.'

Tracy Wilder squinted at Faraday as if he was suddenly a

long way away. 'That ain't a police question! Sure you not a journ'list? You *look* more like a journ'list.'

'He's police, Miz Wilder. You can take my word. 19th Precinct. Homicide Division. I seen his buzzer,' Vergil Wymann said.

'Oh no! Homicide!' Tracy Wilder's face lit up. She stuck her hands into the back pockets of her kingfisher-blue cling-fit pants which had the effect of pushing out the front of her cerise cotton shirt even further than it was pushed out already. 'Oh wow! Where's the body?'

'*Bodies*,' Faraday said.

'What? I don't believe it! Oh boy! A multi! I always wanted to be in a murder 'vestigation. How many?'

'About a wheelbarrow-full.'

'Hey! You want to interrogate me? Like, ask me where I was when it happened? Who I was with? Who I sleep with?'

'It's none of my business,' Faraday said. He made a move toward the door. 'Whyn't you interrogate your*self*? You'd make a better job of it than I would, sounds to me.'

'Oh please!' Tracy Wilder pleaded, pushing out her chest even further, if that were possible. 'Tina won't mind!'

Faraday locked his eyes onto Vergil Wymann's and gave them a yank. It was a look Wymann must have seen before in his thirty-five years on the beat. They left the apartment.

'Lieutenant! Don't go!' Tracy Wilder called after them. '*I'll let you use your handcuffs on me!*'

DELIA SUMMERS, having removed the perforated removable steel panels from the chrysalis chamber, stood still for a moment, taking stock, her skin dappled by the shadows of flying butterflies, their flapping wings agitating the fine hairs on her naked arms and occasionally dusting her face with swatches of their brilliant generic markings. Now that the panels had been removed, the butterflies were free to disentangle themselves from her and each other and return to the restored tropical environment of the atrium, to the specialized plants and companion insects whose existence was essential for their survival. Outside the chamber lay the necessary and sufficient conditions for the continuance of their life cycle; inside, only overcrowding and starvation and eventual death. She could not help smiling at the haphazard way they went about making their getaway, however. They found the exit more by accident than by design, leaving in ones and twos but unable to communicate their discovery, like passengers at an international airport departure dock. And sometimes lost it again, one or two of them flying back into the chamber without knowing that they were. It was as hit-and-miss a process as natural selection itself. She suspected that the insects were probably no more stupid than human beings in this respect: neither of them knew where exactly in the walls of necessity to find the window of free will. Or even that it was there.

Gently fanning the warm damp air, Delia wafted the butterflies in the direction of the open panels. She was relieved to realize that this was the last item on her mental list of things to do that was marked 'urgent'. The atrium was, for the time being, repaired. The temperature and humidity levels had been restored. The team of athletic young architectural artificers had gathered up their equipment – and their check – and bounced away to their next assignment with the élan of a professional dance troupe. Until this moment she had not let herself consider the cause of all the chaos: why someone had needed to blitz Vincent Torelli's couture collection. It had never been her – or even his – main concern. Nevertheless it had become a battlefield. A war had been declared, for reason which she was not privy to. Had she been called to arms? And if so, by whom? Now, in the lull – in the chrysalis chamber where met-amorphosis took place – flashes of the day's drama flitted across her mind's eye like memories of newsreel clips: the stricken look on Vincent Torelli's face when they had stared at each other across the aerial abyss this morning, she bleeding from the wounds in her face and leg, both of them dazed in the first shock of the blast, as if the whole basis of their relationship had suddenly imploded; the police officers with their narrow point of view – first the older Captain who looked like an overweight overworked cop, sweating in his shirtsleeves and his well-worn leather gun holster, then the younger Lieutenant who looked more like one of the Torelli sales personnel hovering about the disaster area with his pointless charm. Hadn't he returned – or had she dreamed it? – to lurk among the undergrowth later, looking at her? And – if Vincent was to believed – *for* her.

Delia Summers knew more than enough about sexual strategies in the natural world to realize that the police detective – the young Lieutenant – had almost certainly wanted to mate with her but also, from his haltingly funny way of expressing himself, that he had not yet fully realized this himself. Later, catching sight of him watching her – hidden from her, or so he thought – she had felt stalked. And trapped. Something had stirred in her. Fear and excitement. She had experienced an inkling of what the female impala, rattlesnake, dragonfly, blue whale, Borneo gibbon, the female of every known species on earth, would have experienced at such a juncture: the urge to show him her most vulnerable part, to reveal herself to him, to turn her back and make herself defenceless and flash that signal which would chemically alter his disposition toward her.

At the time the inclination to do this had taken her completely by surprise. She was shocked by her own naked self-interest, considering all the things that needed doing, and yet even while she was marshalling the team of artificers she had been aware of what was happening inside her and that no female member of any species – except, possibly, certain spiders – ever submits to that dangerous inclination until the male has penetrated her sense of discrimination. So she must have, at some level, selected him. What the Lieutenant possessed that other males around her did not, Delia could not say – perhaps no more than his haltingly funny way of expressing himself. But if she wanted to be honest with herself she had to admit that he had it: she liked him. His display had caught her eye. His was the territory she wanted to enter, his the phenotype she required to combine with her own. She was no different from the female impala or the Borneo gibbon.

It was possible, certainly, that her reaction to him had been hormonal, a biological adjustment to the shock of the bombing. But if this were so, so what? In the contemporary world, shellshock and sexual attraction: what was the difference? The symptoms were virtually the same: the lips pallid, the voice whispering, the pulse rapid, the respiration irregular, sighing, a dry mouth. In a sense she was unable to put her finger on, her sudden tender feelings toward the fake policeman, Maxwell Faraday, had something to do with the shattered atrium, the broken glass dome of Vincent Torelli's insect house, the fragments of butterfly wing floating on the air like pieces of charred paper on which the most beautiful poetry, lost forever, had been written. That moment had triggered all the holocaustic fears of her childhood. After all the talking, the End *had* come. The sky had fallen. She had experienced a pang of fear such as she had not felt since she was a little girl, and not just for herself but for Vincent, the man who had known her mother, whom she revered as a father – who, she suspected, might even be her father. The arrival of Faraday – elegantly crumpled and, no denying it, not bad looking – had plugged the emotional gash the fear had rent inside her. Throughout the day while she had been working to seal up the gaping hole in the atrium roof, he had transmitted to her some kind of inner strength, an ability to cope, not particularly by anything he had said – he had not said anything, particularly – or anything he had done – he had not, later, even approached her – but simply by the fortuitousness of his arrival.

As soon as she was satisfied that the chrysalis chamber was emptying itself of the imagos, she stepped out herself, wondering vaguely whether something nascent inside her had not metamorphosed while she had been in it. A few flashes of color affixed to her tunic, she made her way across the atrium floor in the direction of the external elevator shaft. She noted en route what a professional job the construction team had made of their contract, right down to clearing away the broken glass. The atrium was peaceful as a jungle at close of day. A hush had fallen over it. The shadows had softened now that the sun had dipped past the roof line. She could hear the irregular stridulation of the cicadas and grasshoppers, the steady pulse of the tree-frogs, the males advertising their prescence to the females, the females answering them ever more boldly.

Delia rode the external car to her private apartment. On her mental list of things to do marked 'urgent' she added one last item. A window had opened in *her* horizon of choices. She was not going to be like those dumb butterflies. She knew it was there and where it was. All she needed was to get to a phone. There was no reason why she could not make use of the cordless handheld unit in the top flap-pocket of her fatigues but she preferred to use the one in the seclusion of her own home. She did not see why the cicadas and the tree-frogs should eavesdrop on her call, as she had theirs.

MAX FARADAY, as soon as he arrived home, peeled off his lightweight cotton suit jacket – the one with the custom-tailored zip-in gun holster, for the time being containing his SONY handset – and threw it over the back of the manager's chair. He climbed the stairs and undressed and took a long cool wet shower. Barefoot, with a towel wrapped around his middle and a glass of chilled V8 in his hand, he returned to the back room and stood for a moment in front of the polished chrome and green-glass Wurlitzer, surveying the rows of numbered keys. Most of the paint had long since faded from these but this did not matter because Faraday knew the numbers by heart. He fished one of the old silver quarters from the pile inside the old smoking stand next to the Wurlitzer, dropped it into the slot and pressed the key invisibly numbered D5. The green glass lit up and started to flash. The rocket ship was about to take off. He watched the soothingly slow mechanical rotation of the records on the ancient 78 r.p.m. jukebox until his selection was located and lowered by the metal arm onto the turntable and the sapphire stylus began to scrape over the worn shellac surface of the old disk. It was a sound he loved – the crackly static of minute abrasions that had accrued on the surface of the fragile disk over many decades since its manufacture, a recording of time passing overlaying the more specific information inside the grooves. A piano intro – played in the forgotten 'stride' style – issued from the Wurlitzer's massive speaker.

Faraday dug the SONY from his gun holster, gathered up his tin box, his quartz pipe, his Zippo lighter, and carried them all out onto the back deck. It was time for a smoke and – if he was lucky – a nap.

The sun was already quite low in the sky but it was still damn warm. The painted wood planks felt hot under his feet as he jiggered the white plastic bucket chairs and the table with the umbrella through the center of it. Settling himself comfortably on one and under the other, he let his gaze extend across the expanse of wild timothy grass to the empty reed-beds and, beyond, to the brackish ponds and the hazy horizon of Jamaica Bay. In the windless summer afternoon the yellow reeds had the appearance of uncut corn. A pair of red-legged cranes were working their way along the shallower reaches of the ponds, a female and, alongside it but at a respectful distance, the larger male. Neither of them was paying any attention to the other, pretending that it was not there, like any other courting couple.

Faraday filled his pipe.

The prospect from the back deck – raised on stilts over the lower marshy elevation of the Bird Sanctuary – did not assail the eye with linguistic data, which was the reason the semiologist had bought the house in the first place. There was not a building, antenna, teledish, electric sign or billboard to be seen. In fact, there was nothing out there that needed interpreting – unless you counted the sound-call of the red-legged crane. And Faraday didn't.

> '. . . *Will you come into my parlour,*
> *Said the Spider to the Fly* . . .'

floated out onto the deck from the Wurlitzer, courtesy of Mr Thomas Waller, on scratchy waves of piano notes.

> '. . . *I've got the cutest little living room*
> *That you did ever spy* . . .'

Faraday lit his pipe.

He sipped his chilled vegetable cocktail.

He considered the huge piece of emotional energy that had edged into his life. Yesterday was just like any other day. Today the aliens had landed. He had been invaded by something beyond his horizon, reminding him of the story Charles Darwin had told about the arrival of his ship, *The Beagle*, at one of the tiny uncharted islands in the Pacific. Although the ship had lain in the harbor for some time the inhabitants of the island had been unable to see it. It was too large, larger than anything their imaginations had hitherto needed to take cognizance of. Faraday wondered whether the arrival in his life of the biologist, Delia Summers, would have as devastating an impact on him as the earlier biologist had had on the unsuspecting island community.

> *'Bye-bye! Oh Fly! . . .*
> *Cos you walked into his parlor*
> *Unsuspecting little Fly! . . .'*

The piano music came to an end and Faraday listened to the silence for a while, smoking his quartz pipe. He watched the pair of cranes moving across his field of vision without appearing to move at all, like the hands of a clock, until eventually the silence – of islands stalked by birds since before the Indians ran them – was broken by the sound-call of the SONY handset on the white plastic table in front of him. Faraday listened to the pip-pip-pipping. Then he leaned across and touched the appropriate mode-change key.

A voice issued from the portable communications unit.

'. . . Fine. . . . Well, as well as you could expect. There were a lot of men there. I think some of them were aiming to give me a rough ride. They had me slated as some kind of cheap Canal Street vamp. . . . Here, help me off with this, will you. . . . That's great. . . . But boy, it's big, that place. Did you ever go in it? You know you can lay the ol' Empire State Building on its side inside it? Twenty-two acres! So big – they told me – all fourteen NFL football teams could play simultaneous games and still have room for the Superbowl. . . . Don't worry. It was fine. Unions tend to be natural conservatives so there was a lot of Rocco's supporters in the audience. I'd expected that. . . .'

The unmistakable voice of Tina Rauch – breathy, vulnerable, pregnant with doubt, reminding Faraday of the movie actress Marilyn Monroe – was coming out of the SONY, transmitted by the bug which he had planted in her apartment. The bug, in her bedroom, had voice-activated the moment someone had started to speak.

'. . . I told 'em, Wait a minute. You want the status quo to carry on the same as always, you want a rigid paymaster, you want police pay to increase faster than that of your members, vote for Rocco. Pessimists are always reactionary, they can't imagine things ever getting better than they are. You think human nature is basically corrupt, you believe in original sin, then vote for a fascist like Rocco Da Silva. But you got a spark of life in you, the moxie to change your destiny, you going to have to vote for *me*! . . .'

'How'd they take it?' a second person wanted to know.

'Lying down – kicking their legs in the air!' Tina Rauch giggled. 'I left them howling and dancing in the aisles. I got an ovation! But maybe it was just they could see up my skirt. . . .'

'All eighty-five thousand of them?'

'They had me blown up on this screen. I was like some fucking colossus. A goddess! . . . I told 'em, you ain't seen nothing! Wait till tomorrow!'

'That reminds me,' the voice of the second person – that of Tracy Wilder – broke in. 'I arrived here this afternoon, some police detective was snooping around. Right here in the apartment!'

'Yeah . . .? How d'he get in?'

'Vergil let him in – the dumb fucker.'

'Who was he? What d'he want?'

'I checked with the security channel soon as he left, only it didn't have no reference. It was blank. He must've had Vergil wipe it. He told me he wanted to ask you some questions 'bout the Torelli business.'

'*What*! They think it was *me* did it?'

'Nar. Relax. He was just a Lieutenant. The errand boy. They seriously thought it was you behind it, they'd have sent round the SkyPol. Nar. He just wanted to know what you plan on wearing for the *Vogue* Ball tomorrow evening. . . .'

'Did you tell him?'

'*Me*? You kidding?'

Both women giggled.

'So the police think it's bombed out too, huh?' Tina said after a while.

'Sure looks like it. Why shouldn't they? You seen the news. It's all anyone's talking 'bout!'

Faraday watched the pair of red-legged cranes lift off into the air at exactly the same moment – they must have had some kind of private understanding, or telepathy – their big white wings slapping up and down like shirtsleeves drying on a washing-line as they slowly gained height, circled the Bay, and then disappeared in the direction of the Bronx. They probably had a date with some pals in the Wild Asia enclosure of the Zoo up there.

From the SONY came a rustle of fine-gauge fabrics rubbing against each other. '. . . Thanks . . .' Tina said. 'Boy, is that skirt tight! . . . That's better. You know it was a stroke of pure genius, Tracy. They thought I was going to show up like the Madwoman of Chaillot in a rose faille ballgown and feather boa, they got a shock. A simple short black skirt can't be beat, you want to give a man a hard-on. Kind of took the wind out their sails. Looked stylish *and* professional *and* sexy. . . .'

'It's a fatal combination,' Tracy said. 'Gets the men *and* the women.'

'Right . . . You pass me that peignoire . . .? Now. . . . Let's hit the freezer. I could murder a corned beef . . .' You bring my drink will you, darling . . .?'

The voices disappeared out of range of the bug. After a couple of minutes the SONY clicked itself into an off position.

Faraday's pipe had gone out. His glass of V8 was empty. The cranes had decamped and the communications unit was silent. There was nothing more to be done.

He dug himself out of the bucket chair and padded, yawning, from the deck. On the way the towel fell from his waist. He planted himself, naked, in the swivel manager's chair, leaned across and touched the go-spot on the t.v. As he did, almost simultaneously, the phone handset on the low glass table next to it began to chime and flash its light at him. Faraday hesitated. On the screen the newscaster, Tony Rossini – dapper, wry, well preserved, the male evening counterpart to Bonnie West – was already going over the background to the main story. The picture cut from

Rossini's suntan to a deserted midtown building, a typical old Seventh Avenue factory with modern boutique front entrance, except there was what looked like a body lying in the front entrance of this one.

Eventually the telephone ceased flashing and a voice said, 'Hello Lieutenant? Are you there? This is Delia Summers. . . .'

Faraday opened his mouth and for a moment stared dumbly at the t.v. screen on which a blonde-haired young man in a classy blue cut-silk suit was flitting across Seventh Avenue on rollerskates, then skipped onto the sidewalk and pirouetted delicately over the motionless body on the front steps.

'This piece of film you're looking at,' Tony Rossini's voice was saying, 'is what actually took place this morning at the Torelli Building. The film was delivered anonymously — by courier — a short time ago to the Channel Eleven studio. So don't you say we don't get it to you first and fastest. . . .'

Faraday had kept abreast of fashion directions enough to be able to see that the blue suit the rollerskater was wearing had originated in one of the major couturier houses — the chunky ruched doublet tumbling daringly over the skin pants would never have been bought off the rack. But whether it had come from one of the houses lending its allegiance to Tina Rauch's party or from one throwing its weight behind Rocco Da Silva's gang, Faraday, interestingly, could not say. It was neither extravagantly baroque nor too severely classical.

He watched the rollerskater deposit a bulky black nylon knapsack among the blown litter in the grille of the boutique and, without disturbing the sleeping body or presenting more than a quarter profile to the camera, disappear from the screen, yawing along the sidewalk in the direction of the Park.

'I said are you there, Lieutenant?' Delia Summers' voice said again. 'Is that your t.v. I'm hearing?'

Faraday was torn between the impulse to kill the t.v. and

take the call and his duty to watch the news and log the call on his phonebank.

'. . . Well if you're not, I guess you're not. I just called to ask you what you were doing in the atrium this afternoon. I saw you. . . .'

A white police vehicle ghosted to a standstill in front of the Torelli Building and a pair of uniformed officers cautiously got out of it. They approached the sleeping person – some citizen without a home to go to. Faraday saw that one of them was Officer Rosie Vella, unmistakable with her goldy red locks. He had tried to date Rosie when he had first began to work out of the 19th – it was over two years ago now – without success.

Faraday's left hand cut the sound of the t.v., his right touched the phone-on key.

Officer Rosie Wella and her colleague were crouching on their haunches with their hands on their hips, close to their weapons, as per regulations. The bag person, leaning his head on his hand, stared up at them. He looked mildly disoriented, a gentleman with a hangover at the moment of being woken by his maid and the valet.

'I was hiding,' Faraday said.

'Oh! So you *are* at home!' Delia Summers said. 'I was beginning to think you might still be working.'

'You sound like Captain O'Duff,' Faraday said. 'He thinks the one excludes the other.'

'So – if it's okay for me to ask – what *were* you hiding from?'

'You.'

'*Me*! . . . Oh, I get it. You mistook me for some kind of predatory female arachnid. You thought I was going to eat you. Afterwards.'

'After what?'

There was a pause.

'I guess that's what you dropped by to discuss.'

'I could see it wasn't a good time to discuss anything. All those handsome acrobat construction workers prancing around you.'

'You mean, you want to say something to me in private?' she said as if she were making an invitation – to trick him, no doubt.

'I wanted to know if I could persuade you to meet me tonight. In a club.'

'A club! Hey! You mean, you wanted to *date* me?' Delia's voice sounded amused but not quite incredulous. 'Where did you learn your technique? Creeping up on a girl and peering at her from behind a bush?'

'I must have inherited it from one of my ancestors,' Faraday said. He watched the police vehicle, Rosie Wella driving, cruise off the screen. Seventh Avenue was again deserted. 'If you prefer: How about accompanying me on my investigation. You might find it interesting.'

'You going to be working – or what?'

'You're sounding like Captain O'Duff again.'

'Which club? What time?'

'I have to see someone at Rock's,' Faraday said, improvising. 'If you want to come along for the ride. . . .'

'*Rock's!*'

Faraday had hit the spot. She was impressed. He had clawed back some of the initiative.

'How can you get *in* there?' she said. 'You a personal friend of Rocco Da Silva?'

'I'm a public servant. Paid to keep the peace and not take sides.'

'Oh sure! You telling me you can get into Rock's just because you're a cop? I don't believe it.'

'Nope. Because I was once a professor of semiology,' Faraday said. 'That cuts ice in that world.'

'And a Professor of Biology? How much ice does that cut?' Delia Summers laughed. She had a beautiful laugh.

Faraday saw the front of 700 Seventh Avenue blow out and up. Huge bits of the building fell down and bounced onto the road surface while other, finer fragments floated away. He watched the silent explosion, listening to Delia Summer's laugh, as if the two phenomena were somehow related. There was a coherence to the shape events were taking. They were trying to tell him something. Fats Waller. The red-legged cranes. Tina Rauch and Tracy Wilder. The white flash of explosive light. It was all of a piece. Sections of iron machinery and office equipment became distributed among the rubble of masonry and the shorn limbs of mannequins.

'I'll pick you up in a couple hours,' Faraday said. 'Be ready to jump into a cab.'

'What should I wear? I don't have the kind of wardrobe to go to Rock's. They'll never let me in!'

'Something black, something white. Don't worry. As long as it has *you* in it. Even Rock's can't be *that* choosy.'

They said goodbye and Faraday watched Tony Rossini, looking very pleased with himself, smug even, on behalf of the Raxell Communications Company, sponsors of the Twilight News Show. He was taking as much credit as could be wrung out of the scoop. Faraday turned up the sound in time to hear him explaining to the Channel Eleven audience that the young fella on the rollerskates – presumably the person who had sent in the film tape – had used a remote control camera in order to be certain that there were no innocent passers-by caught up in the explosion – the old bag person, for example. It was a daring and a humane gesture. The way Tony Rossini spoke about it, it didn't sound like a criminal act at all. By the next bulletin the young terrorist would probably be portrayed as some kind of hero – witty, stylish, with plenty of nerve. It was an ugly old building anyway. He was doing the city a favor.

4

Faraday, in his darkest suit, sat in the back of the cab, his face half in darkness, half in the white tungsten light being emitted from across the street by the lamps of the Fire Department engineers who were at work making the area safe. The illuminated scene of destruction that was framed in the black square of the cab window looked too calm and slightly unreal. The too orderly piles of crushed masonry and the stacked too life-like plastic human limbs recalled the scene after a bomb attack in some fictional t.v. film drama. The unreal pin-ball light ricocheted off the engineers' bright yellow hardhats and their cumbersome disconstruction tackle, a minute amount of it ending up on Faraday's lap, making that section of his suit – and half his face – appear silver, exposing it like a piece of photographic film.

Out of the silver side of the cab Faraday watched the hydraulic spider-jointed flying-shore being maneuvered into position according to the commands being radioed between the Fire Department engineers on the ground and those positioned up among the remaining structures of the building. The massive yellow piece of equipment was inching along its own massive yellow gantry, its articulated limbs extended to support critically weak points in the walls while smaller maxillae dislodged and removed the loose material. The items of office furniture and expensive Italian mannequins that Dinah Lazlo and her colleagues had expressed so much interest in earlier in the day now lay in neat piles as if they were just in the way, awaiting removal. Now the brand new-looking flying-shore dominated the scene, squatting over the crater like something that had a right to be there. A vast expensive rarely-seen yellow monster.

Faraday was beginning to wonder what the female of the species looked like when his attention was ensnared by something no less exotic. A medium-sized butterfly floated into the lights, flitting in a slow zigzag toward the enormous spider, vividly incongruous and practically flirting with death.

Delia Summers in a flashy night-black, milk-white silk gown was picking her way carefully over the debris, taking her time. The thin sprung fabric of the garment she was wearing, both concealing and revealing her body, held the imagination for a moment after every movement she made, an afterglow of reflections containing every color in the spectrum from which black and white are theoretically excluded. He watched her falter, pause, look about her as if she had only just noticed that the front half of the building and the way out of it were no longer there. She stood alone among the piles of rubble, slight, hesitant, on the rim of the crater, peering out of the light into the shiny darkness, vulnerable. She appeared to be looking right in Faraday's direction but so far without seeing him. Without even seeing the danger zone she was entering.

The traffic of activity ground to a halt. The engineers froze and their machinery became suddenly silent, hushed by the presence of this luminescent creature, apparently – or by some other factor. Perhaps by the way the fabric of her dress reflected the light as well as allowing it to pass through – which, being engineers, they might have thought was not possible.

Faraday found himself moved by the conjunction of images. His pulse beating faster, he made a grab for the cab door. He had to get out there, for once abandon the *camera objectiva* of his professional detachment, his voyeurism. For once in his life he wasn't watching it on t.v. This was *it*!

the Real Thing. Just across the street was the woman – the one he was getting to like, who sexually and intellectually challenged him – stepping out of the rubble of a bomb-site to meet him, poised, the lights on her, the audience hushed. The chord it struck in him was a poignant minor fifth, almost unbearable. Delia Summers looked splendid – Life issuing forth out of Chaos – but also splendidly inappropriate against the grimness of her surroundings. Where did she think she was? Where did she think she was going? The stylish knee-length Torelli number she had on was a piece of inspired wit – or high folly – considering he was taking her to a club frequented by the fashion adversaries of the dress's creator, people for whom Vincent Torelli's famous shimmer-effect was anathema, vulgar baroque, bad taste. In the circumstances the white and black silk gown was a daringly romantic piece of bravado which Faraday – he couldn't help smiling – hoped the heavyweights in the minimalist black or white tuxedos on the door of the club would have the imagination to appreciate.

The gullwing cab door – in its own sweet time – swung up over the dark sidewalk. Faraday clambered out and felt his way around the dark side of the vehicle towards the light. He crossed the street. This was just the opposite of watching t.v. Fantasy was metamorphosing into fact. He was stepping out of the front stalls of the Opera House, out of the illusion of the performance onto the reality of the stage.

He approached the safety cordon in front of which a pair of police officers, one in uniform, the other in a dark suit, lounged with their hands on their hips. Faraday stood behind them without saying a word. They were also absorbed in the performance. A blue-jacketed yellow-helmeted Fire Department officer was approaching the young woman in the expensive gown who looked as if she was unsure in which direction to turn. It was Wagner in modern dress.

'Faraday . . .?' the police officer in the dark suit murmured over his shoulder, his detective's sixth sense alerting him to Faraday's presence.

'Good evening Captain,' Faraday said.

'What the fuck are *you* doing here?' O'Duff asked in a quiet surprised voice. 'I thought this was your case!'

The uniformed officer standing next to O'Duff guffawed.

'I'm working on it,' Faraday said, his straight face made silver by the artificial lights.

O'Duff gave Faraday's plain but not cheap evening dress suit a sideways once-over.

'Don't tell me,' he said. 'You're taking Miz Summers away for questioning.'

'You got it,' Faraday said.

O'Duff shook his head.

'I don't got shit. I got a hole in the ground and a pain in the ass. It's what *you* got I wish I had. Nerve! Where you intend grilling her? The Waldorf-Astoria?'

The uniformed cop coughed back another guffaw.

'Matter of fact, Captain, I'm taking her with me to see Rocco Da Silva,' Faraday said with a matter-of-fact tone. 'I decided to take Danny Keach's advice and to go armed.'

'Danny knows what he's talking about. What you plan asking young Rocco?'

'Whatever you want me to ask him. It was your idea.'

O'Duff shrugged. 'You'll think of something.' Then: 'By the way, did you watch the News tonight?'

'I sure did.'

'Of course you sure did. Everyone in the City sure did 'cept Police Captain Daniel Clarence O'Duff. He was probably the last person to get round to seeing it, some slick kid rollerskate his way round the Police Department!' O'Duff turned his back on the bright lights to face Faraday. 'How good d'you rollerskate, Lieutenant?'

'Not so bad. I used to be quite good. A bit rusty now, maybe . . .'

'I'm glad. Because you going to get your skates on, Police Lieutenant Faraday, and put in some practice. It would make me happy to see you rolling into the precinct with the little creep who done this chained to your wrist! It would make me *very* happy to see it on the morning News

68

Show!' O'Duff grinned horribly at Faraday. 'Why, you could star in your own favorite t.v. programme!'

'I'll see if I can oblige, Captain.'

Faraday stepped between the two senior police officers towards Delia Summers who was expressing her gratitude to the gallant firefighter for having navigated her safely across the danger-zone. She held her hand out for Faraday to take and, to O'Duff, said: 'Hello Captain.'

'Good evening Miz Summers. You're looking very beautiful. You know I'm relying on you to look after the Lieutenant here. He's the only semi-o-tician I got.'

Delia Summers and Captain O'Duff grinned at each other. They clearly both knew something Faraday didn't.

'You can bet I will!' she said. She drew herself closer towards Faraday's arm. 'He's the only one *I* got!'

O'Duff shook his head, incredulous, and to his uniformed colleague said: 'He draws a check every month from the City Account for doing this!'

Delia Summers, placing her high heels between the bits of rubble, allowed Faraday to guide her towards the waiting cab.

The cab headed toward Broadway which would take them directly to Gramercy Park and the elegant block between Irving Place and 3rd Avenue on 19th Street, where the executives of the Da Silva faction customarily held court.

Having themselves admitted to Rock's turned out to be no great problem. It must have been talent night. When the cab turned out of 21st Street there was already quite a crowd of clubbers in well-tailored suits and dresses hanging around the original stone Old World porch entrance, posing as coolly as people possibly can outside a club they are trying to gain admittance to – about as uncool a situation anyone in style can afford to be seen in. These young hopefuls – beautiful, desperate, infused with the ideals of the New Classicism – were conversing in low voices, politely admiring each other's accessories, giving the impression that they were just taking the air. They didn't look as if they were eating their hearts out, although they probably were. They looked as if they were already safely past the friendly talent scouts on the door, congregating at the bar, having a good time. They were loyal champions of a noble cause. Apprentices learning a trade. They knew you had to start somewhere. Why not here? Next week it might be one of themselves on the turnstile, fingering the lucky ones out of the crowd. Some of the best – not excluding Rocco himself – had gotten started cruising the right clubs and crashing the wrong Art Fashion shows, doing the necessary legwork to catch the attention of other interested parties: designers on the lookout for ideas to appropriate, wealthy patrons who needed someone fresh to look at, to be looked at with. Or simply aspiring club owners who wanted a stake in the game. In the style war these young people were not the combatants, or even the helpless victims. They were the ammunition.

Max Faraday and Delia Summers arrived at exactly the same moment that Sasha – whom some bitchily called the Barracuda – was having her identity processed. She was in the company of the Nigerian textile manufacturer, Osubu Asaba, whose identity was surely beyond question. Sasha was wearing one of his prints, a close-fitting shot-tulle dirndl in a zebra motif of geometric chevrons that flattered her perilously flat figure. In the sparkling foyer lights it almost made her look as if she had one.

Faraday approached the razor-tongued *Vogue* columnist with caution. He did not know what kind of relationship she had with Asaba. That is, whether or not it involved sex. He didn't even know whether or not they had zebras in Nigeria. Fortunately Sasha – aloof among the elegant lost souls in the limbo between the sidewalk and success – noticed Faraday trying to catch her eye. Instead of smiling and ignoring him – as she would have done in the case of almost anyone else – she smiled and came over.

'Max, darling!' she exclaimed. She touched his arm with the tip of her forefinger, as if she were calling for an elevator. 'What *is* this? Business or Pleasure?' The Barracuda flashed

70

a glance at the biologist, Delia Summers. 'Or is it too early to tell?'

'Since when were they different?' Faraday said.

'Since you two walked in!'

Faraday introduced the two women. Delia smiled without opening her mouth. He watched Sasha log the event on the miniature IBM she carried around inside her head.

'So what d'you want?' she said. 'Me to help you steal a base?'

Ten years ago – before Sasha was on single-name terms with the general public and Faraday was still a college professor – they had known each other pretty well, intimately even. Perhaps there still remained, deep down, the sediment of that intimacy.

'Just get us on the plate,' Faraday said. 'We can boff our own homers without anyone's help.'

'You sure you need *me* – to get you in?' Sasha said, arching her voice. She glanced again – but smiling – in Delia's direction.

'You can have my marker,' Faraday said.

Sasha stopped smiling, almost completely, and looked at him with mock deadly seriousness.

'What's your marker worth these days? On the open market?'

Faraday – he didn't have to think about it – said: 'The scoop on the 700 7th Avenue Incident before the Channel Eleven News team get hold of it.'

Sasha – she didn't have to think about it either – took them both by the arm and they all three allowed themselves to be caught up and carried off in Osubu Asaba's party, Delia Summers stepping easily into the difficult situation, Faraday wondering whether he was not promising more than he would be able to deliver.

Once inside the club the affrontery of Delia's gown did not cause a stir so much as a quiet riot of raised eyelashes and knowing glances of appreciation for the ironic homage it paid to the enemy – a Torelli garment that eschewed the extravagance of a Torelli garment. It was witty. It was a joke. It was daring and successful. Paradoxically, the perfect symmetrical black and white dance-dress was not out of place. On the contrary. Reflecting the whites and blacks of the other guests' attire, it magically became transformed into its opposite, one of the factors defining the style of the place. Faraday couldn't help experiencing a certain feeling of relief.

'Why does everyone have to dress so much the same?' Della said over her shoulder as Faraday – he instinctively looked around for some place to hide – guided her in front of him through the crush and jut of flashing revers and square padded epaulettes. They entered the lucite tunnel that traversed the dance area, on the other side of which couples dogged each other around the floor in elaborate stylized embraces appropriate to the tortuous rhythms of the tango whch the DJ was playing, opposite poles unable to escape each other's magnetic field. They were conveyed, stationary, on a moving carpet into the midst of the throng. Delia's dress, flickering under the rotating lights, snagged the attention of one or two of the dancers and she was transformed momentarily into a specimen under glass. When they arrived at the far side of the tunnel, Faraday led her upwards to one of the less crowded – but no less exposed – cocktail lounges looking down onto the dancefloor. The transparent walls and semi-transparent supporting columns of the interior of the building had the effect of opening everyone to the view of everyone else. There was – for those with the power to gain admission – no place to hide. Who you were, what you were wearing, who you were with, what who you were with was wearing, was public property. Almost every chamber in the honey-combed inner shell of the club was visible to every other. This was no doubt the architect's deliberate reference to Da Silva's aristocratic notion of democracy. It was almost impossible to get into Rock's Club but if you did, if you understood his style – you were among equals. There were no differences among those who had attained the élite, so what need was there for concealment?

'Surely,' she said. 'There is only *one* way you can cut a tuxedo?'

They reached the bar and Faraday quickly ordered a brace of Krug Réserve from the attractive young man in silver hair and jet lipglow.

'You're right. There is. But only one. The supreme untoppable evening dress suit exists in the mind of the Creator.' Faraday raised his eyebrows as if it were just a few floors above where they were sitting, in the penthouse, that the Creator was installed, smoking the supreme untoppable cheroot, listening to Wolfgang Amadeus playing cadenzas on the last word in Jap electronic keyboards. This image abruptly brought back to mind his reason for being there: to find the person wearing the best-looking penguin-suit in the house and ask him if he had had any high explosives planted on Seventh Avenue recently.

'I FEEL LIKE a fraud,' Delia Summers said.

And it was true. After the flit of rainbow fragments which were constantly delighting the retina in the world she was accustomed to, the self-conscious austerity of Rock's Club seemed colorless and two-dimensional. And – because its two dimensions were without penumbra – dangerous. There were only sharp edges between categories. The undergrowth of complexity and nuance had been eliminated. There was this and there was that with nothing in between for ambiguity to nest in. The blur that should hedge the categories of reality was missing. It was an environment as natural as a cocktail waitress's smile and as comfortable as a Barcelona chair. It made her wonder whether this was what the hawk moth *acherontia atropos* experienced when it entered the hive of the species of wasp it so closely resembled in order to steal the honey: the brindled conscience of a fraud. An intruder. A social parasite that did not belong there. This was not her territory. She was – albeit by accident – simply mimicking the members of the host community, superficially disguised to resemble one of them, feigning acceptance of their shared assumptions about the clear-cut nature of reality.

If it *was* an accident. Vincent Torelli probably knew what he was doing – he usually did – when he had given her this particular dress to wear.

'Then you should feel at home!' Max Faraday said.

She waited for him to explain what he meant by that.

'This is Art, Delia. Not life. You're looking to get in touch with the chthonic mysteries, you're in the wrong club. You should be working up a sweat down one of the South Side discotheques!'

While he spoke his eyes flickered to and fro like a salamander's, panning the dance floor and the neighboring loggias, and then returned to rest on her. He smiled, uncertainly she thought. Was he a police Lieutenant on the trail of a public felon or a male animal in the presence of a female of the same species, cautious among competitors?

Oh whyn't you shut up Professor? she told herself, returning Faraday's smile.

'You feel like a spy, huh?' Faraday said.

She nodded. Yes. That was it exactly.

'In bad faith. I know. Because your heart is not in tune with your outward appearance. But you have to understand that here – among the New Classicists – an element of deception is necessary. In fact such exquisite alienation is virtually *de rigueur*. It's how these people earth themselves – ontologically. 'I fake, therefore I exist.' Hiding your real purpose, your innermost desires, denying their existence even, is respected. To display emotion is not just bad taste, it's dumb. As Adolf Hitler said: "A man in the uniform of the National Socialist State ceases to be a man. He becomes transformed into the agent of Death."'

'It's the fascistic side of Rocco's style that's going to lose him my vote,' she said.

Faraday nodded. 'Right. A fetish with Power Dressing nearly always coincides with a period of political reaction. That's always been true. Think of the English Civil War, the Cavaliers and the Puritans – it was essentially about style: what shape hat, how long to wear your hair, what kind of collar, fancy lace or plain cotton. In the end the Puritans imposed a dictatorship and the people welcomed back the easy-going Cavaliers. Think of pre-Revolutionary France. Louis Quatorze, the Sun King, the first dandy. But during the Terror it was those who represented the non- bourgeois revolution, the *sans culottes* – those without gentlemen's breeches – who took Liberty literally. Ten years later those same *sans culottes* were under colors for Napoleon. The Revolution was over. Military uniforms – the ultimate in restrictive dressing – were all the rage.'

'It's as simple as that?'

'It's as simple as History – which is as simple as you want to make it. Rocco appeals to people's need for order, their fear of incongruity which, symbolically, is categorized as *dirt*.'

75

'Maybe so, but do we want his avenging angels running the city?'

Faraday made a mock grimace. '*Not so loud!*'

Over his shoulder, two tables away from the transparent loggia in which they were installed, Delia noticed that the young woman nursing the pale green drink, alone, was a person she had seen before, although the way she was gazing over the dance floor through her reflection in the glass panel facing her made her appear to be two people: a pair of identical twins in love with each other.

'Say! Isn't that Bonnie West over there?' Delia said, and immediately felt foolish.

'Yeah. It is,' Faraday said without looking round. 'I saw her soon as we arrived.'

Pale in her white acetate-satin chemise, she looked even younger – thinner – to Delia than she looked on television. And kind of forlorn, out of touch with reality, as if she had finally run out of news items to read.

'Looks like she's in a dream,' she said.

'What do you think of her?' Faraday said.

'Me? I never think of her.'

'It could be you should.' Faraday fingered the stem of his champagne glass. 'You don't want to ignore the idiom of a message. You might find yourself being sold something you didn't want to buy.'

'A virgin – Bonnie West – and a father-figure – Tony Rossini! The anchors for Channel Eleven News programs are custom-designed for the unresolved psychoses of the men and women who watch television! Most the viewers are so screwed up they'll believe anything they say!'

'Uh-uh!' Faraday shook his head. 'It isn't what they *say* is news. It's what they're *wearing*! It's what they *look* like – the image they project.'

Delia noticed the approach of the shadowy reflection in the glass wall in front of her at the same moment that Faraday saw the reflected person herself.

'Excuse me . . .' the reflection said, '. . . if I'm disturbing you 'tall.'

76

Delia turned ninety degrees to face the smiling hostess standing over them. She was a slender fair-skinned brown girl with a huge shock of spun jet hair. She did not need to wear a uniform of any kind to advertise the fact that she was on the payroll. The look in her eyes and the communication handset she was holding in her left hand were enough. She was wearing an open charcoal satin blouson over a white crimped point d'esprit cotton bustier laced nearly all the way up, negligently revealing nearly all of her fair-skinned brown bust, and a pair of semi-transparent striated crepe de chine zouave pantaloons in the same shade of charcoal as the blouson. In her right hand, on a silver salver, she carried a dusty bottle of French wine bearing – incredibly – an 1867 vintage label.

'Lieutenant Faraday,' the young woman said, addressing both of them, '. . . Miz Summers. Hi! I'm Gloria. Mr Da Silva asked me to welcome you to Rock's.' She smiled at both of them. Bending from the waist, presenting a piquant close-up of her décolletage as she did, she lowered the salver onto the low glass table in front of them as carefully as if it had been a loaded revolver. She straightened up, still smiling. 'He hopes you are enjoying yourselves.'

Delia said nothing. This was not her territory. Epinephrine, she noticed with alarm, was being secreted from the adrenal glands in her kidneys, shifting small amounts of blood from her viscera to her muscles and to her brain. Her heart, in the consequent release of glucose, began to beat at a more rapid rate. Her saliva dried up. Her hands began to shake. She understood perfectly what these symptoms meant.

Max Faraday said: 'Well thank you Gloria. Will you please thank Rocco and send along our compliments. You can tell him we're having a great time.'

'He thought you might like to experience some of the range of his cellar, Lieutenant . . .' she went on.

'But . . .' Faraday started to say something but nothing came out. Maybe his saliva had dried up also.

'And . . .' the young brown hostess – she was looking now in Delia's direction – continued: '. . . He would very much appreciate the pleasure of your company.'

Gloria was talking to *her*!

Faraday said nothing.

'Oh . . .' Delia glanced across to him for assistance. 'But, well, I don't know. . . .' But Faraday was not going to offer any assistance. He just looked at her.

Delia rose to her feet.

Young wildebeest, she knew, were often taken by cheetah.

FARADAY THOUGHT hard.

It was very singular.

How had the sommelier succeeded in uncorking the ancient bottle without disturbing any of the layers of dust around the neck? In a situation like this, no doubt, the same old family-heirloom silver corkscrew would have been employed. It was probably thrown in with the price of the bottle, having successfully broached the last three specimens of this vintage in 1882, 1933, 1976 – all of which would have been adjudged sound. Faraday decided that he – for some reason he assumed that the sommelier was a man – had held the bottle in the classic position, from behind, low down between his feet, and applied the gentlest brute force upwards. He would have had to have been good and strong. It was even conceivable, at the kind of price an 1867 classic *premier cru* Haut-Médoc claret would fetch at Christie's, that the sommelier was thrown in with the corkscrew.

But – in a situation like this – was this the kind of question Faraday should be occupying himself with?

He had watched – powerless to intervene – Delia Summers rise from the leather couch, smile at him – bravely, he had thought – and lean toward him, proffering the knuckle of the index finger of her right hand for him to champ on, which he had done until she had cried ouch. She had batted an eyelid at him while the pretty brown-skinned hostess was bending from the waist like a ballerina, making a perfect right-angle of her perfect body, to pour the aged copper-colored wine from the bottle into the glass, lift the glass from the silver salver and place it in front of him. Then he had watched them leave together, disappear down the confluence of glass-walled corridors. What else could he do? He was a semiotician. In any discourse it was not the content of a statement he was meant to concern himself with. His job was to register the formal conventions by which it uttered itself. It was his job to be more interested in the dust on the bottle, the rotting label under the dust, the old cursive script between the dust and the label – signs which bespoke the wine, than in the wine itself.

So what, in this double-edged gesture, was Rocco trying to tell him?

Faraday wondered – not for the first time – how much of his police training had been wasted. Was it as much as Captain O'Duff asserted? More? Or less? Or would the answer to the question be forever hidden from him, as the symptoms of certain neurological disorders are from the patients who suffer from them? Was it something he could ever find out?

Faraday raised the glass and tentatively nosed the bouquet.

Red earth! Blue sky! Fresh-cut marigolds and the odor of ground ochre pigments in seed oil. Louis-Philippe is Emperor, war with Germany brewing. Picnics in hot-air balloons. Charles Baudelaire, in his lover's arms, dying of syphilis.

Faraday knew the names of the five great first growth claret châteaux and in what respects a bordeaux was held to be dissimilar to a burgundy – aside from the shape of the bottle. But – on a police Lieutenant's pay – he was no connoisseur. It didn't seem right that this prized wine, after so long and no doubt interesting a history, should end up on *his* palate. How could he hope to do it justice? Had it survived war, pestilence, acts of God, solely for Max Faraday's delectation? Offering him the experience was a gesture so urbane on Rocco Da Silva's part that it almost made up for the fury Faraday felt at having just had his date so crudely hauled away from him – the fury of a man who has had to surrender his woman to a man stronger than himself. It didn't seem right. It wasn't right.

Urbanity and crudeness – fifty-fifty, in equal proportion. That was Rocco Da Silva.

Faraday – he had no choice – raised the glass and transfered a token measure of Château Lafite de Pauillac, 1867 – *bouteille numéro 2354* – from the glass into his mouth, enjoying the false sense of security that came over him as he did. It instantly became clear that it was of no great importance who died, who lived, who had planted the

80

bomb which had made the African Sorcerer butterfly extinct, what Rocco Da Silva's motives were. Even his own fury was of no great importance. In a moment he was transformed into an epicurean for whom nothing was important. The world – so the wine instructed his palate – was a good and beautiful place. There was nothing he had to fear. He was probably going to die himself one day.

Emboldened, Faraday took another sip of the wine. Nobody – he looked round to see – appeared to find this especially remarkable.

The club was filling up nicely. People were arriving and no one was leaving. On the perimeter of the dance floor the illustrious were strolling among the illustrious. Anton Derutta – the New Wave ad-maker, author of the odd-angle quotation-shot – was being nuzzled by his current skinny young ad-star Maddy Clark who, in a very short black piqué tunic-dress, looked pretty good from just about any angle. The Yankees southpaw slugger, Cody La Renta, this season's Major League highest hitter, in a loose-fitting prince-of-wales check double-breasted jacket, didn't look as if he had just bollixed his third Mets game in a row, the way he was laughing with – or at – Wanda Boëm, the German model, in stretch silver foil heroics. Or maybe it was she who was laughing at him. The hosiery millionaire, Duggie Snaggs, in shiny dacron pro cyclist shorts and sleeveless satin maillot, was in close conversation with his friend, the hair-stylist, Carlton Laplace, also in cyclist chic. Sexy and identically dressed, they looked like one of Derutta's advertisements for their own products. European designers. Musicians. Sport personalities. They were all there. The style-pirates. The demi-gangsters. Faraday recognized nearly all of them. It was one thing he was good at. On the dance floor Ikawa – white-faced, aloof, hair back in a chignon – swayed in an Ikawa belled oyster silk skirt and what looked like an original Burberry geelong top, Faraday could not be sure. He had never seen one for real before.

From where he was sitting – up in one of the glass-walled bars – there was the illusion that the dance floor below was

81

revolving. Whereas – he knew – the opposite was the case: it was the bars that were revolving around the dance floor. On the dance floor the young gladiators were improvising their variations on classic dance steps – merengues, sambas, rumbas, tangos – with a certain refined abandon. They would all have attended dance workout classes and so they knew how to curb excesses, restricting themselves to subtle explorations of the formal conventions of the rhythms. Rock's clientele – elegant, orthodox, diamorphic – expressed the values of their élite social group with a reverence for order, discipline, 'pure' style and the austerity of their dances echoed that of the interior structures of the club. Read as a text, there were certain references in the building that emphasized the architect's preoccupation with the rhetoric of tradition. The paradox of the stationary revolving bars and the motionless but animated dancefloor was probably intended to counterfeit the illusion of History in Time. The dancers on the floor were not simply fashion victims having a good time. They were participants in a rite, dancing on the still center of the turning world, and the rite was concordant with their shared beliefs that all change is illusory because reality is in its essence immutable. The basic laws of the universe – like the steps of the tango – could never be altered. Dancing the intricate and beautiful tangos and merengues was an enactment of this truth and symbolized the dancers' stoical acceptance of it.

On his own level of reality, to his left, Faraday caught sight of Bonnie West again – with the same shock of recognition he had experienced the first time. She had not moved from her table in the glass orthogon parallel to the one he was sitting in himself, her tall lime green drink untouched in front of her. She was staring straight ahead but not as if she were looking at anything in particular, more as if she were watching t.v. because she had nothing better to do. Alone, the gentle-faced young woman whose honest personality attracted forty-five million viewers to the Raxell Communications Channel Eleven News program every day was wearing the expression any woman would wear who was beginning to wonder if he – for some reason Faraday assumed it would be a man – was going to show up, and coming to the conclusion that he wasn't. She was being stood up.

It made Faraday sad to see it. He was familiar with the Bonnie West image – he knew her wardrobe inside out – and here he was being offered a glimpse of the human being behind the image, the person who lived inside the articles of clothing that the wardrobe consisted of. It made him sad to see it because now that he had gotten to know her in the way he had always wanted to know her – existentially – he would no longer be one of the forty-five million carrying a torch for her.

As Faraday stared at her profile – trying to recall if he had ever seen it before – Bonnie West turned and looked straight in his direction. Faraday's heart missed a beat, even though he knew instinctively that he was not the one she was looking at. It was her date, finally, making his entrance. Bonnie West, however, neither stood up as he approached her table nor smiled nor made any sign that it was a pleasure to see him. To judge from her body-language, it wasn't. She was angry. The way she turned her head and gave her date the once-over, he might have been a waiter come to take her order. Her mouth moved. The young man – at the very point at which Faraday wondered whether that was what he was, or a woman – sat down alongside Bonnie and put his hand out to touch her. Bonnie, pulling herself free, let him have it. She gave him a tongue lashing, all the time jabbing her finger in his direction.

The sex of Bonnie West's friend was not particularly ambiguous. He looked enough like a man to be one. Tallish, with a man's swagger, he moved like a man. His fine-boned face, its delicate features, could easily have belonged to a man – or, for that matter, a woman. His shortish wedged blond hair was a style you saw everywhere on virtually anyone – of either sex – who could afford to go to Carlton Laplace to have it cut. In his wide-shouldered two-tone evening suit with fancy revers, he looked like your typical

Rock's samurai – assured and aristocratic. All the same there was that something which Faraday could never put his finger on about crossovers, even good ones: the sexual anima. It didn't quite ring true, but in what respect it was hard to say. Bonnie West's friend, of course, might simply be a not-very-camp – or not-camp-enough – gay male. To make a final decision, Faraday would have to see the man's hands, which he could not do under the white gloves the friend was wearing on them.

Unless it was simply the smile. The man had a pretty woman's mouth that Faraday found attractive, its expression – under Bonnie's verbal assault – remained calm and sexy.

Conscious that he was staring, Faraday turned away from the couple and realized that he had lost the thread. His glass was empty. He should concentrate on the business in hand. He had just poured about a quarter million dollars' worth of nineteenth-century claret into himself without being aware of it.

GLORIA REMOTELY opened the glass door and stood aside to let Delia Summers pass through and, when she had, closed it behind her. Glancing over her shoulder, Delia could see the young ectomorph of mixed race through the glass, walking away, already speaking into her handheld. She took a deep breath – and let it out, deliberately inhaling and exhaling evenly. Her pulse was leveling out at about seventy-five. The epinephrine must have worked its way into her endocrine system. The release of glucose from her liver was stimulating her pituitary which explained the feeling in the pit of her stomach – her diaphragm muscle was contracting. Her physiology was torn between conflicting urges, flight and immobility, either of which might prove to be fatal. In front of her some clean-shaven men in evening dress were lounging over pieces of period Milan furniture, talking and laughing quietly. They glanced sideways at her. She could smell their perfume as they could no doubt smell hers. From the semi-darkness in back came the crack and kiss of colliding billiard balls. She had been admitted to a long narrow barroom. There was a line of stools facing the mirror in which a pair of identical white-coated barmen, back to back, were serving identical drinks to two parallel rows of identical customers. It was a facsimile of a classy Upper East Side martini bar. There was no music, no gambling machines and, she realized, no women.

Determined not to communicate her apprehension, Delia took a few steps into the bar, careful to ignore the glances she attracted. There were black men in white suits and white men in black suits, cut variously on similar lines out of an assortment of expensive fabrics. There were lamp-black and snowy-white pin-tacked matador slacks. There were scooped vests – striped and plain – under cropped jackets in wet slate-grey, pipe-clay and japan black silk, slubbed with china. She understood the strategy behind the contrastive coloration of these costumes. They were intended to serve as a warning to potential predators that it would not be advantageous for them to attack: a sting, something noxious, was sheathed. '*Watch out!*' it told the world.

'*Don't fuck with me!*' A stratagem which worked on just the opposite principles to camouflage. And she also knew that it was not always so simple as that. Certain harmless organisms faked the aggressive signals of dangerous ones, camouflaging their presence among their own enemy for safety or some other advantage. She herself – in the present company – merely mimicked the protective coloration of those around her. But having gained access by deceit, it remained to be seen whether she would be accepted or would be recognized for what she was, an intruder.

The amiable menace of the place recalled, in her physiological reaction to it, other occasions on which she had ventured into the habitat of dangerous carnivores: raw fear distilled into exquisite excitement. It recalled her recurring dreams of jungles – deception, betrayal, copulation and death – that she found so attractive.

Confident in her million-dollar gown, conscious of the open slope of her breasts from inside it, she made her way through the company of men, who watched her with the eyes of recently-fed sleepy cats, placid for the time being. They edged aside to let her pass through to the bar and then they sauntered lazily off in a posse toward the exit. Delia climbed onto a stool. The barman saw her immediately and came over, smiling ever so faintly. The man – bald, squat – had the demeanor of a traffic cop who has caught a respectable citizen committing a trivial violation. She waited for him to crack wise but he said nothing. He merely continued to smile faintly as he poured fizzy wine from a napkin-swaddled bottle into a stemmed glass on the zinc counter in front of her. It did not appear that she had any say in the matter. He knew what she wanted. When the bubbles had settled down he strolled back down the length of the bar, leaving her alone.

In the mirror opposite an attractive woman in a fancy outfit was seated up at the bar. She didn't look like a hooker but that was how the situation defined her, the way she was set apart from the other customers, although suddenly there did not seem to be so many of these as there had been when she arrived. In ones and twos they were slowly moving off. It reminded her of something: the behavior of immature male deer, giving ground at the approach of a dominant stag when a female has strayed into his territory. She had to stop herself from looking around to see where he was. The woman in the mirror smiled at her.

Out of the shadows at the end of the bar a knot of men, one or two of them were carrying pool cues, emerged and strolled with a rolling swagger towards her, joshing each other, sharing some private joke, the way men do when they are among men who play for the same team. When they were level with where Delia was sitting, one of the men – she could see over her shoulder in the mirror – detached himself from the group. 'I'll catch you guys later,' he said and the men carried on towards the exit without him. The barroom, by now, was virtually empty. She wondered how this discreet exodus had been orchestrated, what signal had been given. Unless she herself had been the signal.

The man approached the bar. He leaned his forearm against the edge of the zinc-top next to her, his hands loosely clasped together, and gazed straight in front of him – expressionless, neither at her, nor through her – as if she were the horizon of an ocean which he was inspecting from the deck of a ship, letting his mind slip anchor. Delia, unwilling to betray herself by voice or gesture, said nothing and made no movement. If he didn't want to make the first move, that was fine. She was no hooker. The squat bald barman, meanwhile, was discreetly placing a pilsner beer glass next to the man, and a block of white paper. The pilsner beer glass was full of drawing pens, sharpened lead pencils, various foreign crayons. Without taking his eyes from the horizon, the man took hold of the block, moved the pilsner glass an inch nearer, selected a charcoal-pencil and made some quick slashing strokes with it on the white paper. Delia sat dead still while he sketched her, back-to-front in the mirror – her and her butterfly-sheened Vincent Torelli evening gown.

Rocco Da Silva himself was dressed soberly in an unfussy waisted matt-black silk doublet with plissé satin trim. He wore a broad white tulle cummerbund over black worked-silk ottoman pants. Only the crimped piping of the open bleached-cotton shirt, bloused up like a jabot, softened the severity of the line.

Delia sat perfectly still. She had become transformed into his model. She did not have any say in the matter.

'How is he?' Rocco murmured over his sketch.

'Who?' Delia said, wary.

'Vincent. You know, it's been a while since I saw the old man. I mean, to drink a glass of wine with, shoot the breeze. I kind of miss him. Probably the only person I know can tell an original Worth from a Balenciaga homage without having to check the label. . . . Yeah. I kind of miss him. . . .'

'Oh Vincent's in pretty good shape, considering. A bit tired lately. Considering someone bombed out his factory and his showroom this morning.'

She let that hang there.

Rocco, impassive, sketched with swift confident strokes, glancing from the mirror to the paper and then back to the mirror.

'Yes . . .' he said eventually, '. . . I was real sorry to hear 'bout that. That was a bad thing to do. Real bad. I always liked Vincent. I liked his work. Still do, of course. It's got the finest finish you'll find anywhere.' He grinned at her image in the mirror.

Delia – her heart-rate increased fractionally – looked from his to her own expression. She was relieved to see that it remained as impassive as Rocco's. She was under no illusion that she would be less susceptible to Rocco's infamous charm than anyone else in the city.

'I hope you don't object to me doing this,' he said, still looking at her in the mirror. 'I don't have very many opportunities to get this close to one of Vincent's gowns. Never one as fresh and recent as the one you're wearing – so appropriately, may I say.'

'We had you figured for the brains behind the bombing,' Delia said. She was shocked to hear the words blurt out of her mouth. It was a reflex defensive retaliation.

Rocco shook his head and sucked his teeth to express disdain. 'Is that *all* the brains you figure I have?' he said with what sounded like genuine disappointment.

Delia held her tongue. She was in strange territory. It was a novel sensation to her, to be the object of such unimpassioned scrutiny. And a threatening one. Underneath her clothes, after all, she was completely naked. She could smell the feral sweetness of the man, the deep musk of his cologne – a classic Lagerfeld – cutting across the secretions of his body which, she knew, the chemistry of her own olfactory emission system could not help but react to.

'And that's what your friend's doing here, huh?' Rocco added. 'The Lieutenant Detective, second grade, of the 19th Precinct – to put the finger on me?'

'You're asking me? You know more about him than I do!'

'Oh, Max Faraday has his own reputation. Among the readers of specialized academic journals – like *Semiotext*. I used to read his stuff myself.' Rocco replaced the charcoal-pencil and selected a carmine-coloured waxstick, and then a white one. 'I was you, though, Professor Summers, I'd tell the Lieutenant he's wasting police time. I had nothing to do with that business. It isn't my style. Dammit! *He* should know that!'

He stuck the carmine crayon in his mouth.

'He's up in the bar,' Delia said. 'Why don't you go up, tell him yourself!'

For a while Rocco didn't say anything. He was busy with his sketch. With minute blocking strokes he etched the white light reflecting onto his model's face, concentrating on the delicate work. Then he took the red crayon from his mouth and in two or three rapid touches of it suggested the coloring of her lips. When he had done this he said: 'I start denying knowledge before I'm accused, I'm already halfway to being subpoenaed. It won't make any difference what I say, I'll sound like the President – guilty, whatever they accuse me of. There's a bunch of media people out there – some of them are even my friends – who've been waiting all their life for this story. They can see everything happens. They watch every movement I make. The moment one them pipes to the Lieutenant's suspicions regarding the Torelli bombing, I'm through. They see me in his company – even he just wants to discuss the Mets' chances in the ballgame – by tonight's Late News Roundup I'm a suspect being interviewed by the police. By tomorrow morning I'm just another fucking terrorist. I can't afford any negative exposure right now. Not the smallest whisper of scandal. I have an election to win – tomorrow!'

'Sounds to me,' Delia said. 'You're asking for some kind of favor.'

Rocco carefully replaced in the pilsner glass all the wax crayons he had used – he had finished his sketch – and then angled the block towards Delia for her to appraise.

She saw at once that he had caught it. She recognized the loose confident style which Rocco had made familiar during his years at *Harpers*. He had captured the basic idea of the dress – the bit of it showing above the bar – its flowing line ruched off the shoulders, the discreet invitation of the bust. He had even succeeded in suggesting the scaled shimmer of the sprung silk fabric, hinting at the rainbow spectrum hidden inside the blacks and whites. He had caught *her* too, but looking somewhat younger and much prettier than she ever remembered herself being.

Delia shivered. Something had been taken from her and put onto a page. She felt angry at the loveliness of the sketch, the primitive reaction of a human jungle-dweller who has just been described by someone more civilized than herself. The surface of her skin trembled, the erectile muscles beneath it contracting and expanding in rapid spasms in order to generate warmth.

'You know, I don't think you follow my drift,' Rocco said. His right hand slid underneath the satin trim of his black jacket and reappeared – almost instantly – holding an ivory-handled knife, open. For a moment it lay innocuously in his palm like a surgeon's scalpel. Then he picked up the charcoal-pencil he had just used and with quick flicks of the blade began to put the point back on it.

'I don't know how to say this without frightening you but – ah – you don't really have any choice, you want your boyfriend to see you again tonight. I don't have to kill you. I can, of course, But I don't *have* to. I can keep you – the both of you, if necessary – from going about your business for a while. Say for twenty four hours? Least until after the Election. By when it won't matter. The day after tomorrow he can ask all the damn questions he likes.'

Delia held her breath. If she held it long enough the lack of oxygen to her bowels would put her brain onto red alert.

The blade glinted in Rocco's hand.

'You see what I'm saying? It's not *you* doing *me* a favor,' he went on. 'If anything, it's me doing *you* one.'

With an extra quick flick Rocco Da Silva stabbed the point of the knife into the chest of Delia Summers – into the finished image of her on the top page of the sketch block – between the silver yoke and the shiny black bodice of her gown. The blade stuck upright. The nerves controling the muscles in Delia's intercostal region involuntarily convulsed. Rocco stood up from the bar. He laid a hand gently onto her bare elbow.

'Professor Summers – may I call you Delia? Look – I didn't ask you down here to hold a gun to your head . . .' he said, easing her off the stool as if he already knew that that was her intention. Delia didn't have the strength to resist. For the first time since they had met the two of them looked at each other square on, face to face. He grinned at her, a friendly intimate grin. He kissed her lightly on the lips. 'But I *will*! . .' he said. Holding her hand in his, he led her towards the glass doors that led onto the dance floor. '. . . You don't watch your *step*!'

IT DIDN'T make any sense.

Down on the dancefloor a number of couples were turning skilfully in each other's arms to the music that was being relayed over the system. A female vocalist was accompanying a tight seven-piece band. '. . . *The very thought of you* . . .' she sang, '. . . *and I forget to do* . . .' she sang, '. . . *those li'l or-dinar-y things – that everyone ought-oo do. . . .*' One or two of the dancers were making a stab at the real thing – a bluesy two-step, both fast and slow so that the two persons' bodies were rolling and rocking against each other in continuous jigging friction – but most of them weren't taking any chances, preferring to execute their own tastefully well-rehearsed versions of the number. It was a classic, after all, you could diddle with it, you could kick up its tempo, you could fuck it up completely, but you could never, never change it. '*I'm living in a kind of dream* . . .' she sang, '. . . *I'm happy as a queen. . . . And foolish though it may seem – to me that's everything. . . .*' Because it was unchangeable. Teddy Wilson at piano. '*The mere idea of you. . . .*' Buck Clayton, trumpet. '*The longing* HERE *for you. . . .*' Lester Young on tenor sax. '*You'll never know how slow the moments go till I'm near to you. . . .*' Young Billie Holiday providing the vocals.

Faraday took another slug of the wine.

It didn't make any sense but it wasn't one of the worst moments in his life. Most of the bottle was already inside him and the ancient *grand vin* was begining to infuse his perception of reality. He felt elated – not because of the wine but because of the insight the wine had given him: the thing he suspected Rocco Da Silva was trying to tell him was becoming clearer by the minute. *The message was in the bottle*! In other words, he was telling him that it is the content of the sign which matters, what is *signified*, never mind the bottle, the *signifier*. Rocco was challenging one of the most important tenets of semiology! Just what you would expect from someone running for public office, a politician, a person who thought language was like private property, something that belonged to *him*.

But all Faraday's training told him that this point of view was mistaken – if not mischievous. The interpretation of signs, by this model, was a nostalgic and retrospective process because it started from the premise that there was an essence to a sign – which, of course, only the initiated had access to. It was fallacious logocentrism. Faraday knew that *meaning*, morally and politically, was not something re-covered – from the producer of signs – but something produced and created by their consumer, and deciphering sign-systems should transform the world, not merely repossess the past. Nobody really ever understands anybody else: the thing signified is gone for ever. Charles Baudelaire's lover is dead – and Billie Holiday's. Charles Baudelaire and Billie Holiday are dead, Goddamn it! All we have is the fucking signifier! Isn't that the point?

As soon as you understood this about Rocco Da Silva and his gang you understood his reactionary outlook, his veneration for classical models, stasis, order, economy. It was the appeal the well-turned-out tyrant has always had for ordinary people. People, that is, who are too timorous to interpret the universe for themselves. Where did you find ordinary people these days?

One place you didn't find them was Rock's Club on 19th Street.

Glancing over his shoulder, Faraday saw that Bonnie West and her friend were still not reconciled. Bonnie – in tears – was pointing her finger at him as if it were a loaded .45. The friend – Faraday was now almost certain where he had seen that smile before – was making mollifying gestures with the palms of his hands, unruffled but defensive. Bonnie West wasn't paying him any attention. She had risen to her feet. Batting her blonde hair away from her forehead, her profile tilted aggressively, she looked horribly real. The picture he got of her, a woman, furious, chastising her man, did not in any way fit the image Faraday had of the young innocent who read the news to him every morning – to him and to forty-five million other people. But it wasn't that that was bothering him. It wasn't that which didn't make any sense.

In the meantime, in the time Faraday had been watching Bonnie West and her date, the music had changed and the slow rotation of the bar-mezzanine around the dancefloor had inched into his line of vision a new set of dancers – new in their personal imagery, that is, but identical in every other respects. Carlos Gardel, to his Buenos Aires *orchestra tipica*, was singing his tortuous *tango contado* of love, betrayal and murder, *Tomo y Obligo*. Two of the black and white creatures on the floor, however, were tangoing with such ferocious grace that the other dancers were giving way and making space for them, the way they used to for Fred and Ginger. He had all the steps in the book and a few more. She, willowy in his arms, was sticking to him like a shadow, managing to give the impression that she was a part of him while being apart from him, ghosting him around the floor like a web from which he could not disentangle himself. Faraday gazed at the exotic duel with horror and excitement. Rocco Da Silva and Professor Summers were moving around the dance floor to the rhythm with a combination of arrogance and eroticism that was exactly appropriate to the formal intimacy of the tango – the dance which Da Silva had made synonymous with his attitude to life – severe, elegant, taut with repressed passion. Rocco and Delia glided not as two but not either as one. A pair of insects copulating in midflight.

Faraday became abruptly conscious of an emptiness just under and below the breast-pocket of his evening jacket – where he kept his gun holster. For the first time in a long while he experienced the urge to wrap his fingers around the butt of his police-issue Remington Enforcer. Was Da Silva deliberately trying to humiliate him? He was, of course. He was making a point, a very subtle show of power. If Faraday were a real cop, if he were Captain O'Duff thirty years younger, he would never take this kind of shit. He would kick ass and sleuth, set up an interrogation of the Number One Suspect and put to him those pertinent questions calculated to elicit those impertinent answers, make the man sweat. A real cop would not be sitting on a topgrain white leather bench watching his date being hauled round a dancefloor by the suspect in question while he sat drinking the man's fancy liquor.

Tomo y Obligo!

Faraday – there was no good pretending: he wasn't a real cop – poured the last of the stuff into his glass and swallowed it down to the dregs – as the dance came to an end amid applause. The two dancers disappeared out of his line of vision. The emptiness in his jacket was still there although now it had moved an inch or so to the right of his gun holster. He felt alone. He looked about him and saw that he was. Bonnie West and her friend had left – together presumably. So now he would never find out what Tracy Wilder – Tina Rauch's closest handmaiden – was doing in Rocco Da Silva's private club on the eve of the Big Election. What was she doing there at all? What was she doing there disguised as a man? What business did Bonnie West, of all people, have with her?

It didn't make any sense.

5

He couldn't see a damn thing. It was a gray-green dark kind of light, slimy, the color of mud, marbled with the fears of sleeping creatures. But he could hear a steady deep-throated burp-burping sound coming from every side as he allowed himself to be led, his hand in Delia Summer's, through the unlit undergrowth of the deserted atrium. He was sleepy himself and a teeny-weeny bit drunk. With his free hand he swatted at the moist shadows slapping against his face, depositing on it droplets of water which mingled with his sweat and then ran into his mouth. He followed Delia blindly – she knew, if he didn't, where they were headed – until a black thing swooped out of the mud-colored air and immediately vanished. He started.

'What . . .'

His hand slipped free.

'. . . Was *that*?'

'What was what?'

Delia stopped dead and in the darkness he bumped against her.

'Oh, probably a bat. The fringed-lipped variety, *trachops cirrhosus*,' she said, 'has tuned into the mating call of the male frog *eleutherodactylus fizingeri*. As you can imagine, this faces the frog with a serious dilemma: he has to call loud enough to attract females of his species but if he calls too loud he runs the risk of being eaten. Makes you think, huh?'

Faraday was just wondering what it made you think about when he felt a little tug at his sleeve. Something warm and wet came out of the darkness and brushed against his wet cheek and the open mouth-part of the female of the species *homo sapiens* covered his own. A wet tongue inserted itself into his mouth and its wetness commingled with his own.

'Relax. . . !'

Her breath penetrated the whorl of his outer ear, depositing on his tympanum a cluster of phonemes, minute particles of sound – a semi-retroflex r, a shwa preceding a palatalized lateral and an open-fronted vowel, a final velar fricative. From these small arbitrary signs he was able to reconstruct her meaning. But what it was, what she wanted him to do, was impossible. He was a tense knot of unresolved emotions.

'. . . Bats don't hurt people,' she whispered. 'It's people do.'

DELIA SLID her arms between Faraday's jacket and his shirt and pulled him against her body. The stimulus of his closeness to her – transmitted via afferent nerves to her spinal cortex and to her brain – immediately sent impulses to the nerves of her muscles. They began to quiver. She kissed his mouth again, wondering what he would do, what degree of stimulation would be necessary to trigger the appropriate physiologic response. There was a sensation of butterflies in the pit of her stomach from anticipation. She could hardly wait. She said: 'Darling . . .' conscious that the word would act as a psychological disinhibiter for both of them, that she was deliberately stimulating in her hormone-system the production of sympathin which would – eventually – bring her parasympathetic nervous system into action, and then it would all be outside her control.

Max Faraday, in the meantime, was doing fine. His hand had located the concealed fasteners set into the sidewall of her dress and was fumbling to gain entry. He was breathing deeply, taking down mouthfuls of air, no doubt to fuel the various alterations in his own body chemistry. His mouth made contact with hers and then his hand succeeded in loosening the hooks from the eyes and started to explore the area of skin between the small of her back and the strap of her underslip. She surrendered to the feeling of vulnerability she was exposing herself to as her person, her Self, was being invaded by Other. Almost instantly she became aware of the increase in her body heat and diastolic blood pressure. The soft tissue – the alae – in her nose, her nipples, her anal area and the labia minora of her vagina, tingled as the blood in those places was forced by her arteries faster than the capilliaries and veins could carry it away. Her heart pounded. Her lungs bellowed. There was no going back now. Very soon it would be unbearable.

'Max . . . darling . . .' Delia murmured into Faraday's ear. 'We could. . . .' Her teeth gnawed at his earlobe. '. . . You know, we could lie down right here. But you. . . .' Speaking wasn't easy. '. . . You going to muss up your suit and this dress of mine. . . . Well, it isn't even mine. . . .' She nuzzled her breasts – itchy with tumescence – against his shirtfront. 'Let's see if we can make it up to my apartment. . . .'

A hoarse growling noise came from Faraday's throat. It could have meant anything.

SHE MOVED away from him. The animal moment had passed. He stood alone in the center of the large dimly-lit apartment – her bedroom, perhaps – waiting for what was going to happen next. He was sad and sorry that she had chosen to leave him – already. That she already had something more important to do.

'You should've seen this place this morning!' Her voice came out of the dimness. 'There was glass just *everywhere*. . . .' A small light lit up next to a bed and he saw, despite the big bed and the Navajo rug on it, that it was as much a place of study as a bedroom. There was a top-of-the-line IBM library, the screen shattered. '. . . Boy,' she said. 'I was nearly a goner!'

She was drifting back into her own separateness, talking about it, formulating constructions about the world. Sooner or later he would be doing the same. He would say something, make a comment on the situation, make a pass, a joke, put his feelings into words. Language – the fig-leaf covering their naked intentions – was reclaiming them.

He didn't mind the postponement of the act, however. He savored that. It had been several months since he had gotten anywhere near this close to it. He could wait some more minutes. The cocktail of anticipation and desire – and Château Lafite – coursing through his veins was spiked with dread. Having sexual relations with a person of the opposite sex for the first time was nearly always a tricky business, like trying to read a book backwards – which he had tried. When you had finished you got to the beginning, you knew who dunnit before it was clear what exactly had been done and to whom, and then – often – there was a price that had to be paid.

Delia returned with a glass of something which she put into his hand and lifted to his lips. It was brandy – the liquor to revive the spirits of lost men. 'The bathroom's through there,' she said. 'The t.v., that's over the bed. It's brand new today. And *there*'s the bed, you want to use it. Make yourself at home!'

She disappeared. She had shown him round his motel room and left him alone.

Faraday drank some of the brandy.

He visited the bathroom.

He undressed and laid his clothes out, carefully, on the table at the foot of the bed. He placed his handheld communications console near enough for his hand to get hold of, should it need to, and slid under the Navajo rug and into the bed.

After a while he turned on the brand new t.v.

SHE TIPTOED toward the door. The light was on and there was piano music – *Gaspard de la Nuit*, it sounded like – coming from the other side of it. She pushed her nose into the crack and then edged through it.

'Hi! . .' she called in an audible whisper.

Vincent Torelli – he was sitting up in bed, a book propped against his knees – peered over his reading glasses. 'Delia!' He grinned.

She stepped into the room.

'How you doing?' she said.

'I'm still alive, that's what you mean?'

She took the wine glass out of his hand sniffed at its pungent nose – a Nebbiolo grape, almost certainly – and placed it on the little table. She kissed him on the cheek and then sat down on the edge of the bed.

'Well, I didn't come to see if you were dead!'

They traded knowing smiles. She had not said the truth but she had not lied. They both knew, when the time came, she would probably be the one who found him. She never went to sleep, if she could help it, without looking in on him.

'How was your po-lice-man?' Vincent said with an exaggerated sneer.

'Ask me that tomorrow morning!'

'Don't be dirty! You know what I mean!'

'He was okay. He should've been. He drank a whole bottle of Lafite sixty-seven!'

'*Sixty-seven*!'

'Yeah! *Eighteen* sixty-seven!'

Vincent's jaw dropped.

'You don't say? . . . What – was it like?'

'Don't ask *me*! Ask *him* – tomorrow morning. I wasn't offered any of it. All I had was a couple glasses of Krug Réserve. Yeah – crazy, isn't it? Don't ask me to explain. I'm meant to be the one with the palate. Max knows nothing about wine. It was some kind of calculated insult – or compliment – of Rocco Da Silva's. You know, he threatened to kidnap me, I didn't agree to persuade Max to back off from trying to get an interview with him.'

'Was he scared?'

'After fighting a bottle of nineteenth-century wine all evening? He didn't care.'

'I mean Da Silva.'

'I wouldn't say so. He was taking precautions. He just didn't want any mud to stick to him.'

'What do *you* think? Was he behind it?'

Delia shrugged. 'I don't know. I don't think *he* knows for sure – if he is. He can't be certain what his minions might have been up to, to put themselves good with him. But he can sure see how it can be construed that way. He's uneasy. Afraid of the publicity.'

'Stop it! You're making me feel sorry for him!'

'Yeah. Well – he said to give you this.'

Vincent took the scroll of paper and smoothed it flat against the book already open on his knees. He studied the sketch. He said nothing.

'I like it,' she said.

Vincent continued to study the sketch in silence.

'It only took him 'bout five minutes. He works very fast and, well – I think it's good.'

Vincent nodded. 'I always said that Rocco had it in him to be more'n a clotheshorse.'

'He respects you, you know that?'

'So why'd he want to blitz my operation?'

'You don't know that he did.'

'Till I know he didn't, I know that he did.'

'I don't think you're being fair. I can't help liking him.'

'Oh sure!' Vincent nodded again. 'He's very charming. He has nice manners. He has that way about him, people will cut their own throats, they think he wants them to. They say Adolf Hitler exercised the same power. Rocco Da Silva is a snake, Delia. A rattlesnake. Just as hypnotic, just as slippery, just as lethal. And his politics are the same. When he and Tina separated, he villified my work.'

'That was just a public attitude. You know that!'

'The Torelli Company damn near went out of business, just the same.'

Delia said nothing. There was no point arguing with him. She was pretty sure it was not the survival of the fashion house that Vincent was thinking about. His feelings were hurt. He had not forgiven Rocco for betraying his promise and his vision. An open-hearted exaltation in creation had been discarded for a tiresome retreat into pure style. The promise Rocco had shown during his apprenticeship had, as far as Vincent was concerned, been squandered on self-promotion and the urge to create an Image. Once Rocco had come to the conclusion that human nature is basically corrupt, that it is the duty of one person to exploit another, he was lost. As far as Vincent was concerned, Rocco Da Silva was a fallen angel and his aristocratic posturing, his reactionary pessimism, was the necessary evil outcome of his fall from Grace.

'He doesn't have many qualms,' Vincent added, rapping the sketch with the back of his hand. 'But you can't say he's short on talent!'

'Listen, I got to get back,' Delia said. She stood up and replaced the half-empty wine glass in his hand. 'Good night.'

'I hope it is.'

'Don't be dirty!'

'. . . The Yankees hated to go ahead . . .' the gravelly voice of Art Stukely, the Channel Eleven sport commentator, said over the pictures of the ballgame as they came up on the t.v. screen. '. . . But what choice did they have? Mets reliever Tiny Jolson walked the first man he faced and a pathetic throwing error by third baseman Azzaro twisted the Yankees' arm into an unearned 3–2 lead. Coach Ossie Zhorrer ended the inning by sending young Clark Bryce to his death at the plate. A lousy throw beat Bryce by yards but McEntire's high tag almost let him under. Bryce, however, stuck his arm up and tagged himself out. Nice going fellas! . . .'

Faraday lay inside the bed – sleepy – half-watching the game, half-wondering if he should be. Well, what else was there to do?

'. . . After t'night's fiasco these two great teams are going to be facing each other tomorrow in the game to decide the series – and who knows what they might be asked to do? Something real hard, maybe, like *catch a ball*!' Art Stukely gave a short nasty gravelly laugh. 'Or *throw one* even!' Art was good. Even if you knew nothing about the game, he made you laugh. There were people – Faraday was one of them – who respected his no-frills commentary. He left the fashion gossip to his Channel Nine rival, Harvey Walker.

'See you there!' he concluded with an ironic rising intonation that made his invitation sound faintly ludicrous.

The t.v. went silent. Faraday, his eyelids too heavy to lift, hardly noticed. He was sleepy. He was about ready to say g'night to ol' Art Stukely anyway. It takes two to tango. With the score even so far – and both sides playing so badly – it could be an exciting finish tomorrow. O'Duff would love it – love to hate it. What with Tracy Wilder – switch-hitter for Tina Rauch's A team *and*, it looked like, Rocco Da Silva's! – facing Bonnie West's curve ball, just about anything could happen. It made you think. But what did it make you think about? Bats and Butterflies. Tomorrow – Election Day – one side was going to come out ahead

– but which? The Yellow-Legged Spiders or the African Sorcerers?

G'night Art.

'Hey! . . .'

Faraday's eyelids jerked open.

'. . . Lieutenant!'

He was awake. Professor Summers of the Sherman Fairchild Center for the Life Sciences was standing on the Navajo rug, towering over him, the sheer line of her dress ascending all the way to her bust, her arms symmetrically crooked behind her neck. A caryatid. As soon as she had unsnapped the fasteners she began to wriggle free from the garment, eventually emerging out of the slough of black and white silk as something completely different: a woman, lissom and vulnerable, wearing a semi-transparent libellule camisole-slip. Without hurrying she sat back on the foot of the bed and rolled her smoky-gray stockings off her legs one at a time. Then she kneeled down beside him and pulled the rug off him so that his body was naked, and clasped it to herself so that her own was covered. She looked him over. He lay still under her scrutiny. It was the cool unimpassioned appraisal of a scientist considering from which direction to tackle a problem. He felt like a specimen on a lab-bench.

'Don't look so worried!' she told him. 'I'm not going to cut you open!'

Faraday opened his mouth to say something witty but he discovered that there was not sufficient saliva inside it to lubricate the words.

'. . . But,' she continued. 'You were a spider, you'd have plenty reason to be apprehensive.'

Delia pushed the rug away from her, suddenly impatient with it. The dragonfly's-wing sheen on her slip flashed among the shadows, reflecting the light and simultaneously attracting the eye toward the contours of the body underneath it.

'. . . You know that in some species the female eats the male even while he is in the act of mating with her. She bites his head off while the rest of his body is doing its duty, passing his sperm into her.'

No. Faraday didn't know.

'It makes you think,' his voice croaked.

'Sure's hell does!' Delia said. She grinned down at him. She edged her knees nearer to where he was lying. 'Fact the nourishment she gains from eating him contains nutrients to feed his offspring.'

'It don't sound very fair . . . to the males.'

Delia shrugged. 'They never survive the experience to communicate the danger to the next generation. *That*'s the beauty of it!'

Faraday noticed the transparent hospital patch on her left thigh – he could see the stitches – covering the flesh wound she had received in the explosion. He wanted to ask her about it but now was not the right time.

'In *gorilla gorilla*, on the other hand, the male is twice the size of the female. Copulation is rare and is a very gentle process. She is the one who initiates it – when she wants him, she puts out – so the male doesn't require prominent genitals. His penis, consequently, is tiny.' She demonstrated between her forefinger and thumb how tiny it was. 'Same for the orang-utan. . . .'

She ran the fingers of her right hand along the inside of his right thigh.

'Whereas. . . .'

Her hand took hold of Faraday's own penis and held it gently, raising it slightly for him to look at – as if he might never have seen one quite like it before.

'Compared with all the great apes. . . .'

He saw his member begin to move in her hand, stirring like a pupa in its cocoon, waking up after winter. There was something touching about it.

'Man – so called – the male of the *homo sapiens*, has the largest penis of all the primates.'

Her knees edged nearer still, so that she was now almost on top of him. Faraday, sliding his right leg under him – he needed room to maneuver – lifted himself into a sitting position, his erect dick pointing heroically at Professor Summers' breasts, the nipples of which – he could see through her slip – were erect also.

'Signs . . .' he murmured, his eyes meeting hers as they pulled themselves toward each other. '. . . And signals. . . .' His lips meeting hers. The side of his nose meeting hers. He raised the lace hem of her short slip and gently eased her out of it, drawing it between them, inside out, over her breasts and off her head. 'Everything . . .' he said as she adjusted the position of her legs so that his sexual parts were meeting hers. '. . . Comes down to semiology!'

THE SECRETION of the clear slippery mucus from the Bartholin glands situated in the vestibule of her vagina eased the penetration into it of the chosen male's sexual instrument. As the penis probed the outer petals of her tension her labia minora opened to grant it admittance – holding it caressingly for as long as she could hold off the almost unbearable tenderness it aroused – before swallowing it and its own pre-coital secretions entirely. Her abdominal muscles contracted – air rushed into her lungs – and continued to move in rhythmic spasms, sucking in air in short even gasps. The presence of the solid alien thing inside her immediately plugged the ever-dilating hole in her identity which recent emotional events had created.

From now on she was at the mercy of her own homeostasis. Peaks of neuromuscular tension rolled out of her pelvic region, setting off a chain-reaction of responses throughout her body. The gluteal muscles in her buttocks and the abductor muscles in her thighs convulsed together with coordinated and increasing rapidity as the penis nuzzled against the endodermal lining of her vagina and the hair-trigger of her clitoris. When the moment came – the trigger uncocked – she was barely conscient of the semen shooting into her, of anything except the waves of excruciating pleasure it detonated inside her.

Her muscles relaxed into flaccidity. She lay still, assuaged.

She slept, curled up in Faraday's arms like a soft crab in a borrowed shell, for the time being safe, while shoals of dream-fragments flitted to and fro across the limen of her consciousness.

Faraday – she knew even while she was asleep – slept beside her.

. . . UNTIL A hollow ratcheting sound – a prolonged trilling – began to scrape against the corrugated outside of the parietal lobes of his brain, as if his skull were a pocketwatch someone was winding up. It was a sound both familiar and one he had never heard before. High and intermittent, low and continuous, it was – he realized – two distinct sounds. A duet. The ratcheting was counterpointed by a regular peep-peep tone. Faraday's eyes opened. He hoisted himself up in the bed. He looked around. In the small quantity of light leaking from the bed-lamp he registered the unfamiliar surroundings, where he was, but he could see nothing of a ratcheting nature.

'What – the fuck . . .' he whispered to nobody in particular, '. . . is *that*?'

The woman asleep next to him – disturbed by his movement – adjusted her position and nuzzled her limbs back into the shape of his body.

'Mmmm . . .?'

'That racket?'

The racket continued.

'. . . Oh. Don't worry about it. . . . It's just Simón. . . .'

'Simón?'

'Simón the Bolivian bush cricket,' Delia said into his chest, her warm plosives brushing against the hairs on it. 'The *last* Bolivian bush cricket, you want to know.'

'No it isn't!' Faraday said, turning away from her. He leaned across and picked up his handheld communications terminal – the little red monitor button, he could see now, was flashing on and off in concert with the peep-peep sound it was emitting. He pressed the light, which immediately disilluminated. The peeping ceased. Strangely, and almost simultaneously, the sound-call of Simón the Bolivian bush cricket ceased also. The one must have activated the other. He touched the play-key. There was a pause, followed by the muffled whoosh of fabric crushing against itself.

'So . . . who, ah . . .' a woman's voice, issuing from the tiny terminal, said, '. . . who *you* thinks gonto win?'

'I'd like to say I knew,' a man responded. 'Fuck I would! But – well, *you* seen 'em . . . I never saw the Yankees to play so bad. Jeezus! What a bollixing! And not as if the Mets played much better. But La Renta – he's outta form, sure – but I hadda put money on one team, La Renta even outta form has the class to win a World Series game. I wouldn't put too *much* money on it. But yeah, I'd think the Yankees got the edge. Fact, La Renta, he thinks so too. I was talking with him just tonight. For a man who was struck out three consecutive innings in one game, he sure seems confident!'

The woman who had spoken first giggled. 'You know what they're saying, of course?' she said.

'Whoever *they* are, they're a bunch of jamokes. I never listen to them.'

'They're saying La Renta is hexed by the Mets' new pastel ensembles Zhorrer designed for them. They take his mind off the game, they're so cute. He can't see the ball!'

'It's possible, yeah . . . well . . .' the man said. There was a glum resignation to his voice.

'*That's*. . . .'

'. . . The fuckwit! All that fancy piping . . . shouldn't be allowed.'

'*Hey! That's Rocco Da Silva*!' Delia Summers said in a tense whisper as if Rocco Da Silva was right there in the room and he could hear her. She was wide awake, sitting up in bed, rigid with anticipation.

'There you go! You don't like something, you got to ban it. Regressive, childish behavior, like the doctor told you all those years ago.'

'And that – I don't believe it! – That's *Tina Rauch*! What . . .?'

'Sssh!' Faraday pulled Delia closer to him. 'I have a bug on Tina,' he whispered into her ear. 'In her bedroom. You're accompanying me on my investigation, like I said.'

'You're damn right!' Rocco Da Silva said. 'I'd ban that kinda doctor first thing I do after I swear the oath!'

'Yeah? . . . Darling, can you help me outta this? – Well you ain't going to have the opportunity to ban nobody!'

There was the coarse ripping sound of velcro fasteners becoming detached. 'The Yankees may indeed whup the Mets tomorrow night in the Shea Stadium . . . but it won't make no difference. By then I'll be talking to you from Gracie Mansion!' She giggled. 'Assuming I'm still talking to you!'

'What kind of bug?' Delia piped, still incredulous.

'A cockroach, as a matter fact. . . .'

'*Blatta orientalis*? . . . You're kidding!'

'. . . PD issue, with an FM microtransmitter implanted inside its shell. . . .'

There followed a pause in the transmission. Faraday shut up and listened. Then, in a coarse mock O'Duff whisper, he added: '*Can pick up a fart at twenny feet!*'

'Thanks. . . .' the terminal spoke. Tina — it was reasonable to infer — was disrobing.

'You *say* that, hon . . .' Da Silva finally countered. 'But the t.v. polls, they say different! I'm points ahead of you — as you know. Even the Yankees do bollix the game tomorrow — which I doubt they will — it isn't going to change the result any.'

'You're right . . .' Tina said. ' . . . It isn't!' She giggled triumphantly. 'Cos from the moment they see me, the voters, the moment they see my outfit during our clash on the Robbie Robson Show, who wins the goddamn ballgame will be of academic interest. . . .'

Rocco was silent.

Tina said: 'They going to see me in a gown of such exquisite beauty! One that was fashioned to reflect my policies. Fresh! Romantic! Generous! And boy, is it sexy! I'm telling you, they going to go crazy pressing the vote-facility on their t.v.! They'll understand — soon as I come on — that my 'ministration'll be open to anyone with heart and talent. It's not a club you need a membership card to enter. It'll hit them, the next term, they'll want to look at *me* and people who look like me. 'Stead of you and your storm-troopers and ice-cream sellers!'

'Hold on! Wait a minute! You're so popular, how

come all the polls say it's me in the lead? They want *me*. . . .'

'They want you like a crim wants a probation officer!' Tina jeered. 'They do an' they don't. They don't more'n they do. See, you 'ppeal to their old patriarchic dread of *women*. Nature. Liberty. Sex! You Mister Kleen. You 'ppeal to their old-fashioned symbolic purity rituals. Clean equals good. Me, I offer the illusion of color and danger, adventure. Storm'n Drang. Romance! They want *me* 'cos they know I'm *dirty*! And – sure – they're a tiny bit afraid of that. They're human. It makes'm nervous. And because you and I are in binary opposition to each other, they are half 'ttracted to your rhetoric. Subconsciously they want to be repressed. Maybe we all do.'

'Well, we'll see what they want soon enough.' Rocco gave a short sardonic laugh. 'They knew, I doubt they'd want for Mayor someone who throws her clothes all over the fucking floor when she undresses. You're a goddamn slut Tina, I keep telling you that.'

Tina Rauch sighed. '. . . I guess I am. Still – most folks're attracted to sluts. You got to admit it. Sluts don't give a fuck what anyone thinks. . . . Mmm. Maybe that's my next image-projection. Rumor I open my legs to the garbage collector and the help. Become the Whore-goddess. They all fuck my brains out in their dreams anyway, the good citizens of New York City. What d'you think?'

There was the swish of silk and the sound of air being exhaled in gasps.

'Aaaaah . . Aaaaah . .!'

'*This* is what I think!' Rocco Da Silva growled.

Faraday felt his own dick straighten out – it had a will of its own – and incline itself towards – and against – Delia's thigh until it started to become uncomfortable.

Tina giggled. 'Hey. . . . Get your hands off me! Lemme go!'

A sudden rustling osculation of skin and fabric came from the terminal.

'I hope . . .' Faraday said in a stage whisper. '. . . You're not going to let this come between us?'

'The old gags,' Delia said, kissing his chest. 'Are still the best gags.'

'. . . Listen! I got to cold-cream my face. Just give me five minutes,' Tina said without a shred of urgency in her voice. '. . . Lemme go!'

Rocco Da Silva gave a saloon gambler's chuckle. 'Whyn't you let me help you outta this . . .' he said.

There was the sound of ripping fabric.

'. . . Ahhh! You bastard! . . .'

Delia Summers slid a little way down the bed. She took hold of Faraday's dick in her hand and, in a single motion, rolled him onto his left side and conducted it within herself. It didn't need any persuasion. It snuck in like an elver into a rock fissure.

'Oh . . .' Faraday gasped. '. . . Boy!'

Delia shifted her weight, tipping him onto his back, so that she was on top of him. She squirmed herself comfortable and then lay perfectly still.

The couple at the other end of the transmission must have disengaged from their clinch. Faraday and Delia listened to the silence, but not sharing it. They were enjoying a silence of their own.

'Anyway . . .' Da Silva – now he spoke in a more detached register – said. 'I, ah, want to talk to you 'bout that fancy dress we keep hearing so much about.'

'Talk.'

'Well, I kind of formed the impression – from the t.v. – that it got destroyed this morning – in the explosion.'

'I have to tell you, Rock my sweeting, that you formed the wrong impression. The dress is fine. Tracy went over to Torelli's yesterday to talk to someone about the arrangements for the private Show – which is tomorrow, by the way. Today's event was a security dummy. Tracy's idea. Anyway my gown was not in the atelier when the bomb detonated. It was in that private little catwalk Vincent has in back, among where he keeps all his butterflies and lizards and poisonous snakes.'

Rocco didn't reply immediately. Faraday could almost hear him thinking.

'Your Torelli gown is safe, then, huh?' he said.

'Safe as Staten Island!'

'Well, if that is so, if it didn't go up in smoke 'long with the building – why'd they think I did it?'

'Who's *they* – the jamokes?'

'The police.'

There was a pause.

'What is it they thought you did?'

'Plant the fucking bomb!' Rocco snarled. 'They already got my name on the charge-sheet!'

'You mean you didn't?'

'You think I did?'

'It crossed my mind.'

'And the mind of a certain clever dick from the local precinct who came sniffing round the Club this evening! The cops, they think it was *me* torched the Torelli place, for Chrissake! To destroy your goddamn gown!'

'You *see*! It's like what I was telling you! The cards're falling my way!' Tina said. 'Tracy and me, we heard the news, we figured it wouldn't do no harm, y'know, keep y'all guessing what's Tina Rauch going to be wearing on the Robbie Robson Show for the *Vogue* Ball, her long-waited Torelli being bombed-out and all. Make 'em think. Build up a bit of healthy speculation. So we let them understand – without saying it in so many words – that the dress was part of the fall-out.'

'Thanks hon,' Da Silva said. 'You're a pal.'

'Oh, you're welcome!' Tina said in a dumb waitress voice –then, in her own: 'This police guy, what did he have to say, exactly?'

'Nothing. I didn't give him the chance to open his fucking mouth. I give him a drink and I pass the word, I drop a hint in his old lady's ear, his liberty won't be his for a piece, he even dares point the finger in my direction. In my own club! He didn't take much frightening, you really want to know. He wasn't one of your pastrami-on-rye cops. He's one of the new breed. Wears suits from Valentino.'

'You'd, you're telling me you'd hostage a city police officer?'

'It's not what you do matters. It's what you can get people to believe you will do,' Rocco said. He sounded weary. 'I don't have to tell *you* that. Anyway, It wasn't the threat so much as the bottle of hooch I gave him kept him quiet.'

'Your lawyer, who's your lawyer? Axel Flexner, right? Whyn't you throw him to the PD? Let him worry about it. Flexner'll soon get them reaching for their dictionaries.'

'I'm not worried about the PD. It's the hyenas work for the t.v. networks I gotta watch. Day after tomorrow, after the Election, the Torelli thing won't be news. People'll forget it. I win, Flexner'll be busy pushing his name around the City DA's desk, wondering where's the best place to put it. He'll be doodling his Cartier gold pencil down a string of runners for the vacant position of Police Commissioner. He'll be kicking the wastepaper basket round his new office. Figuring out who planted a bomb didn't kill nobody won't be top of his list of things to do.'

'You win – sure,' Tina said. 'You do, my lawyer, Agnes Wentworth, who I think you already had pleasure of dealing with, Agnes is going to have all the time inna world to start a case 'gainst the new Mayor. Grand Arson. Election Irregularities. The public'll love it, a new Torelligate. Fact, they come to expect it. You lose, it's Agnes Wentworth will be sitting at that desk in the DA's office. Be her kicking the wastepaper basket round it. I guess she might even find the time to put the new PD Commissioner on to the Torelli case. Make it a priority, clean up this city. Whether you were culpable – or some Fast Eddy works for you – won't make a lot of difference. We got you every which way.'

'No quarter, huh . . .?' Da Silva said. 'You'd do that – to *me*?'

'It's not what you do matters, Rock. It's what you can get people to think you'll do.'

There was a moderately long pause during which – Faraday concluded – the two speakers were easing the discourse into another gear, letting the teeth of the contradictions between them declutch so that they could re-engage at a higher, deeper, emotional torque. It was – the intimate whispered phatics passing between them signaled – an effortless change of mood.

Faraday in the meantime – he hoped the terminal was set on record – found himself responding with minimum resistance to the even undulatory motion Delia Summers was initiating. Although she was on top of him he had the sensation that he was the lighter body, a floating vessel, she the ocean he was floating on. He was an anchored sailboat rocking on the flat swell in the harbor at the end of day. Swish. Swish. If the terminal was not set on record, there was nothing he could do about it now.

'Hon . . .?' Rocco said softly. 'Whyn't you come over here?'

'Mmmm . . .?'

Cotton sheets crushed and rubbed against each other.

'How's that, honey?' Rocco murmured.

'Oh . . . That's nice!'

Delia whispered: 'Hey! What are they doing? Don't tell me they're . . .!'

'Sure, they are,' Faraday said. 'Jing-jang. Same as you and me.'

The room was silent except, perhaps, for the distant sound of dead leaves rustling that the male and female Bolivian bush cricket make when they are fucking each other's brains out. Faraday was half-conscious that his little sailboat had slipped anchor. It was drifting out toward the ocean, where the squall was. Until, suddenly:

'*Hey!*'

Delia and Faraday started.

'What . . .?' Rocco started also.

'*Look!*' It was Tina. Her voice had risen in pitch. 'Over *there*, for chrissake!'

'What's the matter?'

117

'A fucking goddamn cockroach is the matter! In my bedroom! I don't believe it!'

'What are you talking about?'

'Over there! You blind or what? Taking a stroll 'cross my carpet!'

'Oh yeah, I see it . . . a big fucker. . . . Wait a minute. . . .'

There was a rustle of movement and then a small dull explosion, then a high-pitched continuous whine as the frequency of the transmitter became inoperative. Faraday leaned across and touched one of the keys on the terminal and the whine ceased.

'Rocco . . .' he said. '. . . Just splatted the bug. With his shoe probably. They nearly always use their shoe. . . .'

'Good!' Delia said. 'Just in time, you ask me. I don't know I wanted to hear anymore. Does it matter?'

'Hell no. It nearly always happens — sooner or later. Roaches are people-tropic but people, well most of them, have this thing against roaches. Nearly always end up splatting them. With their shoe. It's a design feature. Built-in. Means the suspects often destroy the evidence that they were being bugged. Cute, huh?'

'So. . . . We're out of radio contact? There's just you'n me?'

'Guess so,' Faraday said.

Delia — her breasts flat against his chest, her lips brushing against his — rolled her pelvis against the contrary motion of his groin.

Swish. Swish.

The squall was blowing up again.

It made you think. But what — Faraday tried to recall — did it make you think about?

6

Faraday – swaddled in silk, snug, and sleeping faster than light, like an insect inside a chrysalis – gradually became aware of the flickering neon-like quality of his dream. He was dazzled. In his dream he was standing on the perimeter of the world – on the perimeter of the observation deck on top of the World Trade Center in Lower Manhattan, to be precise, looking down onto the plaza bounded by Liberty, Church and Vesey. The light was dazzling. It was a clear day. The sun was shining. His heart – lighter than a bird's feather – was on the point of bursting forth from his skin like a seed from an old pod it no longer had any use for. His spirit – the meaning of the word set free from the word – soared. He was laughing. He was high as a kite. He gave a laughing sideways glance towards Delia Summers, eager to share this with her, and he was momentarily perplexed to see that she was not there beside him. Delia Summers, unaccountably, was not in his dream. He was alone in mid-flight. His heart, recovering its mass and growing heavier than the feather, fell. His laughter petered out. He lost altitude. Then the speed of his descent accelerated. He plummeted. The sidewalk of Vesey and Church rushed toward him and for a split second he stared death in the face. His eyes were opened at the point just before the point of impact by the dazzling neon-like colored images being emitted by the t.v. screen positioned over the bed and decaling the outside of his eyelids.

It was Art Stukely, the sport commentator, looking right at him. When his heart finally stopped thumping, Faraday gave a sideways glance toward Delia but, as he already knew, she was no longer there beside him. He could hear the continuous sound of the water-jet coming from the bathroom where she was taking her shower. He elbowed himself up in the bed and made a brief reconnaissance: the modern sectional sofa and the old comfortable-looking La-Z-Boy, the standard glassplate knee-high leisure-table, the dull light coming in through the film of clear polymol which the deconstruction company's artificers had rigged up over the imploded glass end-wall of the apartment. The artificers had earned their check. Except for the shattered IBM frame in front of the La-Z-Boy, there was virtually no evidence of the explosion.

According to the t.v. clock it was thirteen after seven. The t.v. was tuned, therefore, to the Early Bird News Program. Art – without the sound over – didn't look his old dry humorous self. He was making some strange faces. Come to think of it, he wasn't looking well at all. Surely the Yankees hadn't played so bad last night he was going to throw up. Eventually he pulled a white handkerchief from the breast-pocket of his houndstooth check sport coat and poked it into his eyes. Big Art Stukely – ex-left hander for the Dodgers the year they won the Pennant, with a .330 career average – was crying tears.

Faraday wasted no time hitting the go-pip.

'. . . To say we got no in – Holy Jezzus! – no innication 'tall why this would of happen. Fact is it just. . . . It don't make no sense, no sense 'tall. What . . .? All I can tell you is Bonnie West was found this morning by her transport valet, Miz Margo Pearlis, who is a Channel Eleven employee. Miz Pearlis tried to rouse Bonnie at her usual time the same she does every day, to escort her to the Studio. When there was no response, the security . . . she had the condominium security personnel open up on the apartment. It was Miz Pearlis and Security Officer Youngblood found the . . . found Bonnie's body. It. . . . She was sitting in her living room – Oh my God! This is just too awful! She. . . .' Art Stukely looked up from the piece of paper in his hand from which he was taking his cues. His mouth gagged, unable to get the words out. Finally, in an angry snarl, he bellowed: '*Bonnie has been shot dead!*'

Faraday almost forgot to breathe. The sound of the water-jet in the bathroom suddenly ceased. Did Art Stukely saying this on t.v. mean that it was true? Did hearing that some person was dead – and not just out of town, vacationing in Wap-Wap – mean that they were dead? Did being dead simply consist of the saying it and the hearing it said – and for as long as you went on believing they were still on their vacation or sitting at home in their living room, they were still alive? Faraday realized that he had just witnessed two minutes of the most appallingly momentous television he was ever likely to see in his life.

Art Stukely, after a moment's pause, recovered a small amount of composure. The news, now that he had uttered it, seemed to sink in. He was becoming the professional doing a job of work. He was stand-in anchor for his deceased colleague, announcing her death on her own show. He was seated at her own lilac newsdesk in front of her usual summer flowers, a spray of pink sweetpea in a fluted glass vase. Her signature.

'I'm sorry folks,' Art said to camera. He was stuffing his white handkerchief back into his breast pocket. 'I guess I'm. . . . Y'all know I'm not use to. . . . Well, this is no goddamn ballgame! We all loved Bonnie. I mean *all* of us. Same as you did. I don' unnerstan' who, what kinna fiend, wants to knock off a sweet girl only ever bought happiness inna people's lives. . . .'

Art Stukely's fist screwed the piece of paper inside it into a ball. The fist struck the table-top of the desk, upsetting the glass vase. Automatically Art picked up the vase and righted it and tried to replace the flowers which had tipped out. His huge mitts, which had slugged balls to every corner of Candelstick Park, fumbled to insert the fine stem into the vase's narrow aperture. He just couldn't do it. Finally he gave up. The flower stuck, bent at an angle, awkwardly in the vase. The t.v. camera – a piece of inspired directing, you had to admit – closed onto the pathetic image and stayed there: the sweetpea, like the life of Bonnie West, crushed. It was poetry.

Delia came out of the bathroom wearing a crisp pair of light cotton swamp-fatigues with flapped patch-pockets, identical to the pair she had been wearing when Faraday had seen her for the first time – only yesterday. He could not see her face because she was drying her hair with a hand-blower.

'Hi! You want breakfast? Coffee?' she said through the fall of her hair.

Faraday zeroed the t.v.

'Bonnie West was killed during the night,' he said in a flat take-it-or-leave-it voice. He let it hang there in front of her, a string of words that had some kind of meaning which the words – however you strung them together – could not alter. 'She was murdered.'

Delia stopped. She flicked her hair away from her face and looked up at him sideways. The hand-blower clicked off and the room was silent. Faraday, remembering the last reel of the dream he had just woken up from, experienced a pang of joy, pure and simple. He was relieved to see her and to watch her reaction to the news which he had just given her, how her mouth, her eyes, her whole face, which he had gotten so used to since yesterday, opened – and then closed, her lips and her eyelids clenched tight. She seemed to take in the hard fact, ingesting it whole the way one of those wide-jawed reptiles of hers puts itself on the outside of some larger, once beautiful, now dead thing. It drew a line for him round the futility of it all, the cheap cinematic two-dimensionality of existence in which death was just the flipside of life. Delia's reaction – beautiful, wise – gave him back his hope. Next to her, the senseless murder of Bonnie West almost seemed to make sense, become part of the necessary order of things, part of the price humanity would have to pay.

Almost. But – as Delia Summers approached the bed, again tossing her hair out of her face – he remembered the Second Law of Police Semiology: *You Can Forget What Makes Sense*! Bracket out the content, your feelings, the heart of the matter. Observe how the crime is dressed up. What is it that is being packaged? What are you being sold? A criminal act is a conventional sign like any other act. It makes a statement. Like most laws this one sounded obvious. What it meant – what he told Captain O'Duff it meant – was that the semiologist's job is to tell the world the nature of the statement being made, to decipher it. And sometimes – if you were lucky – it told you where the statement had been made. Who dunnit. Unless the police forensic crew got there first. As they usually did.

It wasn't such a bad law, Faraday considered, considering he had formulated it himself.

Delia, on the edge of the bed, said nothing. She took his right hand in hers and looked into it but there was nothing there. Her silence was perfect – it bounded the ragged edge of what he was feeling, made a map of it on which X marked the spot. She folded his empty palm into a fist as if the thing that was not there were something valuable that he must try to keep hold of. She brought the fist to her lips and kissed it and then gently bit her teeth into it, she bit until he cried out in pain and tears came into his eyes.

Art Stukely's response – Art's and forty-five million other people's – was the right one: blub and raise your voice against God and be damned. It was the *only* response.

When he had showered, shaved, dressed and done what he could not to think about Bonnie West, Faraday stood at the temporary polymol interface at the end of the room while, behind him, Delia ordered breakfast over the phone. He discovered that the play of light and shadow on the atrium viewed from above had a tranquilizing influence on him. The woven intricacy of the jungle greens absorbed, by some optical equivalent of capillary action, the flat un-answerable slab of information he was now in possession of. What was simple gradually became complicated – which was how he liked his information, in discrete bits and pieces, not served up on a plate. It was his phenomenological training. He had already deliberately stashed the various facts of the case in different sections of his brain, the way he had seen cops hold bunches of suspects in separate cells and for the same reason, in order to prevent them from communicating with each other. In Faraday's experience, when one piece of information got together with another piece of information, the character of both pieces — like two amoeba — altered completely. And he was in no hurry, in the present circumstances, to arrive at any obvious conclusions.

'. . . Cawffee? Yeah, sure . . .' Delia was saying in a Flatbush whine. '. . . Well whyn't you put on a fresh pot. . .? That's right. . . . That be wunnerful. . . . Huh? Eggs, I guess. . . . Sure, make that fer two. . . . *Hey Mister*! . . .' she called out to Faraday in a voice from across the River. '*How ya wantcha eggs?*'

Faraday turned from the view of the atrium and looked across to Delia Summers who was standing with one hand on one hip, the hip cocked towards him, making like any all-day-breakfast diner waitress. She winked at him.

'Easy over, sweetheart,' he told her.

'What d'ya know? The same as me. . . . Yeah, you got it. 'Kay. See you in two!'

She dropped the phone into the top flap-pocket of her fatigues. She uncocked her hip and, dropping the fuck-you attitude, said, 'C'mon, Max. Let's go give our amino acids something to chew on.'

FARADAY WAS seated in front of his coffee and orange-juice, his eyes fixed on the rectangle of sunlight that lay on the table in front of him as if it were an open newspaper which he was reading. His face was disturbingly peaceful. He looked like a patient in the aphasic ward of a mental hospital.

Vincent – with a white short-order chef's apron over his faded blue cotton work-pants – hummed along with the hissing of the eggs that he was pushing around the skillet with a wooden spoon.

Delia – she liked the way the two men accepted each other's presence – cut the bread into identical slices. It was good *pane casereccio* from Angiolini's on Mulberry, good for soaking up the olive oil that Vincent insisted on cooking everything in, which in turn he insisted was good for soaking up the *vino da tavola*.

When the eggs were cooked and the sunny side had been eased over, Vincent brought the skillet to the table and slid them onto three plates. 'Tell me . . .' he said, sliding the plates across the table. '. . . What was it like?' He pulled himself up a chair. When Faraday said nothing, he added: 'Lieutenant?'

'You can call him Max, you know that, if you want to,' Delia said. 'He isn't on duty.'

Faraday looked up from his eggs. She watched him. After a moment he said: 'What was what like, Mr Torelli?'

Delia decided it wasn't worth telling Max he didn't have to call Vincent Mr Torelli. Clearly the formal register which they were both adopting performed some male recognition function. It was a display. They were just behaving the way men liked to behave.

'The *Lafite 1867*!' Vincent said, like he was burning to know.

Faraday's left hand moved proprioceptively towards his fork and picked it up. Delia watched him trying to figure out how the old man already knew about what had taken place in Rock's Club last night. It didn't take him long. He looked at her and she winked at him.

'Well . . .?' Vincent said. 'How would you describe it—in a word?'

Faraday ate his eggs and *pane casereccio*, taking his time. Vincent glanced at Delia, waiting. Delia waited also.

'Honest,' Faraday said eventually. 'I guess you could say it was an honest wine.'

'But was it *sound* — for such an old *cuvée*?'

'Old? It didn't taste old to me. Just the opposite, as a matter of fact. *Innocent*. The spirit of a generation before it had to go fight some goddamn war with sabres and bayonets. Tasted of poetry and calf-love. The very essence of youth.'

'Mmmm,' Vincent Torelli murmured — it was no less than he would have expected — and nodded, lowering his eyes to his plate while he did, as if he were trying to recall that period in his own life, his own innocence. 'It waited a long time to be drunk, that wine, Lieutenant,' he added. Maybe he was going to say something else but he left it at that.

The meal was continued to its conclusion in silence, an easy silence containing the sounds of people eating and thinking. Delia collected up the plates and dealt them all a fresh slug of coffee from the jug. After she had done this Vincent said: 'Something on your mind, Lieutenant?'

The two men eyeballed each other across the table. You could not tell which of them was holding the aces and which the eights.

'Nope,' Faraday said. 'Nothing on it. Or in it. And that's the truth.'

'Anything I can do?'

Faraday smiled — for the first time today, Delia realized — as he shook his head. 'There's nothing anybody can do.' He took a bite out of his coffee. Then: 'Except — according to my information — you're expecting a visit from Tina Rauch this morning.'

'*Your* information! I like that! One thing that piece of information isn't is *yours*!' Vincent growled. 'It was hush-hush, I was told. Where d'you get *your* information?'

'I, ah . . . overheard Tina mention it,' Faraday said.

Delia bit her tongue.

'That's funny, because it was Tina told me to keep it hush-hush. But yeah, she is, you want to know. She's due for a final fitting session for her gown. I'll be glad to see the back of it. Which isn't to say it's completely without back-interest. Why?'

'Didn't you tell Captain O'Duff the gown was destroyed? In the bomb attack?'

Vincent looked at Delia. 'I thought you just said the Lieutenant wasn't on duty!' To Faraday: 'I didn't tell the Captain anything he didn't ask me. Didn't seem to me he was too interested in couture. I may be doing him an injustice – if that's what it is. It was *you* I spoke to. Remember? And I told *you* Tina's gown was safe.'

'You know that everyone is under the impression it was destroyed?'

Torelli gave his who-cares shrug. 'Who do you call everyone?'

'Everyone who watches t.v. Which is everyone. I guess you didn't watch much recently.'

'Oh sure! Some crazy kid torches my premises and I spend the rest of my time watching the tube!'

'Yesterday's scheduled fashion show was a security blind – according to my information. In case there was any trouble. Seemed to work too. The real show is this morning. A hush-hush affair.'

'It was hush-hush *before* the bombing. The security arrangements are nothing to do with me. Why?'

'I'd like to attend,' Faraday said.

'You want to see the gown, I can show it you now. We can go down and you can see as much of it you want.'

'Thanks, but it's not the gown on a hanger interests me. It's not Tina interests me either,' Faraday said. 'It's Tina wearing the gown I want to see.'

Vincent looked blank. Maybe he had the aces, maybe the eights. He wasn't going to say.

'Look. . . . Think of a piece of clothing like it was a piece of discourse. What does it say? Language means one thing written down – in a dictionary, as words on a page. When it is uttered by someone in concert with other pieces of language, it comes alive. It becomes a statement. Same with clothes – especially fashion attire. They only acquire signification when they are worn. They tell you things. I want to see what your gown has to tell us about Tina Rauch.'

'She won't like it, she finds out!'

'She won't find out,' Delia said.

Vincent looked at her. 'So you're in on this caper too, huh?' He tapped the table top with the cusped fingers of his hand. 'Just don't let her see you – Okay?'

'She won't know me from a fringed-lipped bat,' Faraday said. He seemed to relax.

At the mention of the word 'bat', a high-pitched almost bat-like peep-peeping call began to issue from Faraday's black evening jacket that was hanging over the back of his chair. It continued until Faraday slid his hand into the inside pocket of the jacket and brought out the neat Police SONY communications unit.

'Sorry . . .' he said. He silenced the unit and dropped it back into his jacket. 'That would be the Captain.'

'You're not going to talk to him?' Delia said.

'I talk to O'Duff now, he'll tear into me for why I'm here and not some place else. I was some place else he would tear in to me for why I'm not here. It's how he likes to start his day – biting my ass!'

THE PERSON in control of the security web was a young woman dressed in antique lingerie, a short 1920s petticoat of peaches-and-cream silk with a flapper waist and wide flounced lace trim. The petticoat was embroidered with tiny flowers and love-knots, the bodice lined with very pale, extremely sheer chiffon through which could be discerned a pair of peaches-and-cream breasts, the nipples rouged. At the neck a shocking pink taffeta scarf had been tied in a flamboyant foulard and, at the wrist, a 1950s chiffon leopard-spotted handkerchief. With corrugated purple suede gauntlets up to her elbows and a pair of flying goggles resting on her forehead, she was dressed as wildly as anyone else, as expensively and with as much witty eclecticism. You could tell she was running the tech side of who was being allowed to join the party and who was not, however, by the way she kept talking into her white and pink Mickey Mouse communications handset without any attempt at pretending she wasn't. You could tell, if that was not enough, because she seemed to be the only person present who was not buzzing with excitement at the proceedings that were about to take place. She wore that far-away expression you see on the guys who stand next to the guys who stand next to the President when he is in public goofing it up for the t.v. cameras.

Delia Summers could tell because she had spent a lot of time – when she was in Brazil, especially, collecting data for her doctorate – observing the diacritical aspects of behavior: different manifestations within a group of the same. Divergence, the mutant phenotype of a species, was always of more interest to her than the species itself.

She couldn't help thinking, then, of Maxwell Faraday – she couldn't help smiling at the thought – before she remembered that he had made her promise to forget about him for the duration of the show. Dutifully she put him out of her mind.

But she didn't see why she should stop smiling. It was fun. She had nearly finished setting out the foldaway plastic chairs around the miniature lake and the rib of concrete –

the catwalk – sprung over it. There weren't going to be enough chairs to go round so people could stand if they wanted to. Most of them, she had a hunch, would want to. Your 1920s *ballet russe* gold sheath gown with attached overmantle of terracotta velvet lined in gold looks its best falling from the perpendicular. It was fun moving in her drab cotton fatigues among the polymorphous crowd of jauntily attired guests, none of whom – like the butterflies that were mingling sociably – appeared to notice her. She was the help – some kind of interior horticulturist, wasn't she? employed to regulate the humidity level and the eco-balance, to set out the chairs and be useful when her employer launched his new collection. The young woman in the petticoat talking into her cute handheld probably had not even noticed her. Delia Summers did not register on the security gadgetry. She was invisible – which, she decided, she quite enjoyed.

It was fun. The warm atmosphere inside the atrium. The guests arriving, greeting, swapping compliments, trying not to sweat too much. The cool expensive champagne the nice-looking waiter was taking round in fluted glasses on a silver tray – the glasses clouded with condensation. The playful rivalry between the vermilion and cerulean silks and cottons among the hibiscus and jacaranda flowers. And, of course, the butterflies – peacock-eyed, slow-flying, long-tailed – slowly eyeing and tailing everybody.

She had to collect the chairs from where they were stacked a short distance from the clearing. On her way to and fro she had to pass between the guests. She had to hear what they had to say.

'. . . It's a real shame! She had such beautiful hair. I cried, when I heard the news, you know that? I cried. . . .'

'. . . Why? My espadrilles? You like them? Oh thanks! They came from a ballet shop in Milan called Orsini. They're in duchesse satin. . . .'

'. . . Well – Coco Chanel wasn't the first, tell me who was. . . .'

'. . . I don't care what Da Silva says. I tell them, they ask me, that her style is pure *flou* – like crepe. It flows, right? So it don't last for ever. . . .'

'. . . Yeah, it's a damn shame. I cried myself. . . .'

'. . . And when I asked him what it was like he said it was like sticking his tongue into a rotten peach. . . .'

'. . . Who d'*you* think's going to win. . .?'

'. . . The cape's in quail's egg blue embroidered with flowers in gold thread on a background of satin appliqué. . . .'

'. . . I dunno, La Renta hits form, they got a chance. . . .'

'. . . Edged by pleated and scalloped flounces in champagne taffetta. . . .'

'. . . I just hope he likes rotten peaches. . . .'

'. . . Don't worry. The Mets'll take 'em. . . .'

'. . . Quails' eggs, I thought, are kinda brown. . . .'

The clearing was the only section of the atrium which had not been laid out purely with zoological considerations in mind. There were soft effervescent flowering evergreens, rhododendrons, azaleas, moonbugs – here and there spiked by vivid carnivorous orchids. There was a circular brick-work area and a few white plastic bar tables at intervals for people to put their drinks on while they applauded. Vincent Torelli had designed the show space himself. It had become associated in people's minds with his 'look'. The bi-annual *Vogue* photosession nearly always took place here. There was something about the contrast between the garments and the vegetation which the photographers liked. Perhaps it was the way the sunlight was so violently cut into tiny pieces by the sharp pinna-shaped leaves, an exhilarating kinetic effect that you could never produce in a studio.

A young woman with very long charcoal-stockinged legs that started inside a pair of pre-legislation snake-skin shoes and extended up into a very short black strapless chemise that would not have looked out of place at Rock's Club, stopped Delia by laying a hand on her upper arm.

'Excuse me . . .' she said. 'Are you from here?'

'Sure am, Ma'am,' Delia told her with a straight face. 'And what 'bout you?'

'Me? Oh, I'm from the *Saturday Review*! I . . . I never been here before. All these bugs. . . . They bring on my anxiety.'

Delia put down the chair she was carrying. 'Why don't you sit down?' she said, taking hold of the young woman by the wrist and sitting her down. Her pulse was up and she seemed to be hyperventilating. She was really just a girl, and a very pretty one. The blackness of her dress against her white skin was in striking contrast to the rest of the colorful assembly. Its presence showed how much more tolerant Tina Rauch's crowd were. The girl was either very naïve or – less likely – a political mugwump.

'I like your shoes,' Delia said. From what she had overheard, this seemed to be the kind of thing you said. She was right. The girl from the *Saturday Review* looked up, radiant.

'You *do*? They're Salvatore Ferragamo – original. From Italy. They were my grandmother's. They're about forty years old!'

'I have to tell you,' Delia was unable to stop herself from saying. 'They're from the old US of A – originally. The Arizona Coral Snake – *microides euryxanthus* – before it was made extinct – about forty-*five* years ago.'

The pretty girl with the long legs dressed up to look like a woman – after a moment – silently burst into tears.

IT WAS ALL a question of light.

The sun was overhead – well, about as far overhead as it was ever likely to get this time of year. Here and there against the silhouetted foliage you could see bright sections of blue sky that looked like they had been cut out with a pair of scissors. Outside it was dry and there was – as the FM DJs would have it – a zero percent pro'bility of precipitation: it wasn't going to rain today. But inside, the meteorological conditions were very different: humid, the pressure several atmospheres higher. You could feel the storm brewing. And as a matter of fact there was one due very soon – with the precision of the tropics – six hours exactly after the last one. Exactly six hours before the next. Green and mud-colored tree-frogs were waiting for it in parts of the atrium where the refracted sunlight merged with the shadows into complex muddy-green colors. Elsewhere – in the brilliant shafts of sunlight – butterflies of different sex of the same species were busy chasing each other up and down invisible spiral staircases.

There were about fifty guests – moving about and making enough commotion to give the impression of there being twice that number. They were all close friends of Tina's, people whom she could trust, who shared her open ideas about fashion, dressing to create an image, a climate. Because – for them – style was an ephemeral act without rules, spontaneous. None of them knew today what they would be wearing tomorrow. How could they know, then, what each other would be arriving in? What would be appropriate? They would say, if you asked them, that it was inspired guesswork. They used their instincts. It was the hour, the moment, which gave the inspiration. Every combination was unique, a gesture calculated to fix in the imagination the poignant beauty of the human condition: the striped chambray cotton that evokes the picnic of *baguette* and *chèvre* and *vin blanc* by the water's edge, of the pretty girl accompanied by her fiancé – Death. None of their outfits, consequently, bore any similarity to anyone else's. There were bustles and boas, jodhpurs, camisoles, smocks, sheaths, trunks, denims. There were pastel shades and bright sporty colors. There was glitz. There was even someone – over by the lake in conversation with Delia – in a sexy black and white number that didn't look out of place. It was all there. Early twentieth century and contemporary. Fortuny and Billy Klein. And yet – despite the provisional, extempore nature of the various garments – there was something about them that made sense, that was concordant with the mood of the occasion: joyous, optimistic, light. They were all in the same key.

Scanning the assembled company was like flipping the pages of a current edition of *Vogue*. Everyone was someone whose face was familiar and – it went without saying – beautiful, all of them striking those unnatural attitudes perfectly naturally. It was a modern Watteau, the rich and famous dressed up like Gods and Goddesses smiling innocently at each other while History was being enacted elsewhere, outside the canvas – on forty-five million t.v. sets, to be exact, where ordinary citizens were at this moment exercising their democratic right to vote. Who they voted for, only time would tell. Tina Rauch's friends, associates and financial backers, were gathered together to express their confidence that it would be for her, that her term of office as 77th mayor of the city was about to start. Among these there was the usual smattering of actors and actresses, musicians, sport personalities – the wives and husbands of powerful men and women – but mostly they were particular buddies of Tina's. There was Tony, the owner of the clam bar on Mott and Hester. There was Tina's factotum, Tracy Wilder, in outrageous anachronistic undergarments and Billy Klein flying goggles, supervising the security arrangements. There was Judy de Haas, Tina's photographer, looking naked without her camera. (Clearly, Tracy Wilder was not taking any chances.) Billy Klein himself was here, the person with him wearing one of his constructivist ensembles sculpted to look like the corner of a room, an oil derrick, a piece of Italian furniture, anything so long as it wasn't an article of clothing. Klein wasn't the only party present who had learnt the art of speaking with a mouth full of pins at the Torelli atelier.

Vincent Torelli – he was wearing an old and crumpled Armani raw linen summer jacket over the same white T-shirt and pair of faded blue cotton pants he had had on at breakfast – was seated at one of the plastic tables. He was talking to an attractive woman with a very straight back of about his own age, making her laugh. She was in a close-fitting black *ciré* evening gown that showed off her superb figure to advantage. They were both drinking out of the same champagne glass.

Faraday – adjusting the unfamiliar weight of the loaded tray on his arm – considered whether their glass was due for a refill. He decided it wasn't. A waiter – a good waiter – understood when, the exact moment, his presence was required, like a priest or the conductor of an orchestra. Professions, after all, for which a black suit was *de rigueur*.

As he moved among the guests, Faraday considered the role of being a waiter, what it meant to be one. He wanted to look right. His movements must be slow and quick. He must approach guests with the casualness of an old friend but by such informality – being a stranger – communicate a certain insolence. He must assume the hauteur of an artist – a champion ice-skater – as if the work he did was extremely dangerous, requiring great skill and courage. He must carry his tray with recklessness – a tightrope-walker – putting himself in a perpetual unstable equilibrium from which he should recover at the last moment, when it came to pouring the drinks, by a light gesture of arm and hand. It wasn't easy, though not because he found being a waiter difficult in itself – it was being Max Faraday and being a waiter, a representation for others, a fake, that was hard. Bad faith – as a rule – was something he avoided like the plague. He wasn't a waiter. He was a facsimile of one.

But the semiology of his black evening suit gave him the dispensation to move among this select, highly-differenti-ated section of New York society, to be a part of the company and yet taking no part in it. The suit was a conventional sign which the guests were interpreting conventionally – if mistakenly – to signify a conventional role. His manipulation of the semiology was a stratagem – he had recently been informed – already adopted by a variety of inhabitants of the atrium, particularly by the lone Peruvian ant spider of the genus *aphantochilus* whose physical and behavioral characteristics mimicked in every respect those of the formidable Peruvian ants *cephalotes* on which it fed, the predator running and living with its prey, indistinguishable from it.

The host of butterflies, meanwhile, attracted to the party by the carefully coordinated colors and perfumes of the floral and human blooms, flitted promiscuously from one to the other, flirting outrageously with Tina's guests who smiled and admired their superb coloration, flattered by the attention and the gratuitous adornment the insects added to their attire. The black and white specimen however, which had settled on the shoulder of Faraday's black jacket – like some futuristic kind of epaulette – had decided to stay put, slowly opening and closing its wings to catch the attention of the identically colored member of its species which had attached itself to Faraday's white shirt-front, cunningly disguised as a bow tie.

'We was two minutes from where I'm standing when it happened, juss across the Avenue, in the park, wasn't we hon?' Bo – the Broadway actor who specialized in agile small person parts – was saying. He was standing among the maidenhair ferns on the lip of a breast-high piece of brickwork, his eyes level with a small gathering of fellow showbiz personalities and his pretty, familiar-looking girlfriend – didn't she do the *Neutrogena* complexion cream ads on the t.v.? Bo was holding forth about how he was right there when the explosion took out the Torelli Building yesterday morning, how he heard the blast and saw the smoke. On one leg he leaned across to exchange his empty glass for one of the full ones on the tray that Faraday was holding out. His balance was perfect. '. . . Nearly blew me over, didn't it hon?' Hon smiled and nodded while the fellow showbiz personalities laughed at the self-deprecatory joke. Obviously it would take more than a little high explosive to blow Bo over.

As Bo was speaking the light inside the atrium thickened, the sharp-edged bits of blue sky lost their sharp-edged quality, the emerald luminescence in the elephant-ear fronds disappeared into thin air. A cloud must have passed overhead. Alone, a single finger of sun-like light pierced the gloom. Faraday, taking care to keep his back to it, could make out its pale reflection on the faces of the guests. He studied their reaction to what was happening, amused to see how quick they were to abandon their conversations and, childlike, so surrender their identity in a communality of expectation, like a cinema audience – or, more realistically, the court of the Sun King at the commencement of a Lully *masque*.

In the hush that followed you could hear the gasps of surprise, the sudden collective intake of breath. Resolute, tray in hand, his face in darkness, Faraday kept his back to the object of everyone's attention. It was part of his practice, a tool of his trade, not to see what he was looking at – to bracket out the *what* of a statement in order to take a closer look at the *how*. If you didn't – it was his theory – you could end up being sold something you didn't want to buy.

In his field of vision he could see Bo and Bo's acquaintances, the stages between shock, disbelief, understanding, belief – the classic stages of enlightenment – register on their faces. He could see – on the other side of the miniature lake – a biologist standing next to a slip of a girl in black he had never seen before, the biologist's smile of recognition. He could see a woman with flying goggles on her head staring in his direction.

Faraday decided it was time Vince Torelli's glass needed refilling.

'There you are!' Torelli growled. 'Wondered where you got to.'

Faraday, bowing from the waist, silent, filled the glass from the iced bottle of Bollinger Blanc de Noirs and then stepped back into semi-darkness. It was, he realized, all a question of light, the laws that made it work. Optics: refraction and reflection.

Tina Rauch – she stood alone on the catwalk among the lepidoptera attracted to her – was appareled in a garment that flowed out of her body and, apparently, into it. The line did not fall conventionally from bust and hip but instead, by-passing these, soared upwards from a narrow pedestal hem, above the knee, in a single uninterupted whoosh that arrived in a décolleté crescendo, a pair of gossamer petals sprung off the bare shoulder, and then finally evaporated into particles of light. The sweep of the dress above and the kinetic angularity of the legs below were in deliberate apposition to each other, subtly drawing the eye away from – and also, therefore, drawing it towards – their erogenous confluence. It was an erotic touch. Almost incidentally the gown became an extension of the wearer's sexuality. It was an invitation – to the appropriate member of the appropriate species – to mate. The iridescent sheen of the fabric – a patina of complex high-molecular tiny scales overlapping each other, splintering the light into fragments of the spectrum – seemed to be made up of alternate layers of silk and light, revealing the body without exposing it.

But that wasn't what arrested the attention and caused the sudden intake of breath. A mere description of the form, the cut of the gown, ruched out of the woman's sexuality, took no account of the Torelli Effect, the optical illusion which conferred onto the image a startling two-dimensionality. However Tina moved, from whatever angle she was viewed, the minute pleats concealed inside the fabric of the garment, responded instantaneously and tricked the eye away from the roundness of the movement. Tina became flat, without depth. She ceased being a person and became the image of a person. There, not there. Beautiful and unobtainable. An icon that flickered from different points of view like a 2-D printed holographic construct.

And was not this what Tina Rauch represented? What she was iconic of? It was a faithful portrayal of the reality she projected: provisional, ever-changing, one which did not possess dimensionality for psychological factors to gain purchase in. For Tina and for Tina's followers there was no room – no time – for the so-called interior life. There was this. There was this. There was this. And that's all there was. Personality consisted of what was here, not of what was not here, of appearances, of what the world could see and get hold of. The Great Eternal Questions she left to Rocco Da Silva and his tired classic look hinting at depth and complexity.

In the present surroundings, among the atrium's gradations of lucidity and obfuscation, the effect of the gown was impressive. It was ironic and paradoxical. Fragments of applause broke out among the guests, smatteringly at first like droplets of rain falling on a glass roof, gathering momentum, until it was more like a downpour. The audience was going wild. Nobody, in Faraday's opinion, would be wanting to make a grab for anything for a while. With one hand he placed the tray onto the nearest piece of brickwork and with the other hand helped himself to one of the glasses of wine from it as if he were waiting on himself – and thereby stepping out of his role as waiter.

He caught Delia's eye at the very moment she caught his, raised his glass to hers in recognition of the triumph, then lost contact with her as people, in their eagerness to maneuver themselves into a better position from which to judge, interposed themselves between where she was standing and where he was. There was some whistling. On the catwalk Tina Rauch, ignoring the ovation, was moving in the traditional manner, with slow dispassionate grace, as though she were only modeling the gown for someone else, letting it speak for itself. Letting it speak for both of them.

As soon as the pretty girl with the long black-stockinged legs and extinct Arizona coral snake skin on her feet burst into tears, the sun – on cue – appeared to lose its lustre and a dullness descended on the party. By a controlled adjustment of the solar-reflecting devices positioned over the atrium, a small amount of light trapped in the well of the building was lured onto the miniature lake and the raised catwalk over it. The crowd hushed. Butterflies – also on cue – made for the sunny glade in their own apparently haphazard way. Tina stepped out of the undergrowth – incandescent against the greens and a funny growling noise came from the collective throat of the party.

Tina looked lovely – no getting away from it. She caused a pleasurable reflex tingling sensation in the pelvic and sacral areas of the autonomic nervous system. She possessed one of those rare personalities that makes use of obscure physiological signals to trigger – below the threshold of consciousness – obscure physiological responses in those around her. She did not need to rely on special effects. She would look lovely in Duck Head bib overalls from the utility store. When she smiled, when she turned it on, she created the illusion that it was for you – no other son of a bitch – that she was smiling and turning it on. You became – for the instant – the one that mattered, the centre of the universe. Sure, it was only an illusion, but wouldn't it be a cute project, Delia mused, to investigate the chemistry that made it happen?

The dress was lovely, of course, too – that went without saying – but Delia was not bowled over by it. Even before she had come to live with Vincent she had been surrounded by couture. She took it for granted. The Torelli reputation, after all, had been built – literally and metaphorically – on her mother's back. He had created some of his most intimate gowns for her. The new Style Wing in the Metropolitan contained items of clothing Delia had been cuddled in, fallen asleep on and in all likelihood, thrown up over. Neither her mother, before she died, nor Vincent after, had ever encouraged in Delia anything except a disdain for fashion. That was probably the explanation for why she was such an undistinguished dresser herself.

Besides, she had had to live with Vincent during the months which he had spent working on Tina's dress. It wasn't exactly a surprise.

The girl from the *Saturday Review* however, stood up – still holding onto Delia's hand – and stared, blinking through her tear-glazed eyes, open-mouthed, at the spectacle.

'Oh *my*!' she said. 'Oh *my*!'

People started to applaud.

Tina was radiant. She smiled at everyone and at no one in particular. The dress shimmered as it moved, its surface manufactured to replicate the effect produced by the minute coned structure on the scales of butterfly wings. In particular – in its coloration and general detail – those of the *papilio fulgurans*, the African Sorcerer. Delia caught sight of Max Faraday across the tumult and waited to see if he was going to see her. He did – on cue. He grinned. He raised the champagne glass in his hand to salute the grand success.

Then she lost him.

It wasn't a stampede, but people abandoned their friends and closed in. There were calls of 'Bravo!' and '*Bien fait*!' The tinkling nineteenth-century piano music had given away to the melodic strains of a tenor saxophone in a combo laying down a golden carpet for a female vocalist to step out onto.

'*Evening, every night you come and you find me. . . .*'

When she finally succeeded in picking Faraday out in the melee he was still on the other side of the miniature lake. He was in conversation with someone – a woman, it looked like. It was hard to tell at first, through the crush. Then, without warning, Max turned and stepped through the wall of foliage just behind him and disappeared from view. The woman followed him. Delia noticed a sudden leap in her pulse rate. The muscles in her lower abdomen shrank. Was it an instinctive urge on her part to prevent a rival female from approaching too closely to her mate?

Or was she jealous?

'HI! SO WHAT you think?'

Faraday turned on his heels.

Smiling, the flying goggles now resting on the bridge of her nose, she came at him out of the sun. Bandits at three o'clock. Unable to see her eyes clearly, he returned her smile – taking the bait, tasting the hook. But you couldn't help smiling, looking at her, her bizarre mélange of periods and styles, semi-transparent lingerie and silly pink chiffon, the auburn perruque, the rouged nipples. How could you take her seriously?

'I think Rocco's got a surprise coming to him, he sees this,' Faraday said. 'To tell you the truth I feel sorry for him.'

'Don't waste your sympathy,' Tracy Wilder said, raising the flying goggles onto her forehead. 'No one ever felt sorry for a snake, that I heard of.'

'A mongoose?'

'What's that?'

'It isn't anything anymore. It's extinct.'

'That's what Mr Da Silva's going to be this time tomorrow morning. Most the people're just waiting for the Robbie Robson Show before they register their choice. Tap in their voting number is all they have to do. They going to take their time. Sit down front the t.v. with a cold Bud. Cop Tina's tits. Mellow out ready for the ballgame.'

'The Mets don't have the necessary poke this year to whup the Yankees, I hear,' Faraday said.

Tracy Wilder shook her pretty auburn false hair at him. 'Uh-uh! So the Mets lose! It won't make no big difference by then. The ballgame – when does it start? Seven thirty? They gonna have to wait till 10.30 for who wins. The voters, they going to commit themselves soon as they *see* Tina! Take a look the effect she's having on that crowd over there – and they're all pros, in the business! I tell you there isn't a person in the Five Boroughs isn't wondering what she's going to be wearing!'

Faraday nodded. Typically, Tina Rauch was betting everything on a single throw of the dice.

'Especially,' he said. 'After the terrorist attack on the Torelli headquarters yesterday. They're wondering what Tina's going to be wearing now that her latest creation by the old wizard has been bombed out!'

Tracy grinned.

'C'mon! You can't blame us for *that*! Taking advantage of a teeny bit of free publicity?' She wrinkled her nose at how teeny it was.

'Hell, no. I don't blame you,' Faraday said. 'Good luck to you.' And left it there. If she thought he was going to add anything more on that subject she was going to be disappointed. He took the opportunity to look at her, at her flying goggles – they were in matt pink soft plastic but in every other respect authentic Second World War US Navy issue – and at her nipples, rouged the same shocking pink as the absurd bow tied around her neck.

'Okay I ask, then, why you're here Lieutenant?' she said. 'You're not on my guest list.' She gestured with one hand to the invisible guest list which she was holding up in the other hand.

'It's not *why* I'm here you want to know, Tracy, is it? It's *how*. How'd I get through your security web?'

With a shrug she said: 'You laid the pretty lady biologist is *how*.' She grinned. She wrinkled her nose at how pretty she was. 'You took her to Le Zinc and she invited you back to look at her butterfly collection. You got the hots and she put out. Right?'

'Hey!' Faraday said, indignant. 'Who do you take me for – *gorilla gorilla*?'

'What?'

He nodded. 'But that's about the shape of it. Yeah.'

'Right. So you don't *have* a reason to be here. You're invited by the management. That's fine. You're welcome. I just wish they'd tell *me*! How'm I expected to access-control the joint, they letting Tom and Jerry through the back door?'

'Except,' Faraday continued. 'It wasn't Le Zinc we went.'

She gave him a blank look. Eventually she said: 'What, you want me to guess outta fifty thousand restaurants on Manhattan which one you took her to?'

'No. I don't mind telling you. Matter of fact we went to Rock's Club.'

Faraday watched Tracy Wilder weigh the small piece of information that instantly changed everything.

'Lively, wasn't it?' he added.

She hesitated. She was watching him watch her make the calculation. She let him have her pink innocent smile. That was all she let him have.

'I really liked your slubbed silk suit,' Faraday said. 'The tulle revers were just right.'

'I didn't have the pleasure,' she said finally. 'Of seeing what *you* were wearing.'

'Well, you were kind of busy explaining to your date why you kept her waiting,' Faraday said. 'But your explanation, far as I could see, didn't seem to impress her.'

They stood there smiling innocently at each other.

'So you see,' he said. 'The interesting question we should be asking is not what am *I* doing *here* but what were *you* doing *there*.'

Tracy Wilder looked him straight in the eye. 'That just depends who's asking it.'

'Anyone with an interest why your date is currently lying with a plastic police tag tied round her foot down the forensic morgue on 28th Street.'

Tracy made a good stab at looking pained. But not quite good enough. She was improvising. If he had had any doubts before he didn't have any now. She was remorseless. A lifetaker.

'And – of course – why you killed her. That's a question that has to have some kind of answer.'

She slid a hand into a placket in her undergarment and fished out a white handkerchief. Was she going to go for his weak spot and burst into tears? Her other hand slid into the handkerchief and fished out a small handgun. Putting a brave face on her pained look, she screwed the handkerchief into her fist and pointed the gun in Faraday's direction.

They were standing on the edge of the party, in the shadows. '*Evening* . . .' a female jazz vocalist – he didn't know which one – was singing. '. . . *Every night you come and you find me. Must you always remind me. That my man is gone.* . . .' The guests – along with the butterflies – had all been drawn toward the flame of Tina Rauch's gown. Tracy Wilder had the light behind her. Faraday had the jungle behind him. She was holding an antique four-shot revolver – a .41 single-action rimfire Colt, it looked like – one of the rare models with the stock silver-inlaid and engraved by Tiffany. All he was holding was a chilled glass of Bollinger Blanc de Noirs.

> '. . . *Shadows fall – Upon the wall*
> *That's the time I miss his kisses most of all.* . . .'

'You can't prove I even knew her. Nobody can. It wasn't even *me* she was in love with. It was some other guy.' Tracy Wilder cocked her head. 'Mind telling me how you rec'nized me?'

'By your style, of course!' Faraday said. 'I had an attack of déjà vu. Bonnie West's lover hit different notes but in the same key, the same ironic coherence, as the Barbie Doll I just met a few hours before in Tina's apartment.'

'I thought you was police!'

'I'm a police semiologist. That's my job.'

'It *was* your job.'

'What are you pointing that at me for? You can't fire it in here,' Faraday reasoned. 'Everyone will notice. They'll hear it go bang.'

'No one will hear *this*, don't worry. You think it fires lead bullets, forget it. The shell – that's original, sure. But the inside's been hollowed out and replaced with modern Japanese parts. Just like near everything else in the USA. Comes with a Mitsu silencer built-in.'

'What about when I fall over?'

145

'What difference that going to make to you? You'll be dead!' She grinned. She wrinkled her nose at how dead he would be. 'Anyone's curious, I'll tell 'em I challenged your legitimate right to be here. That's *my* job. Access-controller. Say I took you for an intruder – going for a weapon. These days you can't take no chances. A case of mistaken identity. Happens to cops every day. No DA would touch it.' She threw him her innocent look. 'What other motive could I have?'

Faraday, showing the empty palms of his hands – the conventional sign of non-aggressive intention – took a half-step towards her. *Phut*! Tracy – she didn't seem to move a muscle – fired the gun. He felt the minute turbulence stir about his ears and he heard the zip of the projectile as it penetrated the foliage behind him. *Phut*! She fired again. He froze, his hands conveniently in the slightly raised open position which signifies surrender.

She was right. The guests clamoring around Tina Rauch would never hear such a damp fart-like little plunk. He only just heard it himself.

'Has a spur trigger,' she said. 'Classic looks. In fact, has everything you could ask from a modern high caliber handgun.' She might have been demonstrating the weapon to a potential customer. Then she motioned with her chin to the spot just over Faraday's shoulder where the gun was pointing, into the thick of the jungle. 'Seeing as you're self-conscious, Lieutenant, let's us take a hike.'

IN HER YELLOW-and-green jungle fatigues, Delia Summers –
Professor of Arthropod Behavior at the Sherman Fairchild
Center, Harlem – scuttled through the yellow-and-green
artificial rain forest behind Seventh Avenue in midtown
Manhattan with the single-mindedness of the agile lynx
spider which jumps its prey after running it down, often
over a great distance. Delia – she was in her element – did
not pause to ponder on her course of action. She moved
instinctually, with rapid sure-footed strides through the
vegetation, making use of her knowledge of the atrium to
traverse it circuitously, her body close to the ground,
balanced between the razor-edged *comosos ananas* cactus
and the treacherously spiked *cyperus prolix* grasses. The
swiftness of her movements was a reflex response to the
colossal amount of epinephrine being discharged from her
adrenal medulla gland into her blood stream and stimulating her muscles to rapid action. It was a warm uncomplicated sensation – just the opposite of fear. She was a
warrior. An Amazon. Fearless. As she raced along pathways
known only to herself, she recognized that she had been
here before. It was an emotional landscape already familiar
to her from her dreams. She knew what she had to do next.
It was a combination of circumstances for which she had
unconsciously prepared herself all her life – in her research
and in her dreams – to face: the intimate inescapable
embrace of sex and death.

She heard the two humans a moment before she saw
them, locating their exact position by the variable pitch of
their voices in contrast to the regular hum of the atrium at
midday. She stopped in her tracks and approached with
caution, stalking. All species engaged in display with the
opposite sex are at their most unpredictable. She was calm
now, doing what she was best at. Rapid action had
displaced all fear. She eased her nose between the heavy
fronds of the tree-fern *cyathes fugax* and glimpsed, on the
other side of it, part of a beautifully dressed young woman
and part of a man in a tuxedo. They were chatting with each
other as if they were at a cocktail party, displaced from their

natural habitat. The woman was doing the speaking. On the brown mossy trunk of the fern level with where she was concealed, Delia noticed the eight brown hairy legs of a giant tree-dwelling mygalomorph – a Trinidadian trapdoor tarantula – the female of the species, waving her maxillae in a friendly come-hither gesture.

'You know you're right! I say I found you poking around out here,' the woman in shocking pink chiffon was saying. 'Who's gonna blame me, I shoot you?'

It was Tina Rauch's assistant, the one who was in charge of the security arrangements for the show – the one in the flying goggles and her nipples rouged shocking pink. She had exchanged her cute Mickey Mouse communication handset for a little handgun which she was holding on the man in the tuxedo.

'Pity though, you're not carrying a gun yourself. That would just clinch it!'

Max Faraday – she couldn't see his expression – was silent.

'I thought all cops had to carry one,' the woman said. 'Isn't it what they're paid to do?'

'You sound like my boss,' Faraday said. 'The Precinct Captain. He's always telling me, one day I'll wish I didn't leave it in the drawer.'

'You should've listened to the Captain, Lieutenant. This is the day he was talking about!'

'C'mon Tracy! Give me a break!' Faraday remonstrated. 'He's going to cuss me blind, he sees me bumped off without my gun in my hand! It'll go on my record!'

Tracy giggled.

Faraday made a sudden grab for the gun – but not sudden enough. The gun phut-phutted rapidly. Faraday's arm recoiled. He let out a gasp of pain.

Delia did not stop to think. The DNA structure of the chromosomes of her as-yet-unborn offspring was about to be removed from the gene-pool of her species by a process known – for some reason – as natural selection. What was there to stop to think about?

She scooped up the hand-sized female mygalomorph in a single swipe – the only way to catch hold of one – from the trunk of the tree-fern and pitched it at the strike zone of the woman. The large hairs on the legs – and the large legs themselves – clung to the air and seemed to float on it. The spider righted itself and then settled delicately on the pink chiffon bow tied over the woman's chest and stuck fast. Immediately it took up the rigid threatening posture on straightened legs, maxillae waving, that most female tarantulas adopt when they are under attack or courting – apparently perceiving little difference between the two activities.

The woman Faraday had called Tracy let out a squeaking-squawking noise and began hitting out at the giant arachnid with the barrel of the gun.

Phut! . . . *Phut*!

She was taking pot shots at the helpless dumb animal!

Delia stepped out from behind the leaves of the tree-fern, uncertain whether her first instinct was to protect the human male or the female spider. Tracy saw her and froze but she could not now see Faraday who had ducked to her right, out of her field of vision. When, realizing this, she turned back to put the gun on him, he came at her from a crouched position and struck her a glancing blow on her right cheek with his left hand.

Tracy sat on the floor of the atrium, dazed enough to be unaware of the large spider affixed to her scarf like some marvelous lifelike broach. Faraday, whose right hand was covered in blood, held the woman's gun in his left, examining it. It looked like a rich child's expensive toy pistol.

Delia stepped from behind the leaves towards the woman, careful to approach the spider from behind. Like a lot of mygalomorph tarantulas this species did not take kindly to being shot at with a high-caliber pistol. A pelt of fine hairs covered its abdomen which, if persistently tormented, it lifted and from it scraped free a puff of the hairs. These many-barbed hairs were extremely unpleasant

149

– Delia knew from experience – once they became entrammeled in the mucous membranes of nose or eye.

'You know, you want to be more careful!' she told Tina Rauch's security officer. Cupping the mygalomorph – not strictly a true spider – in two hands, she lifted it off the shocking pink bow. She let it rest on the flat of her open palm for the woman to look at. 'This is an endangered species. Destroying one of these is an arrestable offence. Can put you away for twenty-eight days!'

Tracy slowly picked herself up from the atrium floor. She was blinking, sniffling, from the irritating urtication caused by the trapdoor tarantula's defense system. For a moment she stared, aghast, at Delia Summers, the Spider Woman, before fleeing into the jungle.

7

But her body was not lying in the forensic morgue on 28th Street with a plastic police tag tied around one of her feet, in fact. It was still reclining over a modular grosgrain tan leather ottoman in her twentieth-floor apartment in the New Barbizon, her arm resting on the back of the ottoman, her head resting on the back of her arm, where she had died. She was facing a blank t.v. screen. She had presumably been killed in this position, while she was seated. She looked very comfortable. A glass of orange juice stood on the lily-stemmed Jason Mo side-table beside her, where she had presumably left it. A Cindy Loewe print silk peignoir styled by Etienne D'Offay was loosely wrapped around the body over a white cotton camisole-slip and smokey bas-collants. A pair of classic black slingback high-heeled shoes stood at right angles to each other next to the stockinged feet. The rest of her clothes were folded under her arm, where she had presumably left them. She also had on a pale Number 3 Dior skin-combination and a sweetpea pink lipgloss. Her white Porsche chronograph-09 was attached to her wrist – it read 2:13 p.m. – and a plastic police tag was tied around one of her feet. Except that the police – when they couldn't stand it any longer – had killed the t.v. picture and silenced the alarm on the watch – set for 6:15 this a.m. – everything in the room was fixed at the moment when time had run out for the Channel Eleven News presenter, Bonnie West, and she had become News.

As well as the dead body there were five live ones – three men, two women – also present in the room, four of them on their feet, one of them seated. Aside from the representative from the District Attorney's Office, they were all police personnel. One of the three men out of the four people standing was Captain Daniel Clarence O'Duff. He was in his shirtsleeves. Unshaven, he looked tired, ragged, a man who had been up all night. He was needling Lieutenant Dinah Lazlo who, in her immaculately pressed regulation egg-blue pantsuit and white wet-plastic gunstrap and holster – looked as if she had recently stepped out of cryogenic storage.

'I'm *not*. . . .'

'I never said you was. . . .'

'You just said. . . .'

'I said you *thought* you was. Giving off-the-record interviews, letting those jamokes follow you round the lab with their cameras, making a fucking drama production outta the 'vestigation! If you didn't *think* you was a t.v. show star, you sure's hell acted like you was in one, is what I'm saying.'

Dinah Lazlo was doing her best to return the Captain's service while at the same time overlook Counselor Sue Connolly in her task of videoing the evidence-gathering activities of Sergeant Kriwaczek. Seated on the ottoman alongside Bonnie West, Sergeant Kriwaczek looked like a bored make-up artist, which he wasn't. He was a bored city employee painstakingly gathering fragments of human and air-conditioning detritus from a dead person's clothes and skin and fingernails by some kind of electromagnetic process. It was – the fourth police official present, the one standing over by the door with his hand in his pocket, could see – the 19th Precinct's forensic team hard at work. They could probably tell you, as soon as they were through snarling at each other, whom the victim had recently been associated with and where on the basis of the chemical composition of the fragments, and – from their molecular weight – who had murdered her.

'All I did was, like, show them round the Forensic Department facilities, demonstrate some of our techniques. You know, give the public a true picture of what police work is really like. You're always saying. . . .'

'That's *all* you did, huh?' O'Duff growled.

'Right.'

'When I heard you – let me tell you something, Lieutenant, I was in a bar with half a dozen other guys when I heard you, right? – you were telling the public, me and the half a dozen guys drinking beer next to me, you were telling them things *I* didn't know!'

'I . . .' Dinah Lazlo faltered. 'Well, I may have let them have some hunches I have. . . .'

'I'm old-fashioned, Lieutenant. Shit! maybe I'm just old! But I kinda got used to the procedure, which is a fuck of a lot older than I am: officers report their hunches to the Precinct Captain without he has to sit around bars waiting to hear them from the Channel Eleven News Show!'

'Captain, hold on, I only said what. . . .'

'And that dress you was in! I never seen so much your chest all the time you been working for us. I don't even think I ever saw you in a dress. It stopped before it even got started!'

There was a hollow silence. The unconscious contradictions between the Captain and the Lieutenant were looming into consciousness. The silence – you could hear everyone in the room listening to it – lasted until Dinah Lazlo said what had to be said: '*Well you liked what you saw didn't you!*'

O'Duff – he caught sight of Faraday in the doorway and threw him a look – said, deadpan: 'We got a procedure in the NYC PD to deal with incitement to sexual harassment, you know that?'

Dinah Lazlo – she almost stamped her foot – turned her back and put her hands on her hips and glared at Sergeant Kriwaczek.

'Aw, C'mon, Dinah. I was just joshing!' O'Duff said, obviously pleased that he had succeeded in warming her cool up some. 'Anyway,' he chuckled. 'You're off duty. Max Faraday finally arrived.'

The forensic PhD swiveled the upper part of her body without moving the lower part – the way they get the models in *Vogue* to do sometimes – in order to squint at Faraday.

'Morning Dinah,' he said from the doorway. 'Didn't the Captain have any breakfast today, or what?'

'Sure he did!' She made a face. '*Me!*'

'Well I'm here now. It's my personality he really likes to gnaw on.'

O'Duff bared his teeth and snarled. Dinah Lazlo shook her head, half-smiled – resigned. And that was that. The cops were through joshing each other over the corpse.

Almost simultaneously Sergeant Kriwaczek was through gathering his evidence. He had began to put away his evidence-gathering equipment. Counselor Sue Connolly was almost through videoing him. All she had to do was to record the transfer of the specimen-containers into her own custody and transfer them, under the forensic Lieutenant's supervision, to the senior technician at the laboratory to analyse, and her job was over. She could go get something to eat. Fuck these guys. She didn't have to do what the fat unshaven bully said, laugh at his jokes. A different department at City Hall to the one that paid the police paid her to represent the person whose name would be on the arrest sheet which these guys – they ever get round to it – would serve on the citizen accused of Murder One.

Faraday took in the whole scene – O'Duff's picky sense of humour, Dinah Lazlo's ambiguous sexy professionalism, the DA Counselor's barely concealed contempt, the bored expression on Sergeant Kriwaczek's face. He took in the interior décor of the apartment – expensively constructed for a person who had the cash but not the confidence to construct it herself: burnt sienna and ochre yellows crumbling into each other from upholstery to carpet to light-fittings. It was – the 'Home' section of the Thursday edition of the *Times* would have said – cogent. Faraday could almost put his finger on which one of the Canal Street personal ambient auteurs had given expression to this particular client's taste. Jasper Clarke or Xavier Bon aventura, it had to be one of those two. Teddy Gallagan, maybe. It had the currently voguish juxtaposition of ultra-modern construction materials with classical line and art objects: the Vuillard terracotta crayon sketch of the servant-girl stepping into a bathtub set behind light-absorbent Pilkington lucite flush with the wall, that did not come between the viewer and the picture and would require a steamhammer to crack. What it said to the world about the inhabitant was: 'I am sensitive and wise. I respond to Art and I know a good investment when I see one. I can afford a servant-girl but my sensibilities prevent me from owning a servant-girl. I own the picture of one.'

But no. It wasn't true that Faraday was able to take in the whole scene. The discrete bits that made up the scene—the tan leather ottoman, the glass of orange juice, his Police Department colleagues, the Vuillard sketch—he could take in these but the whole scene, as such, made no sense because the collective reason for everything's being there was missing. It was an emptiness, an absence of being, that held it all together. Her body was there, her D'Offay silk peignoir was there, her Number 3 Dior skin-combination was there, but she, Bonnie West herself, had been removed before Faraday had arrived. It was like looking at one of those advertisements for life insurance where they show you a photograph of a group of people from which the one that matters, the one they all depend on, has been cut out of the picture. Everyone carries on as usual, unaware of the existential void at the centre of their lives. O'Duff and Lazlo, they could josh each other all they liked, the DA's counselor could tape the proceedings. What the fuck difference did it make? They were hollow people, irreal, beautifully constructed high-affect robots, going through the motions. Their lips moved and words issued from their lips but—when you added them up — they didn't mean anything. And that went for Max Faraday, the same as everyone else.

The only things in the room that existed — so far as Faraday could see — were the two little holes neatly drilled side-by-side in the white bodice of the camisole-slip revealed by the open peignoir on Bonnie West's cadaver. They were there. You couldn't argue with them.

Faraday had never met the t.v. personality Bonnie West although — along with forty-five million other people — he knew plenty about her. He knew what caliber watch she wore and what combination of makeup she used and where she shopped for her clothes. Along with forty-five million other people he was shocked and saddened by her death, but he was careful not to encumber himself with spurious emotion. Two could not be parted who had never been joined. What he experienced, chiefly, was the hollowness inside himself, the absence of emotion. The signifier 'Bonnie West', about which the public system of knowledge existed, had been arbitrarily and drastically altered from what — only last night — it had signified. What was there was not there — and yet it was. Her being was full of nothingness. It was as if a cherished volume had been stolen from a library, leaving on the shelf the space it had always occupied. The emptiness that remained possessed the exact shape and form, the identical dimensions, of what had been taken away.

'Well . . .' O'Duff, crossing the room toward where Faraday was standing, said with a barbed rise-fall intonation. When Faraday, refusing to be drawn onto it, said nothing, he added: 'I see you're still wearing your penguin suit.'

'I haven't been home,' Faraday said. 'To change.'

'You don't have to tell me that, Lieutenant. I'm a detective. I can *see* you been working on the case all night.' He grinned sourly. 'Like the rest of us.'

'That's right. I have,' Faraday said. 'But it looks to me, Captain, you could do with some shuteye. You don't mind me saying.'

'I don't mind. It's the truth. But don't let it worry you. I'm in better shape than I look. I even grabbed a couple hours sleep. I was sawing wood in the back of Kriwaczek's vehicle when they woke me up to give me the news.' He jerked his chin over his shoulder toward the dead newscaster without looking at her. 'And for once we was here before the t.v. crews. They couldn't believe it. They gave me a rough ride, I told them, No they couldn't come in and take pictures of the deceased. They said some very uncomplimentary things about the Police Department within my hearing. They asked why they couldn't. I told them because it was against the law is why, which of course they already knew. They said some uncomplimentary things about the law. I told them they should be more respectful. And then – you believe this? – one these jamokes throws a punch at me.' O'Duff snickered. 'The way a old lady throws a stick for a dog. I told Lieutenant Lazlo to draw her weapon and warned the bastards to toe the line or there was going to be another sudden outbreak of mortality 'mong t.v. news personnel. And you know what?' O'Duff lowered his voice and continued in a loud stage-whisper. 'You know what the Lieutenant had in her holster?'

Faraday shook his head. How would he know?

'*A can of hairspray and a eye-makeup kit!*'

'So what did you do?' Faraday said in a normal voice. He was unwilling to collude in the Captain's conspiratorial attitude toward Dinah Lazlo.

O'Duff tapped his own weapon-case. 'I gave them a peek at the old airweight .38 Chief Special! The sight of that took the fight outta them!'

'It would. Yes.'

'I regret to say it did. I was almost looking forward to winging one those ghoulish bastards!'

'Don't be too hard on them, Captain. Bonnie West is one of their own. It's like – for them – the way cops feel when another cop gets in the way of one. They take it to heart.'

'If by their heart you mean their wallet, I agree with you. Those bastards, they'd point cameras at a cancer ward, they thought it would sell fucking news space!'

'Bonnie West *is* news. She was popular. Everyone – even Captain O'Duff – has heard of her. Right?'

'Sure I heard of her. Where you think I live, Week-hawken?'

The Captain lived in Weekhawken.

'Because,' Faraday said, 'she didn't have a position. She just *read* the news, which meant people didn't have to approve of her. Men, women, you were with Tina, you were with Rocco, didn't make any difference, your politics or your sexual orientation. Bonnie West cut across the map.'

'But.' O'Duff raised his finger to make the numeral 1. 'Someone didn't like her. She had enemies.'

'She didn't have any.'

'Everyone who doesn't have enemies has enemies. That's the *reason* they have enemies.'

'Uh-uh. Not Bonnie West. She was innocent.'

O'Duff shrugged. 'That's where she went wrong then,' he said. 'All we have to do is find the one who was in love with her enough to point a gun at her and pull the trigger – twice!'

'Someone . . .' Lieutenant Lazlo, joining them, said on cue: '. . . who is male, dark-haired, white, a hundred, a hundred twenty pounds, owns a black suit.' She almost smiled at Faraday. This was his department. 'A supporter of Rocco Da Silva, I'd say.' She was beating him at his own game. 'And some kind of foreign high-velocity automatic did the damage. Korean or Japanese, I'd say.'

There was a funny kind of silence – full of meaing. It was a signal to Faraday that he was being invited to initiate the next phase of the conversation. If he didn't, they weren't going to tell him anything. Faraday – appropriately – looked to O'Duff for an explanation.

'Didn't you know?' O'Duff grinned. He was loving this. 'There was an autonomic security video of the pair of them – Bonnie West and the killer – entering the condo at 1:56 this a.m. Everyone comes or goes is filmed.'

There followed another silence – even funnier than the first. If Faraday wanted to know more, he would have to ask. He would have to admit the superiority of old-fashioned police work. Lazlo and O'Duff were enjoying

158

themselves. Faraday, for his part, was enjoying the metalin-guistic level of what was being said: the triumph of the forensic method over the semiological.

'Let's get this straight,' Faraday said. 'You're telling me you have an ID of the assassin?'

'We don't have a face, as such, yet,' Dinah Lazlo said. 'He took care to keep it away from the camera. So it's a good guess he was here before. But don't worry, we got enough to go on. The computer'll locate him, soon as we feed in his dimensions.'

'*Her*!' Faraday said.

'What . . .?' O'Duff started.

The dialogue stalled. It was Faraday's turn to look dumb and give nothing away.

'I beg your pardon?' Dinah Lazlo said.

'The killer,' Faraday told them. 'Is a *her*. Female. A woman.'

'Did you see the video yet?'

'. . . Blonde. Nearer a hundred than a hundred twenty pounds. A Tina Rauch supporter, you really want to know – although she moves from one party to the other without difficulty. And the two slugs that killed Bonnie came out the end of a .41 Colt revolver.'

At first Lieutenant Dinah Lazlo and Captain Daniel Clarence O'Duff said nothing. They glanced from Faraday to each other and then, when they saw that he was being serious, they started to laugh politely in his face.

'Oh no! . . . Please! . . . Don't make me laugh. . . . You know it makes me break wind. . . . Don't. . . .' O'Duff, laughing, broke wind steadily.

In the toneless tone of a police witness filing an affidavit Faraday continued: 'She – the killer – was wearing a double-breasted two-tone wet-slate grey suit with shot silver tulle gored revers and her blonde hair spiked and glitzed à la mode. She was also wearing cotton gloves – which is why there are no prints – and she used an original revolving chamber .41 caliber rimfire Colt with Tiffany silver-inlay work on it, factory-modified to take a Mitzu recoilless automatic firing mechanism with built-in silencer and spur-trigger – which is why there are two gunshot wounds on the victim. It's almost impossible to fire a single shot from this weapon. Least. . . .' Faraday withdrew his right hand from his hip-pocket. '. . . In *my* experience it is.'

He held up the punctured cuff of his black jacket – and underneath it, the white dressing Delia Summers had applied to his lower arm – for them to inspect. Exhibit A.

He left Exhibit B – the Colt .41 – inside the pocket.

Dinah Lazlo opened her lips as if she was going to say something. O'Duff closed his – *he* sure wasn't.

Faraday lifted his arm out of the way and took a step backward to allow the sudden traffic of police and forensic personnel to pass between him and his two colleagues. The snooty District Attorney's Counselor and Sergeant Kriwaczek were leaving – silent – in each other's company. Faraday watched the nonplussed expression on Dinah Lazlo's face flicker behind the toing and froing of people – and on O'Duff's face no expression at all. Kriwaczek was signing the body over into the custody of a trio of SkyPol officers who had just arrived to transfer it to the heliport on top of the condo tower and, from there, to the morgue on 28th Street. They weren't in any hurry but they would probably get there before Kriwaczek did. Tall, handsome, wearing the anti-glare mirror-visors of their white helmets down over their eyes, they looked almost identical in their identical skyblue uniforms. They said nothing. Strapped against their thighs they carried prestigious blue-steeled Kalashnikov 9mm. parabellum machine-carbines capable of stopping a small tank. They did not especially ignore Captain O'Duff and everyone else in the room. They probably did not see O'Duff – or anyone else. The SkyPol were a law unto themselves. They would conduct the transfer of the body without seeing the licensed news-hounds waving cameras and Public Right of Access to Information warrants over the cops' shoulders at them. You couldn't help admiring them, their polite arrogance. Faraday himself had passed with some difficulty through the police cordon keeping the bastards – as O'Duff always called the media people – from entering what they would soon be referring to as the Kill Chamber.

In the time it took O'Duff to detach himself from Dinah Lazlo, take Faraday by the elbow and, placing his trigger finger over his own closed lips, edge him away from the melee, the two SkyPol officers had lifted Bonnie West's body from the ottoman where it looked so comfortable and placed it inside the aluminium and zinc stretcher-trolly they had brought with them. The third SkyPol officer had folded the authority-chit, signed, back into his breast-pocket. They did this with the slow easy confidence with which they did everything, without wasting any words and without any ceremony. The victim was a television personality or she was a bag-woman, it made no difference to these guys. These guys had scraped their buddies off the field of battle in combat zones – under fire, probably. Nothing, after that, made any goddamn difference. There weren't any words to waste.

Without releasing Faraday's elbow, O'Duff waited for the two SkyPol officers to wheel past their loaded bier – the capsule's lid mercifully lowered over its contents – and then he steered Faraday out of the apartment behind them. With the third SkyPol officer bringing up the rear, the cortège proceeded in silence along the carpeted corridor. The uniformed police stationed outside the entrances of the neighboring apartments – a guard of honor – looked on.

'I figured,' O'Duff said out of the side of his mouth, 'that Lieutenant Lazlo didn't need to hear the whys and wherefores of the case. Yeah? The t.v. people are on her tail already. I mean that literally! They'll have the top button of her shirt undone and the latest Police theory outta her before she has time to powder her nose.'

Faraday let himself be guided by his superior officer and said nothing. As they reached the end of the corridor they came abreast of the row of elevators and also, at the contiguous elbow of the corridor, face to face with the full fury of the t.v. company employees engaged in arm-wrestling contests with the cordon of Police Department employees. Each party was only doing its duty by its employer. Guns and cameras had been drawn but so far neither had been fired. Faraday – he recognized one or two of the top journalists present, and they probably recognized him – snuck behind the large framed SkyPol officers and kept his head down.

'Faraday!' one of the media tribe called out to him. '*Faraday!*' It was Sasha, the *Vogue* society columnist whom they called the Barracuda and to whom he owed a considerable favor. 'I won't forget this, Faraday!' she yelled after him. If she didn't forget this he might as well kiss goodbye to his career right here and now.

O'Duff and Faraday followed the immaculately laundered skyblue uniforms into the elevator. There was just enough room to accommodate the five of them around the stretcher-capsule. The gates closed, immediately shutting out all the swearing and clamor. They rode toward the roof of the building in silence as if – flanked by these imperious agents of destiny – Bonnie West was leaving earthly concerns behind, setting out on the first stage of her rocket-trip to her resting place in the everlasting t.v. program in the sky.

'You know, I think one these boys musta forgot to deodorize hisself this morning,' O'Duff remarked in a casual voice.

The remark ricocheted around the tiny aluminium cabin. Faraday could hardly believe his ears.

'Which one them you think it is, Lieutenant?' O'Duff continued.

Three mirror-visors turned fractionally towards O'Duff. Faraday saw the Captain's and his own distorted reflection looking back at him.

'Must be me, Captain,' he said. He grinned as foolishly as he was able. 'I was on duty all night. Don't you remember?'

'Nar. So was I. It's not you. I know the smell of good human sweat. Can't beat it. This. . . .' He sniffed the air. 'Nar. This. . . . This is more like rat. This is your rat smell.'

One of the SkyPol officers moved his elbow just a fraction of an inch and O'Duff already had the man covered with his stubby Chief Special which somehow was already in his hand.

'This is a single-action mechanism, Officer,' O'Duff explained. 'So you hear the click means you're dead.' He added: 'I got you all 'fore any you lay your hand on the fucking erections you keep strapped to your legs.'

'Captain O'Duff. Ain't you got no respect?' the third SkyPol officer said in a soft desert drawl, smilingly. 'I don't see as you have any call pointing a gun at us. We have the authority. . . .'

The man slowly moved his hand in the direction of his breast-pocket, where the authority was. O'Duff – before it had gotten halfway there – had the barrel of his weapon six inches away from the man's smiling mouth.

'You ratfuckers'll give me, my staff, the time o' day or I'll be talking my way outta a multiple gunshot accident. Won't be easy but with the help of the Lieutenant here, I could beat it.'

The elevator hummed.

O'Duff sweated.

Faraday didn't know where to look. Everything was a reflection of everything else.

After about twenty years the elevator stopped dead with a soundless bump and the gates opened. A current of warm afternoon city air breezed into the icy cabin. No one moved.

Eventually the third SkyPol officer – the one who was paid to look after the other two – said: 'Apologies, Captain, we was discourteous.'

O'Duff backed out of the elevator, his gun still in his hand. He jerked it the way you do when you are holding a weapon on a person and you want that person to start moving in a particular direction. 'Get lost, ratfuckers!' he sneered as only O'Duff knew how.

The three SkyPol officers, neither slowly nor fast, left the elevator cabin and conducted the trolley containing the corpse of Bonnie West toward the revving skyblue jet-helicopter in which a fourth officer was waiting, idling the controls. The revving accelerated as they approached.

'Best to hit these guys where it hurts most – their pride!' O'Duff said. 'The poor ratfuckers! Think they're the only ones seen combat! They was trapped in there, you see that?' The Captain – ragged, unshaven, overweight – looked strangely animated in spite of the fact that the sunlight seemed to bleach all the color out of his face and his thinning hair was being buffeted by the random turbulence of the downdraft. 'They didn't have room to clear their weapons! Those foreign 9mm. popguns are fine, you want to take out a auto at fifty, but in a clinch. . . .' He raised his open palm containing the worn metal Chief Special as if he were trying to gauge its weight. 'Gimme a old American handgun.'

About fifty yards away the team from the crack air-defence unit of the NYC PD was already aboard their chopper, the last one to enter the craft throwing a salute – it looked like – towards where O'Duff and Faraday were standing on the edge of the tarmac. Almost absentmindedly, O'Duff acknowledged the gesture with the barrel of his gun.

'Bonnie West was killed by the person she left Rock's Club with last night,' Faraday said.

'Yeah?' O'Duff said, without looking at him. 'And who *did* Bonnie West leave Rock's Club with last night?'

'That person's identity does not exist. Which is the reason Dinah Lazlo'll never find him – assuming *he* shows up on her computer scan of the condo's security file.'

'This person's got a name though.'

'Her name's Tracy Wilder.'

O'Duff – still watching the SkyPol helicopter preparing to lift off – repeated the name: 'Tracy Wilder . . .' as if he might have heard it before some place. Then: 'How come she – this Tracy Wilder – makes out like she's a man?'

Faraday shrugged. 'It's the territory she occupies. *Entre deux mondes.*'

'What . . .?'

'The twilight zone. Neither one thing nor the other. She works both sides of the street – for Tina Rauch and, I suspect, for Rocco Da Silva. A double agent, if you like. She lives in a world of betrayal.'

'Yeah, but how's she, ah, *built* . . .?'

'She owns a bona fide pair of female breasts, that's what you mean. I can vouch for that because I've seen them myself. That don't mean much, of course, these days. With a TS like her, well maybe Dinah is right after all. She *could* be a man.'

'But Bonnie West, wouldn't she, ah, like. . . .'

Faraday grinned. 'You're out of date, Captain, you don't mind me saying. However she's built, that's how Bonnie liked her. You'll have to have a gynosurgeon examine her, you want to get the truth of the matter.'

The helicopter – its retro-motors screaming – lifted off the ground. The wind velocity suddenly increased and banged about the heliport, forcing Faraday and O'Duff to incline their shoulders towards it in order not to be bowled over backwards. The helicopter tilted its axis by about five degrees. Then it drove, only a few feet above the tarmac – as if it were a heavy fixed-wing jet, taking off – towards O'Duff and Faraday. It came at them fast. They could do nothing, when it was on them, except throw themselves onto the tarmac, face down, in a gesture of supplication. The chopper, inches above, almost blew the pants off them and the roar was almost loud enough to drown out the double explosion – *boom-boom* – which sounded when the machine was directly overhead. The ground shuddered. Then the helicopter was gone, veering away from the elevator stack.

The wind dropped.

Silence.

Faraday helped Captain O'Duff to his feet, careful not to look too hard at the symmetrical pair of craters, each about two feet in diameter, placed in the blacktop a yard away on either side of them. A friendly demonstration of the firepower of your Kalashnikov 9mm. parabellum autocarbine.

'Oh no . . .' O'Duff was laughing. 'My wind . . .!'

He ignored their little brush with death.

'So. . . . Now I suppose you going tell me why the mintie had it in for Bonnie West. Let me guess. She was Bonnie's lover?'

'Very good Captain. How did you work that out?' Faraday said without a hint of irony in his voice.

O'Duff nodded and grinned. 'Had to be.' He finally holstered his Smith .38 which was still in his hand. 'Had to be. Eighty-seven percent murders where there is no intent to commit a robbery are matrimonial – or amatory, as they say now.'

'Tracy Wilder didn't kill Bonnie because she was her lover but despite the fact. She didn't have any choice. Bonnie was in a position to tie her in with a serious crime and – it's my belief – she was about to do that.'

'You been doing your homework, Lieutenant. I can see that. So what *was* the crime?'

This was the moment Faraday had been waiting for.

'The bomb attack on the Torelli Building,' he said.

O'Duff, his hand still shading his eyes, continued squinting into the cloudless blue sky at the skyblue helicopter disappearing into it, upwards and onwards, becoming a speck, then half a speck, then a quarter of a speck, and so on into infinity. It was the very last they would see of Bonnie West.

'Bonnie knew how to read television. Fewer people do than you would think,' Faraday continued. 'She sees the man in the video-clip sent to the Channel Eleven Studio. She sees him plant the bomb outside the Torelli Building and she recognizes who it is. Even from a back shot. Of course she does! He's her lover. It's not just his ass she recognizes, it's his *style*. She wants to know what the fuck he thinks he's doing. So she confronts him – Wilder – whatever name she knows him by. Bonnie West is unable to countenance the crime because . . . because she's Bonnie West!'

'How d'you know this?'

'Because I was there when she did – when she pointed her finger at her boyfriend.'

166

'Oh boy! This is too good to be true! Max Faraday playing the detective!' O'Duff chortled. 'So Tracy Wilder decides to get rid of Bonnie West and the shit Bonnie has on him – her?'

They reached the balustrade rimming the heliport of the New Barbizon. They leaned against the steel safety-barrier. Below them lay the city of New York – wild, beautiful, hopelessly free – anyone's for the taking – that for which Sin had been the price: the Big Apple. Three blocks East – Central Park like a map of itself. The aerial view of unplanned rusting air-conditioning units and water-towers appended like afterthoughts onto expensive buildings, an unsightliness which the visitor on the street never guessed the existence of. A skyscape of semi-derelict baroque and modernist and post-modernist scrapers, neoplastic excrescences that had metastasized throughout the city and from which part of it had already died. The miracle of capitalism regenerating itself on its own corpse. It was an exhausted overfinanced landscape that still, nevertheless, had its charm.

'. . . This shit would include, yeah? why she chose to bomb Torelli's inna first place,' O'Duff said. 'Was it Rocco paid her to?'

'She's Tina Rauch's campaign manager, for Chrissake! It's not Rocco stands to gain from the public believing Tina's gown was destroyed. It's Tina does! Think about it. It concentrates the attention of the voters onto *her*. Couple hours from now, they switch on their t.v.s, they're not going to even look at Rocco Da Silva!'

'A publicity caper – that's all it was?'

'Nothing so crude as that Captain. How shall I put it? We live in an age in which all human expression has to pass through the filter of the t.v. image. A person wants to make a statement, he has to grab the camera. You shoot the President, you're a celebrity. The artist today has to compete with the soap star and the criminal.'

'Tracy Wilder is an *artist*?'

'In a modern sense of an old term, yes. Why d'you figure

she took such pains to vid herself in the act of planting the explosive device? And then to send the vidfilm – potentially incriminating evidence – to the t.v. stations?'

'As an act of humanity?' O'Duff suggested. 'To make certain the public knew she had taken every precaution that no one would get hurt?'

'That's one reason, for sure. Violence against people and Art are incompatible. People don't care about buildings, they care about people. It means they don't have to disapprove of her, they don't want to. It was also an elegant way of pointing at how a t.v. statement – this statement in particular – works. We call it a metalanguage – a statement that makes a self-conscious comment on itself, on its own process. All art, if it *is* art, has a metalinguistic angle. To get her message over, Tracy Wilder made use of a vocabulary which the majority of t.v. viewers were already familiar with: terrorism. She hijacked the rhetoric of conventional news-imagery for her own purposes so that people would take on board ideas which they would never normally entertain. Like the Trojan horse – you know the story. It's an old story. It's not new. More or less, it's what the artist's been doing since the beginning of history.'

'Breaking the law?'

'You put your finger on it!'

'Slow up there a minute. Let me get this straight,' O'Duff said. 'We're talking here about terrorism as Art – right? As an Art form?'

'You got it. We're talking about its impact on people's consciousness. What it *says* to them – not its criminality or its morality. That's not my province. Look at the business – the unauthorized destruction of a top couturier's atelier – as a discourse, just like it was any other piece of speech. Try and forget the rights and wrongs of the matter for the moment.'

'Give me a break Faraday,' O'Duff said. 'That goes against my nature – and my training.'

'Of course it does. But you consider the *linguistic* nature of what took place inside the Channel Nine News Quiz format and you'll be able to understand it. The event denotes one thing immediately – has the standard indices of what the public conventionally recognizes as a *terrorist act*. Sure. But it also *connotes* a secondary level of meaning: the stylish perpetrator – his skates, his snazzy one-off skating outfit – says he's a stylist. It's an inside job. The act is meaningful even if the meaning is not clear. He records himself in the act, he's saying, "I'm making news and I'm making a t.v. program about what I'm making." He sends the film to the t.v. companies, to tell them, "I'm ahead of you" but – more to the point – to say, "Here is the code. Here is the key to the code. Work it out. Content is a function of form." Now listen very carefully, Captain, try and stay awake for this bit. When you have used the key to deconstruct the code, what it says is: "I do what can't be done. I unite opposites. In this artifact contraries meet." Am I going too fast for you?'

'It's not the speed you're going at, Faraday. . . .'

'The transitoriness of existence – all things are in flux – such as is celebrated in Tina Rauch's romantic imagery – is in dialectical opposition to the continuance of *form* embodied in Rocco's classicism. Right?'

O'Duff almost nodded.

'Both these philosophical points of departure are yoked together in Tracy Wilder's construct: the ephemeral nature of the explosion and the permanence of the recording. She is mediating between the two. At the same time, more obviously, by levelling a fashion house to the ground she is – as a terrorist and as an artist – challenging one of the bases on which our society is built. Most people, at some level, will understand this. It's a solution only Art can make.'

'I don't believe this. This is a dream,' O'Duff said. 'I'm going to wake up any minute. I'm not really here listening to Max Faraday's semi-logical horseshit. . . .'

Faraday suddenly got a flash of his own dream he had woken up from this morning – looking down on the city from a great height. Only it wasn't the World Trade Center on Vesey and Liberty he was looking down from, and it wasn't Delia Summers he was standing next to. Seventy percent of the dream had come true. It's always the thirty percent that makes the difference.

'But you *are* here. No getting away from it. And you're begining to see what the fuck I'm talking about,' Faraday said. 'Aren't you?'

O'Duff shook his head. He wanted to disagree. 'The way things look,' he said. 'You could be right. I got to admit you done the legwork on this one. It hurts me to say so.' He grinned. 'I dunno.' He laughed. He shook his head. 'You think it's time I retired? I coulda killed those boys in there.'

'You coulda killed *all* of us,' Faraday said.

'That's what I mean.' O'Duff turned his back on New York City and leaned his elbows against the safety-rail. 'It's crap what you're saying but these days that gives it the seal of approval, there's so much of it talked. Please don't think I don't 'ppreciate your work, Faraday. I do. I guess now all we got to do is apply for a arrest warrant soon as possible. You thought where you aim making the collar on Mister-slash-Miz Tracy Wilder?'

'Not so fast, Captain. It's not so simple as that.'

'What? What you saying? Making the collar is the most easy part!'

'I'm talking about who runs this city. Who did you have in mind to sign the warrant?'

'The Police Commissioner – who else?'

'Liebman?'

'Sure. A case like this, you don't want to take any chances.'

'"Black Fats" Liebman isn't going to be Police Commissioner much longer'n tonight – tomorrow afternoon, the latest. After the swearing in of the new Mayor.'

'Oh no!'

'Oh yes. Whoever wins the mayoral race, "Black Fats" Liebman's going to be cashing in his annuity. He's probably got his desk cleared already. Day after tomorrow he'll be an ex-Police Commissioner playing with his yacht up in the Hamptons along with all the other ex-PCs. Liebman's not going to stick his neck out for us, not if he's planning on enjoying his annuity. Tina wins, Agnes Wentworth is in the saddle and she is not going to be in any hurry to pin a terrorist bombing charge plus Murder One onto Tina's agent, right? Be more'n her job's worth. In fact, that's exactly what her job *is* worth. That'll be the vig. But if Rocco wins, it's the same difference only we take our orders from that cheap crook Axel Flexner. Flexner knows a witch-hunt among Tina's people is sure's goddamn going to jump back and hit him in the face. Don't forget, Captain, that Tracy Wilder can always say it was Da Silva put her up to it in the first place. Make more sense — way any jury would see it — he did. She can jump both ways. That's her style. The last thing Axel Flexner wants is a dirty tricks trial dragging on through Rocco's administration. He won't sign your warrant, Rocco gets in, because he knows they're not going to pull any percentage on who gets nailed for vandalizing some old stone building in the garment district. You can take your warrant to Flexner, you can take it to Wentworth, won't make any difference. It's going to end up in the same East River.'

Faraday stopped speaking.

The light was dazzling. It was a clear day. The sun was shining.

'Lieutenant Faraday,' O'Duff said. 'You're saying we have a murderer we can't arrest?'

'I'm saying we have an arrest warrant we can't apply for.'

'Shit!'

'I thought you'd appreciate that,' Faraday said. He grinned at the ambiguous panorama of Manhattan. 'It's cute, isn't it?'

'Shit!'

8

It was almost twilight. Alert, she crossed from the stationary cab to the opening in the iron railings where the iron stairs descended into the lower level of the old building. West 32nd Street was hot and humid. The steel shutters of the licensed small firearms boutique were rolling down for the night just as the sex show next door was turning on its lights. This – she knew – was the lawless intermediate zone in which a person needed to be alert, the one area that was accessible to everyone in the city, even to those who did not have access any other place, especially any place that could not afford air-conditioning: pimps with guns with girls with habits, bums with philosophy degrees from NYCU, bag-persons with Tourette's Syndrome, foreign bodies with nothing except hard unforgiving eyes. Streetpeople – a permanently transient species with its own strict classification of sub-groups. This was their home, their front room and their backyard. But where were they? In the short distance she had to cover she did not get balked, rolled, mauled, propositioned, attacked, sung to, heckled, hawked at. She did not even get stuck for the down payment on a pint of sunshine. It caused her to wonder whether the city sidewalk was the perilous region it was cracked up to be.

The cab – when she had reached the steps and okayed the driver – slowly accelerated in the direction of Sixth Avenue, leaving her alone. She climbed one step at a time down the cast-iron stairway which seemed to have been specifically

172

engineered to trap the narrow gauge of a lady's high-heeled shoe – a subtle device, she wondered, to discourage any person wearing such a shoe from proceeding further.

Undiscouraged, she waded through the swing-doors into a tunnel of a room in which some low-wattage lamp bulbs were burning. The current from a noisy window-fan situated above her, over the doors, pleasantly interposed itself between her clothing and her skin. There was a shade and a silence, a scrubbed coolness about the room which she associated with places of prayer. Rituals took place here. Mysteries were revealed. She paused in order to allow the pupils of her eyes, contracted to restrict the daylight glare, to dilate sufficiently for her to take her bearings in the poorly lit interior. When they had done this she saw that she was not alone. A broad-framed man in a white shirt and a black bow-tie, untied, was shaving his face in front of a mirror that ran almost the length of the wall. The man's eyes, as she stepped down the short plank stairway, swiveled in their sockets without the sockets appearing to move. His hand continued shaving. At the furthest end of the bar a t.v. was on with sound adjusted to zero.

'Well, hello!' the man said without turning round, addressing her reflection in the mirror. 'Glad you could make it. . . .' But then, when he saw her, her shiny fuschia pink satin fuck-me shoes and her short cobwebby cocktail dress of re-embroidered black lace over a fuchsia purple slip – all by Romeo Cavalcanti – when he saw her obvious *class* – he left off shaving and turned to face her. He grinned out of the map of Alaska covering the lower part of his face. 'What can I do for you Ma'am? You lose your way?' he said. He held a soaped shaving brush in one hand and in the other an old-fashioned steel safety razor. 'Or you just suddenly came over all thirsty?'

She marched right up to the bar.

'TG with Roses,' she said, hiking her dress up in order to climb more comfortably onto one of the vacant stools. There were about twenty of these to choose from, but to be friendly she chose the one directly in front of the man.

'Three to one. Straight up. In a thin glass – preferably one I don't need two hands to lift.'

'*Roses*? D'I hear you say *Roses*? Oh, no! That's my luck for you! Will you believe me I tell you my bottle of Roses broke yes'day morning? No kidding. Some local jamoke let off a sack of very high explosive inner next block. 'Cept for some glasses and my nerves, my bottle of Roses was the only casualty. Now you come by, sweet as you like, and ask for the stuff. And I don't get asked for it every day.'

'So what *do* you get asked for every day?' she said.

'I get asked for beer. I get asked for whiskey. Whiskey with beer back. Beer with whiskey back. Beer with beer back. . . .'

'Gimme a beer, just as it comes.'

Carefully angling the glass, he started to draw off what looked like used engine lubricant, black and slow-moving. The process took about three minutes. Neither of them spoke until he had placed the full glass onto a paper coaster in front of her. She looked at the creamy white head floating on the top of it.

'What' this?' she said. 'Your shaving mug?'

'Hey! C'mon now! They were making this stuff 'fore George was more'n a twinkle in Mrs Washington's eye! Don't knock it! I got some Potsville piss back here, you prefer,' the man said.

She shook her head. She took a bite out of the beer – if that was really what it was. What it was was slightly chilled, but not so much that you couldn't taste it. She had to admit it was dry, clean even to a palate habituated to Sancerre and Petit Chablis. It had an intense hoppiness married to a roasted barley finish, with just a hint of sharp quenching sourness. It was very interesting.

The barman watched her.

'It's very interesting,' she said.

'The day they stop making it, we're finished,' he said.

Without asking who 'we' were – or whether it would include herself – she said: 'It's very good.' She was glad she did not have to lie.

'*You're* telling *me* that?'

After a moment the man – he had returned to the mirror to complete his shave – enquired: 'You, ah, meeting someone particular or, like I already said, you just happen to wander in off the street?' He eyed her over his razor. 'Dangerous habit, walking into joints without a invite.'

'I'm looking for a man name of Danny Keach. You know where I can find him?'

'Ow! Goddamn! You shouldn't do that!'

It took her by surprise.

'Do what?'

'Make a pass at a guy when he's shaving his face!'

'I was told to ask for Danny Keach and he would see me okay,' she said. 'Until my date arrives.'

''ll be a pleasure! Your date . . .?'

'Maxwell Faraday.'

'It's the Lieutenant you're meeting?' Danny Keach looked relieved. He grinned.

'Yeah. And he's late. Or, I guess, I could be early.'

'You couldn't been much earlier. I only just opened the doors before you came in.' He dabbed at his jowl with a paper coaster. Danny Keach was probably nearer seventy than sixty but he still possessed his teeth and enough of his hair that you wouldn't call him bald. He had the build of an ex-pugilist. It would be a brave man, she suspected, who would call him anything he didn't care to be called. He began to tie his black bowtie with thoughtful precision, the same way he poured beer. The same way, she suspected, that he did everything.

A couple of men wearing identical uniforms – transit employees – entered the bar. They leaned against the counter and traded insults with Danny Keach while he stuck glasses under the tap. He didn't wait to ask whether or not it was beer they required. He already knew. Then some more people came in – also men – and almost the same routine was gone through. She noticed that they were all pretending that the classy broad in the sexy dress at the bar was invisible, but she could feel the electricity in the air that her presence engendered. The t.v. sound came on although no one was especially looking at the picture. It was only Harvey Walker, the Channel Nine sports reporter, trying to work up some enthusiasm for the ballgame, scheduled to start any moment now, that would decide the Series one way or the other, however badly the two teams played. People continued to arrive singly and in groups – even one or two women, she was pleased to see – and in no time the bar was humming. It was Election night, the climax of both candidates' campaigns. Tonight the issue was going to be decided one way or the other. Bets had been placed and soon money would be changing hands. The odds were shortening by the minute.

Danny Keach replaced her glass, when it was empty, with a fresh one without asking her whether or not any more beer was what she required. Evidently he belonged to the rare class of barmen who could read minds. She made to pay for it, he shook his head. He looked at her with mock fearsomeness, rapped his knuckles on the bartop and jerked his thumb in the direction of his own chest. 'Seeing as you's a hon'ry member of the Precinct, Miz. . . .'

'Summers. Delia Summers.'

'Please to meet you, Miz Summers.' He leaned across the bar and shook her hand. 'Any these roughnecks try anything, you sing out. 'll give me pleasure to personally dispose 'em to get in line.'

'You mean behind Max Faraday?' she said.

Danny Keach jerked his thumb toward his own chest again. 'I mean behind me – behind Lieutenant Faraday!'

The old cop knew how to pitch a compliment. You couldn't help liking him.

'Who you got your money on – to win?' she said, motioning with her chin towards the t.v. screen.

'The 'Lection?'

'The ballgame.'

A pained expression crossed Danny Keach's face.

'Everyone says Cody La Renta hits form, it's a shoo-in. But I'm not so sure. La Renta's playing as bad as the rest the team added together. I wouldn't like to have to place a bet either way. I saw better baseball played at the ol' Ed Koch High School. They used to coach you good when I played. How to catch a ball. How to throw it.' He leaned back to face the t.v. in time to see Tim Bryce – in a replay of last night's game – grabbing a softball bunt and, with the lead man dead by yards, throw to first. 'And . . .' Danny Keach groaned, '. . . *where* to throw it!'

'A lot hangs on this game, all the same – for all the undecided voters,' she said. 'With Tina and Rocco running neck and neck – Rocco just ahead. A win for the Mets might make the difference who ends up signing the checks. You know how folks like to identify with success.'

'Yeah. Well. Maybe. Inner ol' days a political party wasn't the kind you attended to have a drink and a dance with your ol' lady. The voters were influenced by what the can'dates had to *say*. Like their proposals how to run the city. They had *ideas.'*

'Ideas are too abstract for people to relate to,' she said. 'What the candidates have to say is encoded – Max would say – in their imagery. How they present themselves to the public.'

'I'm 'quainted with the Lieutenant's theories, Miz Summers,' he said.

'Alvin Cooler and Teddy Haynes . . .' Harvey Walker was saying, '. . . were ecstatic when the New York Mets rallied with two out to beat the Yankees last night . . .' over a picture of Alvin Cooler and Teddy Haynes looking ecstatic. Immediately the t.v. cut to right fielder, Billy Boscacci, it looked like. 'But Billy Boscacci could only show dejection after he committed the error that allowed the winning run to be scored off the 10th and the Mets to level the Series.' Picture of Billy Boscacci looking dejected.

The t.v. was suspended over the dead-end of the bar so that you could enjoy it from just about wherever you sat. A majority of customers, however, had chosen to congregate as near to the screen as they could edge their stools. You could see they had arrived early in order to do this. They were getting settled in, ready for the ballgame. Hamburgers and tacos and club sandwiches were appearing on the top of the bar. The tone of the conversation was becoming audibly disputatious. Orange and blue Mets caps and blue and white Yankees' caps were about evenly distributed.

'Dress the poor bastards like minties – how d'you expect 'em to play?' Delia Summers said. 'Even Harvey Walker knew how to make contact with a straight ball in his time.'

Danny Keach glanced away from the t.v. to look at her with respect, either at her grasp of the mysteries of the game or at the appropriate register in which she had expressed it. She spoke his language.

'The rot set in . . .' Harvey Walker continued. 'In the ninth when Yankees shortstop Gaylord Macnamara kicked a grounder, but the next batter hit a double play. The Yankees, in their half, were offered a win. Ozbec walked the leadoff man. Cody La Renta laid down the night's sixth pathetic sacrifice bunt, and catcher Lucien Bickler threw wildly to second. . . .'

Danny Keach shook his head and wandered away in disgust.

Two stools down from where Delia was sitting a scruffy, past-middle-aged man growled, 'That was one for the Hall of Shame' to no one in particular. The man was wearing a twenty-four-hour beard and the sort of colorless suit your wife buys you from Syms. In the mirror she recognized Police Detective Captain O'Duff immediately, even though he looked more than twenty-four hours older than when she had last spoken with him.

'But that's a cute kingfisher-blue silk blouson he's wearing, Captain, you have to admit that,' she said.

Their eyes locked in the mirror.

'It's Miz Summers,' he said, surprised. Perhaps even pleasantly surprised.

She smiled at him. 'You look like a man who could use a drink, if I ever saw one,' she said. 'Allow me to buy it for you. So long as you don't want something with Roses in it.'

'Roses? I want a bed of the damn things!' And then: 'What's happening? La Renta's playing like a rookie.'

Delia slid her glass and her pile of money along the bar and, at the same time, climbed off her stool and onto the vacant one that stood between them. A pilsner glass of used engine lubricant appeared in front of O'Duff without his asking for it. Without even acknowledging its presence – or that of Danny Keach – he picked up the beer and drank half of it down. She gave the sign to Keach and he picked up the exact money from in front of her and returned to the t.v. end of the bar where most of his business was.

'What's a nice girl like you,' O'Duff said, a white mustache of foam on his upper lip which he carefully licked off, 'doing in a dump like this?'

'I have an assignation with one of your officers. He's late.'

'Faraday? He's always late, he turns up at all. Claims the habit of punctuality is bad for the brain. I never knew anyone to talk more crap than Faraday!'

'That's funny. I thought his timing wasn't bad.'

O'Duff looked at her, probably wondering how dirty he was meant to take her remark.

'Oh no! Please don't start singing Faraday's praises!' he said. 'I might end up joining you. I don't think I could survive that!'

O'Duff – she was fairly sure – began to break wind quietly to himself. It was hard to tell. His gravelly belly-laugh sounded so similar to the reverberation of methane gas involuntarily escaping from the rectal passage.

'I'm glad to hear he's risen in your estimation,' she said.

'Let's us say he isn't drawing a minus score anymore,' O'Duff said while he clawed at his recent beard. 'Yeah. Hurts me to say it but he's doing good, though I don't mind telling you I never agreed to having him join the Precinct. In fact, I 'pposed it. Nothing personal. I *like* Max Faraday. I just didn't see the need for a Professor of Semi-Logy in police work. But I was overruled. They even gave him two 'pprentices to train. Maybe I been mistaken. It's not the same world it was when me'n Danny Keach chased crims up'n down 41st Street. Faraday, he's looking for something I wouldn't know what it was you showed me first and then

hit me over the head with it. He's dealing off a different deck.'
O'Duff shook his head. 'I came *this* near to killing three guys
today.' He measured with his thumb and forefinger for her to
see how near it had been—about half an inch. 'Four, you want
to count Faraday. And I guess you do.'

'He was in one piece when I left him, Captain. I'd like him
back that way,' she said. She looked at her wrist watch. It
would be seven-thirty in two minutes' time. In two minutes
the Channel Eleven coverage of the *Vogue* Election Ball
would get under way. The majority of the clientele in the bar,
however, seemed content to watch the ballgame on Channel
Nine. On the t.v. screen the pre-match discussion was taking
place. The Mets' new jodhpur-style pastel uniform trousers
were coming under the scrutiny of the panel of style-experts.

'He'll turn up, Miz Summers,' O'Duff said. He glanced at
his own watch. 'Funny, though, he didn't say nothing to *me*
when he told me to meet him at Keach's, 'bout *you* being
here.'

It took her by surprise.

'You're meeting Max too?'

'No.' O'Duff grinned. 'I'm meeting Lieutenant Faraday.
He said it would be a good place to watch the Tina-Rocco
clash over a few beers. He said it would be instructive. I
might learn something.'

Faraday, like O'Duff said, was obviously dealing off a
different deck.

'If you were planning on watching the show here, Captain,
you might be disappointed. There's a couple dozen guys
down the end of the bar, cops and transit workers mostly,
been waiting all season to watch the Mets-Yankees clash
over a few beers in Keach's.'

O'Duff peered around Delia, assessing the situation. He
caught Danny Keach's eye. Danny glided over, his clean-
shaven face expressionless. They were back in the squadroom.

'Danny. Listen,' O'Duff said. 'Miz Summers and me and,
he ever turns up, Lieutenant Faraday, we was hoping to
watch the Election Ball on t.v. You know, the Rocco Da

Silva—Tina Rauch ding-dong.' He said this with a straight face. 'Only.' He nodded towards the t.v.-end of the bar. 'Some your customers, they 'pparently got other ideas.'

Danny Keach didn't say a word. He walked the length of the bar and immediately jigged the t.v. control to the appropriate channel. Zhorrer's delicious pastel combinations disappeared and the horribly groomed features of Robbie Robson filled the screen. He killed the sound.

The guys in the baseball caps paused just long enough to swallow the hamburgers and tacos in their mouths, then all hell broke loose.

'. . . The fuck you doin' Keach?'

'. . . Shit! Turn it over. . . .'

'. . . You playing at?'

Keach tried to make himself heard but no one was listening. Glasses were banging on the oak bartop. Someone must have heard, however, because a glass sailed down the bar and splintered close to O'Duff. O'Duff didn't move. He continued clawing his twenty-four-hour growth in the mirror as if he were considering whether he should borrow the barman's shaving tackle.

'Now cool it, fellas . . .' Keach was saying. He held out his hands as if he were warming them at a fire. 'Let's keep it civ'lized. This is business. Can't be helped. . . .' It didn't do any good. The fire was getting out of control. The bar was going wild. It was developing into a miniature riot. Another glass flew, smashing against Robbie Robson's face on the t.v. screen. Keach turned away. As he did, the thrown half-hamburger caught him on the back of the head. Ignoring the assault, he went to his till and, from underneath it, Delia watched him draw out a small piece of shiny black metal. Keach levelled the stubby-barreled revolver over his head so that everyone in the bar was able to see it – exactly as prescribed by Police Regulations. He cocked the hammer and then he pulled the trigger. The report was deafening.

The hush which followed the report was so quiet that Delia wondered whether she had, in fact, gone deaf. The acrid smell of cordite irritated the membranes situated inside the concheal cavities of her nostrils. For a moment she thought she was going to sneeze.

Keach, his police-issue revolver smoking at the end of his bent arm, pointing toward the ceiling, stood waiting.

'Be obliged,' he said. 'You gentlemen take some air.'

The smoke cleared. In ones and twos the dozen or so customers collected up their junk food, stood up and left with solemn dignity. No one spoke. It was like watching a jury leave the courtroom in order to decide what verdict to bring in. No question, however, if this were the case, which it would be. In the space of five minutes Danny Keach had gotten rid of the best part of his regular customers at pistol point. Except for herself and the Captain, the barroom was empty.

And quiet.

The window-fan hummed noisily.

'Don't worry 'bout *them*,' Keach said. He carefully cleared the spent case from the chamber of the gun and replaced it with a fresh shell from the supply under the till. He spun the barrel to make sure it sat true. 'They'll be back.' He snapped the barrel into the stock. He didn't look worried. 'They know it, I know it. And no hard feelings either way. We both know they don't have no choice. They'll have to travel a long way to find a bar sells better stout'n Keach does.'

He put the revolver back to bed under the till.

Delia and O'Duff, while Keach swept away the taco chips and french fries, decamped down the counter to be in a better position from which to watch the t.v. Keach fished up three fresh glasses of stout and, pulling up a stool for himself, he turned on the t.v. sound.

'I locked the door,' he said. 'The Lieutenant'll have to ring the bell, he wants to join the party.'

ROBBIE ROBSON — unctuously affable, hideous in his peroxide wig-hat and pomaded jowls, was taking the t.v. audience on a tour of the *beaux arts* charm of the old St Regis-Sheraton. The Old World hotel, built at a time when money didn't have to talk at the top of its voice, was in pretty good shape — high marble walls, fancy gilt pargetting, crystal chandeliers — although, like Robbie Robson, it had undergone its share of face-lifts since then. There were period frescoes on the walls — white-skinned blond-haired jailbait sat naked on the peaks of mountains, hugging their ankles, gazing longingly into the pinky-blue haze. John Jacob Astor IV's idea of tasteful interior decoration.

Robbie Robson — at a hundred and eighty or however old he was — was wearing the same hideous emerald green suit with pale emerald shirt, lemon display handkerchief and purple necktie that he had worn every day for a hundred years, or however long it was since his show became a National Monument. He had the same mannered facial expressions and the same cheerful philistinism that still cued paroxysms of hilarity across the country. You always knew where you stood with Robbie — whether it was the new orang-utan from the Zoological Park he was interviewing or some for'ner thought he could write po'try, there were never any surprises. He was a pro. He was sitting right there in your t.v. room giving shit to some monkey thought he was clever'n you. *Give him shit, Robbie!*

Robbie was standing on the balcony circling the entrance lobby of the hotel so that he would be in a position to look down on the celebrities as they made their entrances. These — Tina's and Rocco's guests and the few unaligned among them — were arriving strictly according to protocol, kissing each other, exchanging compliments, ignoring allegiances and the t.v. cameras. They all possessed the easy familiarity of royalty whose governments happened to have declared war on each other — it was nothing to do with them. There were designers, photographers, models, film-makers, fabric-creators, artists, some of the biggest in the business, some especially flown across from Europe for the evening, and some who had simply bankrolled their way in. Robbie was leaning, saurian, over the balustrade – his emerald suit an exemplum of bad taste. He was reading off Who was Who from a list for the benefit of the less *au fait* among the t.v. audience. Clarence O'Duff and Danny Keach.

'So, ah, who we got here . . .? Ben – wazzat? – Rizzoli? Makes socks, says here. . . . Can you beat that?' He gave his can-you-beat-that? leer to camera. 'This guy designs *socks*!'

Ben Rizzoli, a tall silver-haired gent in his fifties wearing a monocle and a nonchalant white cotton blazer, cloth-buttoned and slashed in white satin, passed up the staircase. You could tell he was European just by the way he walked, without a trace of a swagger. It must be in the blood. He was accompanied by his wife, the beautiful svelte English tango dancer, Kate Horner. She was as tall as he and also dressed in whites, vanilla and cream taffetas, an ingenious cut-in-the-round short fan-pleated skirt that showed off her slender dancer's legs. The couple ascended the grand staircase with great aplomb, like a pair of swans.

The t.v. cut to inside the ballroom, already quite full. Ben Rizzoli and Kate Horner were just entering through the main door. We were into the *crème* now.

'Well, as a matter of *fact*, Robbie darling, Signor Rizzoli is *rather* more than a socks manufacturer. . . .' Robbie Robson's co-host added helpfully. The picture cut to the *Vogue* columnist, Sasha, vivid in a fluorescent zigzaggy off-the-shoulder African print sarong. She was sitting with some friends at one of the tables on the edge of the dance floor. Smiling, she explained: 'Rizzoli's fascination with the laws of geometry has produced some of the boldest asymmetries in dress in recent years, as well as technical achievements like the laser-stitch and the bias-cut in-the-round-look. . . .' The picture closed on Miz Rizzoli's laser-stitched bias-cut gown. '. . . He is an innovator and an inventor and at the same time a traditionalist, an ardent neo-classicist. His designs reflect his pleasure in clean Greco-Roman lines and the fluid fall of drapery. Rocco Da Silva is a great admirer of his work. When I worked with

Ben recently, he told me that he acquired his love for the classical when he played soccer as a boy with his friends in a ruined Greek temple in Southern Italy. . . .'

O'Duff groaned.

Robbie Robson made his well-you-don't-say grimace to the folks at home. 'Now don't say you never learn nothin' on my Show! A'right?' he said. He threw in a malicious we-don't-believe-this-crap-do-we wink for good measure.

'Oh my balls!' O'Duff groaned again. 'I think I'm going to have to throw up! You know, I didn't look at this suckoff for least twenny years – till now!'

'Shsh!' Delia elbowed the Captain's elbow.

The t.v. panned the *salle de bal*. It was noticeable how intimately the members of the two principal faculties in the New York School were acquainted. Everyone knew everyone. Opposites rubbed shoulders. Contraries met. The moderate elements in both parties melded into each other so that it was sometimes hard to tell them apart. The inky garnet-hearted blues of Katya Shiburi were almost indistinguishable from the Tyrian purple-to-black of Ramón. The two of them stood holding hands – she was laughing at something he had said – even though they had both publicly endorsed opposing candidates. They were style polemicists, they weren't mortal enemies. You had the feeling some of these people went back a long way together. A snow-bodiced black-skinned dame-fatale danced cheek-by-jowl with a no-longer-young perruqued cavalier frothing in florid silks like a Louis Quinze armchair. (What was *their* relationship?) Ben Rizzoli's wife was kissing Billy Klein, the matt white cloqué silk of her ensemble in apposition to the shiny white ciré of his. Zhorrer, petalled in pastels – he had obviously abandoned the Mets to their fate – was walking arm-in-arm with a dead ringer for a nineteenth-century Neapolitan secret policeman. Everyone was having a good time. The Cuban orchestra was playing – alternately – tangos and polkas, the foxtrot and the watusi. You could take your pick.

'I'm doing this,' O'Duff explained to Keach, 'because I

promised young Faraday. He tol' me I'd unnerstan' what he's doing in the Precinct — his angle. I guess I owe him that much. . . . But, shit, can you tell me what's happening?'

Keach shook his head, speechless.

Tina — heralded by Robbie's most horrible salacious leer — and Rocco made their separate entrances almost simultaneously. Rocco, characteristically, slipped into the hall unannounced from a side-door. He stood apart, erect but not stiff, one hand in the hip-pocket of his evening suit, the other holding a lighted cheroot. The lights dimmed. A spot picked him out, his suit looking very black in the white light, its tulle revers flashing like a pair of blades. Noticeably, he was not surrounded by minions, look-alikes, hangers-on. Nobody approached him. He was just standing there — alone, separate. He seemed to smile faintly. The smile — of the handsome gangster who knows how the movie will end — had already decided a proportion of the city voters.

Tina, on the other hand, went for the grand entrance. Colorful in her *trompe l'oeil* Torelli gown — you could hear the gasps of delight it aroused — she swept down the grand staircase in a bouquet of colorful well-wishers, sexy young romantics in crazy diverse tailoring. She took the Ball by storm. It was very impressive. The eyes of everyone in the room, including those of Rocco Da Silva, were on her, on her gown, the beauty of which could not be gainsaid — and Tina didn't look bad either. A hush fell on the assembled company, on Robbie Robson, on Sasha, on Danny Keach and on Captain O'Duff, probably on everyone in the city who was tuned into Channel Eleven. Everyone else — they would be tuned into Channel Nine — was probably roaring the Mets' leadoff man onto the plate as the Yankees' pitcher prepared to go into his windup. Tina and Rocco, likewise, faced each other from opposite ends of the style continuum: polymorphic, contradictory. The t.v. had to split-screen in order to accommodate simultaneously the grandeur of his lonely stoic posture and the flashy splendour of her devil-may-care gesture. The aristocrat, the populist. You could take your pick.

'Well – there you go, folks. Now you seen everything.' Robbie Robson said over. He sniggered. 'If you can't tell from the cut of *this* man's jib how he plans to balance the Budget and deal with the Labor Unions, you been watching the wrong channel!'

'. . . Hold on there, Robbie darling. . . .' The crisp voice of Sasha cut in. '. . . If it's *economy* you want to talk about, take a close look at Rocco Da Silva's classic dress suit. . . .'

The t.v. left Tina and closed onto Da Silva. He had been joined by a small group of friends, handsome men and women – no children here – wearing, between them, a historiography of formal evening-wear that went back as far as Dior and Chanel. These superb garments, some of them museum pieces, contained obvious references to each other, but presumably that was the point, to demonstrate the coherence in the development of the classic style. There were certain basic principles that should always be observed.

'. . . You won't see anything in the Five Boroughs more economical than Rocco's ensemble. Look how the line of the jacket sways rhythmically from the shoulders into the hips and the narrow fall of the drapery of the leg. The design is all in the cutting. It has the economy of a Doric Greek column – the Golden Mean. There's nothing superfluous here, when you consider the expensive multi-discipline media artwork that is required to produce Tina's wonderful effects. And don't forget this, Robbie, Rocco created his *nonchalance de luxe* from nothing – himself – with his own hands! He didn't rely on *anyone*'s help or advice. *He* carded the silk, *he* wove it, *he* dyed it, *he* cut it and *he* finished it. Right? What he has done is to take responsibility for every stage in the process. He has reintegrated into the designer's role *all* the procedures. And there you have it: Rocco Da Silva's philosophy, his social policy. This suit is his manifesto. We are all separate individuals in this world, he's saying. You're on your own and you have to look out for yourself, make your *own* mark. Don't expect handouts. Don't rely on the next guy because – let's be realistic – the next guy's going to screw you. It's only human nature. This is nothing new, of course. What Rocco is saying is just a modern expression of an ancient truth: the Old American Way. What you're looking at is, in every sense, a pillar of Western Culture!'

Sasha stopped talking and smiled at the Channel Eleven audience. She looked pleased. This was not Robbie Robson's Show. It was the Barracuda's.

'Be nice to know how much Rocco's paying her to come out for him!' O'Duff sneered.

Danny Keach shook his head.

'Nothing, Captain,' Delia said. 'He doesn't have to pay her anything. They have the same interests – to keep *style* the preserve of a minority. *Vogue Magazine* has always been a conservative force in the fashion world and it only ever endorsed the least innovatory candidates for Mayor.'

The house lights in the *salle de bal* were coming back on. The t.v. scanned the guests, pausing to close in on the more spectacular or familiar individuals among them. For a few moments Tina Rauch and Rocco Da Silva disappeared from view in the visual diapason. Then – the band hushed, the guests hushed also – the pair of them emerged. They stepped out into the open space of the vacated dancefloor. Tina, in her petaled African Sorcerer gown that combined eroticism and regal splendour, looked both available and unobtainable. She was a romantic dream. If she got herself elected, the city officials would be falling over themselves to please her. Meanwhile Rocco – cool and aloof and, apparently, without emotion – stood waiting like the Executioner of the Royal Personage. In his white gloves and black swallowtails, he reminded Delia of the largest and most deadly of the *scorpionida*, the Mexican desert variety, its black body honed to perfection by evolution into a sheath to house its lethal sting. She had once seen a scorpion – strictly speaking an arachnid – stab its own carapace when a large-winged day moth alighted on its shiny back. Reflexly the scorpion's sting had whiplashed, crushing a portion of the moth's wing. The moth had flown free, almost unscathed, leaving the scorpion writhing in its own venom. Delia remembered this as Rocco crossed the floor, held out his hands to Tina and the two of them clasped in the traditional tango clinch. The band struck up. The two Mayoral candidates fell in with the intimate this-way that-way rhythm of the most deadly dance known to Man.

They danced with the passion of irreconcilable opposites. Physicists call it electricity: the spark engendered when alternately coiled copper wire is rotated in contrary directions. Materialist historians, when the contradictory forces in a historical period collide, call it revolution. Lovers, of course, have their own name for it.

Ben Rizzoli and Kate Horner were the first to step out and join them. Kate knew how to tango as well as anyone did. Others soon followed. Henri Ribèc and, white-faced, Ikawa – he wearing something from her collection, she something from his. Anton Derutta and pretty Maddy Clark . . . Cindy Loewe and Etienne D'Offay . . . Duggie Snaggs and his friend Carlton Laplace. . . . Soon the floor was milling as guests climbed down off the fence and embraced José-Maria Varga-Lopez's latest composition in the classic meter. Tina's supporters were doing it with Rocco's, Rocco's with Tina's. One couple was even showing how it should be done on rollerskates. There were many different styles but every pair of dancers was careful to ignore every other pair, conscious that the tango, in its essence, is a dance that only two people can do at any one time.

'Well, this the moment y'all been waiting for . . .' Robbie Robson said. 'Ain't that so Sasha sweetheart . . .?'

'Yes indeed, Robbie.' Sasha's deep voice answered his treble. 'What you're about to witness'll take your breath away. I guarantee. . . .'

The dancers moved in and out of each other without colliding, sensing each other's presence like hive insects. Tina and Rocco swayed as one – two gametes fused into zygote. The *Vogue* Ball was under way. Slow and quick, quick-quick and slow, the two rollerskaters moved so skilfully that they appeared to be not two but three people, spinning expertly backward and forward in and out of the dancers. He was wearing black glasses and a black suit like a lot of Rocco's guests. She – one of Tina's – was a petite black woman in a frivolously short fringed scarlet shimmy-dress, so petite she looked like a girl. They made a terrific pair. With immaculate timing they separated and – suddenly there *were* three of them – spun in opposite circles. At exactly the same moment something black and shiny appeared in their right hands. What the something was, Delia – and probably everyone tuned to Channel Eleven – half-guessed even before the t.v. camera closed onto the skaters' right hands and showed clearly that all three were wielding long-barreled machine-pistols.

'What . . . the fuck! . . .' Robbie Robson shrieked.

HE HAD made a mental list of the necessary steps in a course of action which would lead up to this point and he had numbered each step – as he had been taught to do during his training. Having considered the ethical dimension and practical considerations involved in each step he had proceeded to carry them out from Number One through the sequence without considering the steps further. It was a program and he became a robotic machine obeying the program's commands – One, Two, Three – without emotion, as if they had nothing to do with him. He had – Number One – obtained the arrest warrant from 'Black Fats' Liebman, notwithstanding the outgoing Police Commissioner's reluctance to part with it – perhaps one of the least enjoyable moments in old Liebman's fat black life. He had returned, numb, to Cross Bay Boulevard. He had showered. He had put on a fresh white dress-shirt under the same tired black dress-suit, easing it over his hurt hand. He had exchanged the light-weight murderer's drawer pistol for his more conspicuous regulation Remington. He had checked and double-checked the magazine – as he had been taught to do during his training. Four . . . Six . . . Nine. . . . He had spent an hour dismantling and lubricating and reassembling his old Veriflex trucks and a further twenty minutes whiting up the white leather of his Bauer skateboots. Ten . . . Eleven. . . . He had spoken over the police channel with Cadet Officer Danielle Tornova and apprised her of the situation and given her a number of instructions. She had said, 'Right Lieutenant.' Then: 'I'll wear my mother's red shimmy dress. It's dynamite.' He had had an almost identical conversation with Cadet Officer Ed Conway. He had taken a cab to the Condé Nast Building on Madison Avenue – Eighteen . . . Nineteen . . . and he had persuaded Sasha to hear him out, patient while she calculated the personal advantage she would gain from his proposal. Twenty. It was a program – arrest by numbers. And now – the Remington in his hand, the skateboots on his feet, the warrant in his pocket – now there was just one more thing on his mental list of steps that had to be taken.

''Scuse my French, folks. But does anyone know who these guys *are* . . .?' Robbie Robson was saying – his voice shrill, piqued. His Show was falling apart.

On the screen two of the skaters – one of the men and the black girl – were pointing their weapons inches over the heads of the surrounding guests. Some of these had stopped dancing and were looking on bemused and amused. The third skater, meanwhile – the one in the white skateboots and the black glasses – was aiming his pistol directly into the face of a young woman in an amethyst silk wrap over a flared dance-dress in hunting pink. He was prising her away from her partner. Behind him, the other two skaters continued to circle the action, isolating it from the rest of the pack.

'*These guys*,' Sasha drawled, taking her time. She was in no special hurry. She had put one over on Robbie Robson on his own Show. ' . . . *These guys* are on-duty plainclothes police officers. Making an arrest. They have a warrant.'

'Oh shit!' Captain O'Duff muttered. '*Faraday*! The fuck's he doing? I don't believe this! What warrant she talking 'bout?'

Delia shook her head, speechless.

' . . . And, I'm not mistaken,' O'Duff continued. 'That's Faraday's two rookies, Conway and Tornova!'

'They. . . . Let me get this straight . . .' Robbie's voice piped, incredulous. 'These police officers are making an arrest, like, *now*? *Here*?' Nothing like this had ever happened to him. That's how he came to live to be a hundred and ninety, or however old he was.

'And you. . . . Are you in on this caper?'

'My cooperation was requested by the New York Police Department, sure,' Sasha said. 'Naturally I would not refuse. . . .'

'That's how they got in, huh? These cops?' Robbie sneered. He was turning nasty but there was nothing he could do. 'You helped set this up!'

'Calm down Robbie. . . .'

'I don't believe what I'm hearing here. . . .'

The dance band had ceased playing. Max Faraday was holding his weapon on the yellow-haired woman in the purple and vermilion silk tango-dress while, at the same time, holding his PD badge high above his head. His two colleagues, spinning on his heels, were doing the same. The guests – Tina and Rocco were nowhere to be seen – stood around like film extras waiting for something to happen, upstaged by the drama.

'You are watching. . . .' Sasha said, but she was no longer speaking for Robbie Robson's benefit. She was addressing the millions of potential *Vogue* customers out there watching the Show, 'Lieutenant Maxwell Faraday of the 19th Precinct who is about to legally make an arrest on a person by name of Tracy Wilder. Tracy Wilder who is Personal Assistant to Tina Rauch. . . .'

'*Tracy*. . . .!'

Tina – she had reappeared – stepped forward but no further, unable to get past the leveled pistol barrel of the black femcop in the sassy shimmy-dress.

Tracy Wilder stood gazing at Faraday, her mouth opening in disbelief.

'*Get her down onner floor! Fer Crissake!*' O'Duff was hollering at the screen as if Faraday was able to hear his advice.

HE DIDN'T want to look at her. There were tears in her eyes.

'Christ, Faraday! . . . Whyn't you leave me alone? You don't understand! It's not just . . . a question of justice!'

He didn't want to listen to her. He wanted to be a machine carrying out a program of commands, just as he had been taught to do during his training.

'Get down on the floor,' he said mechanically.

Tracy Wilder – she looked like a dumb animal, cornered beseeching him – did not move.

'Don't fuck around, Tracy,' he said, motioning with his Remington toward the floor. He noticed that his hurt left hand – he must have transfered the pistol into it in order to exchange his badge for the warrant with his right hand – was no longer shaking. Its numbness had spread throughout his whole body. 'Just lie on the floor. It's the drill.'

Tracy crossed her arms in front of her and then uncrossed them. She raised her hands which held onto the border of her dress so that the drapery fell like wings, opening the front of the garment with a measured flourish to reveal her body underneath.

It was just a body – human, vulnerable, now unclothed for the rest of humanity to consider. It possessed the usual two arms, two legs, two female breasts, slender neck, spiky yellow hair, one head, belly, omphalos, and, looking unnaturally congruous among the pubic area, a dick.

A male's scrotum and penis.

A murmer rippled through the hushed crowd, first of awe, then degenerating into an indignant hiss.

She's a . . . .

He, you mean. . . .

Is she a he?

A what?

A fucking hermo!

This –

for the fashion curators present you could break the rules, that was permitted: you could wear brown shoes with black trousers, you could examine the dialectics between one style, one sex, and another, you could ridicule them

– but this, this was outrageous. It didn't break rules. It created a category outside all rule-systems, the very existence of which sneered at the conventions that fashion depended upon, struggled to make sense of. What Tracy revealed under her dress homogenized the least experimental and the most outré among the guests. It marginalized the notion of Fashion itself.

Tracy took a step forward, proffering the paradox of her body for Faraday to make head or tail of. Did he, perhaps, have the key to it? the ambiguity of her nature? Was this what he wanted from her – the dismemberment of her personality? Her humiliation? Here, then, take it.

Faraday tried to recall which number came next on his mental list of commands he had given himself.

'I loved her too, Max Faraday. And *she* loved *me*!' Tracy murmured with quiet reproach. 'For what I *am*. Can you understand that? The innocent t.v. newscaster you were in love with – you and forty million other people – loved *this*! This body! You're so clever, maybe you can explain me why.'

He said nothing. Speech had its uses but explaining this – whatever this was – was not one of them. Here was the person who had murdered someone he had loved, naked before him. At his mercy. He had reached the point to which a career in semiotics had brought him: the arbitrary nature of signs cruelly exposed as the conventional signifier – Tracy Wilder's social identity – was stripped from what it purported to signify: her, her sexuality, forcing him to witness the failure of language to clothe the animal and revealing a terrible meaningless truth. A piece of raw meat. Unutterable. Something which only God had to answer for.

Tracy looked at him, waiting. Any moment now she would be in his arms. He would be stroking her hair.

'Get down on the floor, Tracy,' he told her quietly, as he had been taught to do during his training. It was the drill.

TRACY WILDER – gathering her dress around her – lay down on the dance floor in front of Faraday.

'An *hermaphrodite*!' Delia Summers said. Something her biology could explain in the aphid and the garden snail but which in human beings was an aberration, a tragic mutant conjunction of opposites.

'Oh beautiful . . .!' O'Duff said, his voice husky with emotion. 'Just beautiful!'

Danny Keach, bug-eyed, said nothing.

The t.v. audience watched Sasha rise from her seat and cross the crowded dance floor, a silver spotlight tracking her progress – dancers, no longer dancing, stood aside to let her pass – until she reached the epicentre of the disturbance and she was standing in back of Faraday and between the two rookies, Conway and Tornova. Faraday didn't move.

'What's . . . happening . . .?' Robbie Robson muttered.

Sasha said: 'I'm live Max. . . .' She unclipped her clip-on mike and held it toward him. 'Go 'head. Make your arrest. Tell Robbie what's happening. Tell the world!'

There was a pause while Robbie listened. While the world listened.

'Tracy Wilder . . .' Faraday's voice said over the picture of Faraday holding the big police pistol on the person spreadeagled at his feet. '. . . With the authority invested in me by the City of New York I am placing you under arrest on a charge of complicity in an arson attack on a city building, 700 Seventh Avenue, the Torelli Design Factory, on the eleventh this month . . . .'

The ballroom became suddenly restive. Faraday – he had pocketed his buzzer – was holding up a white document although Tracy Wilder was not in a good position to inspect it. People began to jostle each other in order to obtain a closer view of the excitement. Robbie Robson said nothing. Tina Rauch put her hands to her face. She was weeping, it looked like. For her, too, it was all over.

'. . . And you are further charged on a count of murder. The murder last night of Bonnie Karbowska West. . . .'

The ballroom went wild. There were some angry cat-calls. Maybe someone shouted, 'String her up!' Cadet Officers Conway and Tornova kept everyone present at a respectful distance while Faraday read Tracy Wilder her rights.

Sasha stood facing the camera.

'You have just witnessed,' she said into her mike, 'an historic event, Ladies, Gen'lemen. The arrest – live – of a ruthless assassin, the person charged by the police for the slaying last night of the Channel Eleven News personality, Bonnie West, someone we all of us deeply loved. This has been made possible for you by the sponsors of this Show, *Vogue Magazine*, and the cooperation the Police Department received from the Channel Eleven Broadcasting Syndicate.'

Sasha could not help looking triumphant. This was her big moment. She had ridden the tiger. She had gotten her scoop.

Blue uniformed police officers were entering the *salle de bal*, dozens of them, several with their weapons drawn. A chunky female sergeant stepped between Faraday and his prisoner. She eased Tracy Wilder's arms behind her back and slipped on the bracelets, then – she must have understood how hard it is to rise from a belly-down position without the use of your hands – gently helped her to her feet. The sergeant wrapped Tracy's body inside her dress, careful not to expose it any more than could be helped.

Faraday had turned away – Delia could see why he did this – and approached the two cadets, his gun hanging down, pointing to the floor. He looked wrung out. It was hard watching him, unable to go to him. He spoke to Conway and Tornova but what he said to them, no longer in range of Sasha's mike, was not audible.

A smattering of applause – possibly ironic – erupted among a section of the crowd. The t.v. slowly panned across the room. Fist-fights were breaking out. Guests began to leave. Tina Rauch was nowhere to be seen. The party was over.

'Well, Captain,' Delia said. She looked sideways at O'Duff. She looked sideways at Danny Keach. But neither of the two men took their eyes from the t.v. screen. 'He seems to have pulled it off, our semiological detective! And boy! Can he skate! Did you ever see anything like it?'

O'Duff shook his head, speechless.

SWISH. SWISH.

The tiny roar of sealed nylon bearings rotating inside skate-trucks swished in a counter-direction to the swish of nylon wheels against the black road surface, made shiny here and there by the lighted storefronts. It was four o'clock in the morning. The sidewalk was deserted. At the intersection of Park Row and Center the signals were on red but he didn't pay any attention to them. There was not very much traffic moving in either direction – a few medallion cabs, some private limousines. In his white shirt he was visible plain enough. And, for fuck's sake, he didn't particularly feel like paying attention to any goddamn red lights! He felt like playing Russian roulette with the cross-traffic. He was free. At last the cool night air was on his face, pleasantly chilling the sweat inside his shirt which he had worked up several hours before and had sat around in several hours since. Swish. Swish.

It was a good reckless feeling to be skating alone, fast and with finesse, across the city at night, cruising the sportcars, dodging the bandits, concentrating on staying alive – although not concentrating too hard. There was nothing like it to clear the head. It felt good to be away from the tired lined faces, the quiet voices, the bad coffee, the whir of recording tape, the smell of the Interrogation Room, the hard functional plastic furniture – to get the fuck out of the old NYC Police Headquarters building on Pearl Street. Good, most of all, to be away from Tracy Wilder and Tracy Wilder's ironic smile and Iago-like silence. He could skate away from all that – for the time being – but never from the consequences of what had happened to take him there.

His black jacket hooked over his shoulder, he swished down Chambers, heading east, careful as he skirted the perimeter of City Park to keep his head turned away from the nineteenth-century French Renaissance-style building lit up inside the darkness of the park. City Hall was an elegant approachable building, worthy of a second look under normal circumstances, but he had seen enough of it for today. Sooner or later what he had gone there and done this afternoon would catch up with him – and probably shoot him in the back.

But not tonight.

Tonight it seemed like several thousand years since he had entered the building, tracked down the outgoing Police Commissioner – he was at a Let's-call-it-a-day junket in the outgoing Mayor's office – in order to persuade him to put his name to a police document which would authorize the arrest of a public felon and, incidentally, alter the course of history completely. (And for the worse, some might say.) Commissioner 'Black Fats' Liebman, the moment Faraday had gotten him alone, had, of course, procrastinated. He had hemmed and he had hawed as soon as he understood the implications of what Faraday was asking him to do. His full attention, Faraday could not help noticing, had not seemed to be on the matter in hand. Perhaps he was a little bit sleepy, a little bit drunk, a little bit thinking about the deluxe condo apartment he had his name down for up in one of the Hamptons.

Faraday swished down the middle of Chambers as if he owned it. The young cop leaning against the parked prowlcar must have recognized him because he smiled and threw him a salute. Faraday – it was a strange sensation – found himself smiling.

I can't do this just like that, 'Black Fats' Liebman had said. I need to see a full report. I need to talk with the Precinct Captain. I need to see some hard evidence. Faraday, to oblige, had taken out of his pocket Tracy Wilder's modified Tiffany inlay .41 fourshot rimfire Colt revolver and let the Commissioner see it. The Commissioner had said that was, um, cute and he reached his hand out to make a closer inspection of the piece. Yes, ah, this was indeed material. But Faraday had not let him take hold of the gun. Instead he had given him a demonstration of the discreet little popping tone its Mitzu firing mechanism made, after which the Commissioner had looked very shaken. A love of life had suddenly filled his fat brown eyes as if someone had just roused him from a bad dream, reminding the old cop what guns did to people. Yes, um, I see your point Lieutenant. It may be in the public interest for the City to, ah, put a suspected assassin into custody, but. . . . Faraday had let off another round, splintering the rosewood cornice just behind where the Commissioner was standing. He apologized about the accuracy of his aim but, you see, he was using his left hand. His left hand was shaking. In the face of the overwhelming piece of evidence Faraday was in possession of, 'Black Fats' Liebman had come round to Faraday's way of thinking and had obligingly written his big fat signature on the warrant with his big fat Dunhill fountain pen. Faraday had had difficulty taking it out of the Commissioner's hand with his own wounded right hand, but he had nevertheless taken it.

When he hit Broadway, Faraday hung a right and headed uptown. The traffic was still light although figures sometimes moved on the sidewalk, loading or unloading off the backs of trucks. There was always something that had to be done at four o'clock in the morning in Chinatown. At Canal he tacked through Soho until he was on West Houston. Groups of people without ID sat singing and playing music – classical, popular, Latin, you name it – frying food and kidding each other. They were good people, most of them, but they had fallen through the net. He returned their waves and swished away from their lewd invitations. Washington Square was partying under bright white lights. It might have been four o'clock in the afternoon. Young men wearing only shorts threw frisbees back and forth to each other, demonstrating fancy behind-the-back catching techniques. A lot of folks, notwithstanding, were bedded down for the night, trying to get some sleep. Faraday zigzagged through the Village, crossing the Avenue of the Americas, until he hit Seventh. All he had to do now was keep going for about thirty blocks. That's all.

It was warm work. He was begining to work up a fresh film of sweat. His shirt was sticking to his back, but his head was clearing. At 12th Street he gave away his black jacket to a girl who asked him for it. Whatever they tried to do to him now – take away his shield or hang a citation on him – it made no difference. He had no use for either. He was through. Finished. He had pointed enough guns in enough people's faces to last him a good while.

At 28th he threw away his shield.

Maybe Rocco would have won the Election anyway, even without a helping hand from Max Faraday. It was possible. But Cody La Renta, apparently, had bollixed for the Yankees once again – struck out on 3 and 2 in the 11th with the bases loaded! – to let the Mets off with a win to clinch the Series. So it wasn't likely.

It was all the same to Max Faraday who won – Tina or Rocco, the Mets or the Yankees. The significance of either did not lie in 'Tina' or in 'Rocco', as they liked to think, but in their relationship, in the space between their apparent differences – their contradictions. Who won or who lost was no more interesting than which of the contestants was victorious and which vanquished in a t.v. games show. The interesting object of study was the rules they agreed to play by, the conventions that governed the system. The lovely-lovely style-dictators, Tina and Rocco, were little more than conventional ciphers within this arrangement. The fact that they were also lovers simply underlined the conventional nature of their relationship. They had found it as hard as anyone else to escape the arbitrariness of signs – the otherness of meaning. Language, after all, is – always would be – public property. It was the artist, as always, who understood this and who consciously sought to evade the semiotic codes, who violated the rules of the system. The semiotician's job was to call attention to the evasion, particularly in the *oeuvre* of the artist, just as it was the job of the police detective, second grade, to blow the whistle on the citizen who contravened Federal and State Laws. It was Faraday's misfortune – and Bonnie West's even more so – that in this instance the artist and the criminal happened to be the same citizen.

700 Seventh Avenue when Faraday arrived there, wet with sweat but with a clear head, was deserted. Temporary

plywood siding fenced in the demolition work. The t.v. crews had left. The Fire Department engineers had left, taking with them their bright lights and their science-fiction deconstruction equipment. Even the police presence had been withdrawn. The Torelli Building was no longer news – it was just another midtown construction site. He buzzed through the temporary intercom to the temporary security guard and had him open up. The temporary steel-mesh gates clicked open. He stepped between them and thanked the guard who, without leaving his cubicle, waved aside Faraday's thanks and remotely clicked shut the gates after him.

'I saw you tonight onna Rob Rob Show, Lieutenant . . .' the guard said. The young man – he was wearing a blousy flying-jacket in black parachute-silk, his hair skilfully cut and tossed into a daring plumed shock – grinned at Faraday. 'I got to tell you, you was looking real good in there, you know that? You looked like some real ace cop. A pro.'

Again he batted aside Faraday's thanks. Young and clean-looking, he himself looked like some real ace hair-dresser's receptionist. Still grinning, he wished Faraday a good night.

Faraday, curious to know how a security employee could afford such a recent Carlton Laplace hairstyle, skated cautiously over the temporary flooring of the corridor that led to the atrium and the elevator which would take him to the apartment of the resident arachnologist. The quiet swish-swish of his recently lubricated skate-trucks, amplified by the hollow surface of the flooring, echoed noisily down the empty corridor.

Too noisily?

Instinctively Faraday glanced over his shoulder. Behind him, at a respectful distance, he saw his echo. Black against the light, a young man in a bomber-jacket was skating after him with a lazy alternating switch of the hips. The sight of him on skates told Faraday everything – it wasn't a sign you needed to be a semiologist to interpret – even before the thing the man was carrying in his right hand, swaying across his rhythm, defined itself in the silhouette: the wire-framed stock of a machine-shotgun.

Swish. Swish.

The security employee in the expensive experimental haircut, whatever he was, was not a security employee.

Faraday, when he reached the atrium, welcomed the obfuscation it offered. Its shadowy foliage, layered with the invisible wings of sleeping butterflies, would conceal him. He struck into the black undergrowth, his white skateboots appearing intermittently green in the dull chlorophyll-colored night-lamps set into the ground at intervals. Straight ahead, on the further side of the atrium, the lighted external elevator-shaft rose out of the forest like a rocket gantry. His shuttle to safety, on countdown to liftoff. He skated warily toward it, reasonably certain that in the intervening distance someone was waiting for him – either the candidate who had lost the Election or the candidate who had won it – to ambush him with the threat of death. Or, maybe worse, an offer of employment.

Swish. Swish.

The ex-Lieutenant in Homicide switched his weight into a semi-crouch position. Elbowing up momentum, his arms swinging as if making use of invisible ski-poles, he slalomed through the darkness, fast, surrendering himself to his intuitive fears. Before he gained the elevator-shaft and the security of his lady's chamber there lay a maze of danger and moral choices to be traversed. Behind him, a fashion thug with a gun. In front, a predatory member of his own species concealed inside a simulated jungle environment in order to pierce his body – or his integrity.

And to Maxwell Faraday – no longer armed, shorn of public authority – it seemed only right, appropriate, that it should be like this. The meaning of anything that meant anything must be hard and hard to find. There was a formal symmetry to the situation which appealed to him. The beautiful biologist, safe inside the treacherous atrium, stood in the same relation to him, her lover, as Meaning inside the

faithlessness of Language stands to the student of semiology: elusive and irrecoverable. To attempt to recover it — to
recover her — was a perilous enterprise. And probably
hopeless.

With expert technique he skated swiftly away from his
armed pursuer into the densest section of the atrium.

Swish. Swish.